The
SECOND
SON

PRAISE FOR THE BETRAYAL PROPHECIES
BOOK 1: *The Third Daughter*

"Immersive and intense; hand this royal fantasy to readers of Kendare Blake's *Three Dark Crowns* and Victoria Aveyard's Red Queen series."
—*SLJ*

"My only complaint about the book is that I wish it had been four times as long."
—Heather Hogan, *Autostraddle*

"An enchanting YA.... A riveting star-crossed romance as well as a story of two teenage girls embracing their emotions as a source of strength."
—*Shelf Awareness*

"Subtly vicious and achingly tender, with a charming cast and delightful twists to boot.... At the novel's gentle heart is a story about the healing magic of being known."
—Allison Saft, *New York Times* bestselling author of *A Far Wilder Magic*

"Spectacularly emotional and majestically dark, *The Third Daughter* is a glittering jewel of a novel certain to win over even the most hard-hearted readers."
—Morgan Rhodes, *New York Times* bestselling author of the Falling Kingdoms series

"This sprawling fantasy...features frothy romance and charismatic, take-charge heroines."
—*Publishers Weekly*

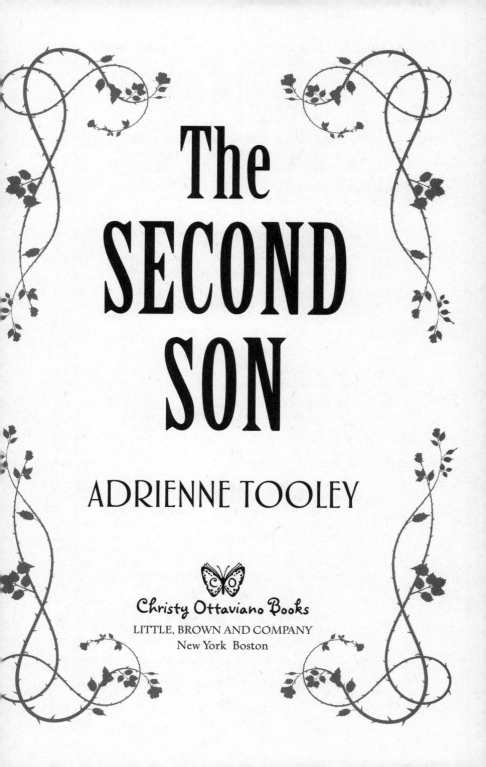

The
SECOND
SON

ADRIENNE TOOLEY

Christy Ottaviano Books

LITTLE, BROWN AND COMPANY
New York Boston

Copyright © 2024 by Adrienne Tooley
Vine art © Anton Dzyna/Shutterstock.com
Fleur-de-lis art © Naddya/Shutterstock.com

Cover art copyright © 2024 by Gemma O'Brien. Cover design by Karina Granda.
Cover copyright © 2024 by Hachette Book Group, Inc.
Interior design by Michelle Gengaro-Kokmen.

Christy Ottaviano Books
Hachette Book Group
1290 Avenue of the Americas, New York, NY 10104
Visit us at LBYR.com

First Edition: July 2024

Christy Ottaviano Books is an imprint of Little, Brown and Company. The Christy Ottaviano Books name and logo are registered trademarks of Hachette Book Group, Inc.

Library of Congress Cataloging-in-Publication Data
Names: Tooley, Adrienne, author. | Tooley, Adrienne. Third daughter.
Title: The second son / Adrienne Tooley.
Description: First edition. | New York : Little, Brown and Company, 2024. | Series: The Betrayal Prophecies | Audience: Ages 14–18. | Summary: "Book 2 in a dark fantasy duology about leadership, betrayal, male rage, and politicizing female emotion—with an undercurrent of sapphic romance." —Provided by publisher.
Identifiers: LCCN 2023036902 | ISBN 9780316465908 (hardcover) | ISBN 9780316466103 (ebook)
Subjects: CYAC: Magic—Fiction. | Birth order—Fiction. | Fantasy. | LCGFT: Fantasy fiction. | Romance fiction. | Novels.
Classification: LCC PZ7.1.T6264 Se 2024 | DDC [Fic]—dc23
LC record available at https://lccn.loc.gov/2023036902

ISBNs: 978-0-316-46590-8 (hardcover), 978-0-316-46610-3 (ebook)

Printed in Indiana, USA

LSC-C

Printing 1, 2024

For anyone who has ever known the darkness.
You are not alone.

ALWAYS AN ANGEL, NEVER A GOD

—BOYGENIUS

The
SECOND
SON

PART ONE

The Second Son was not gifted his name, he was born with it. His father was the leader of the Lower Banks, his elder brother poised to inherit the family's titles, land, and legacy, leaving him with nothing. So when the riverbanks shriveled and dried, when their camp was invaded and burned to the ground, when the townspeople decided to move on, to rebuild elsewhere, the Second Son saw a chance to rewrite his destiny.

When Sebastien would not follow his kin beyond the Lower Banks, his father spat at his feet.

"Only a fool would fall victim to idolatry and bright smiles." His father pointed to the girl of seventeen who stood proudly on the scorched earth and swore to restore her homeland. "There is nothing for you in these ashes."

The Second Son did not flinch, despite his patriarch's raised hand. Where once his father's disregard had shamed him, it now fueled his vision.

"There is opportunity," the Second Son insisted. "There is a place for me by her side." His eyes were fixed hungrily on the girl who would become the New Maiden.

She met his gaze. In her eyes, Sebastien's future was clear. Together they would bring the world to its knees. And then his father would see how wrong he had been to spurn his second son.

—Psalm of the Second Son

1

On the thirty-first day of Her Second Ascension, the wind shifted east, and the New Maiden gave a sermon on the bell tower's front steps.

Sabine's skin prickled beneath her elaborate robe. The expensive silk—hand-dyed in the New Maiden's signature aubergine—rippled like water and shimmered like a jewel in the afternoon light. It was the finest thing she had ever worn. The fabric was light as a feather along her pale arms, the cuffs of her sleeves hand-embroidered with tiny white stars. The young woman who had stitched it, a member of the clergy in the Arts District, trembled when she handed the garment over to Sabine.

"I cannot believe the New Maiden stands before me." The woman was only a few years her senior, the same age as Sabine's older sister, Katrynn. Her deference made Sabine uncomfortable.

"We are not so different." Sabine busied herself with admiring the delicate handiwork. "Thank you for sharing your gift with me."

"No, thank *you*." The woman looked up at her with wide, marveling eyes. "For coming back to us."

Sabine did not know how to respond. She was constantly being thanked, praised, and extolled for things far outside her control. She had not asked to be born the third daughter of a third daughter. Her role as the New Maiden reincarnated was no more than happenstance.

Yet happenstance meant nothing in the face of a miracle. That miracle of her ascension, her public calling forth of the darkness, was the reason so many had gathered in the city square to hear Sabine speak.

"Maiden?" A gentle hand came to rest on Sabine's shoulder. She turned to meet the soft gray eyes of Silas. "It's nearly time."

Silas was a bishop, returned from the small province of Adeya to run Harborside's recently reopened house of worship. Tall and broad, her gray hair shorn short to reveal a striking, hawkish face, the woman was Sabine's favorite member of the clergy. The bishop taught Sabine about the rites and responsibilities of her new role, introduced her to the Church's hierarchy, even organized this inaugural sermon. The size of the crowd was a testament to Silas's influence.

"I still can't believe this many people want to hear anything I have to say."

"Not *you*, Sabine," Silas corrected her, gently. "The New Maiden."

That's right, Sabine could practically hear her darkness mutter. *No one cares about* you, *only what you stand for.* But the darkness was gone, absent from her veins, which now shone blue beneath her skin. The voice that had once haunted her every waking moment—infiltrating her judgment, suffocating her confidence, poisoning her actions—had gone silent, too. Her tears no longer held magic—now, they were nothing but salt. Where the people of Velle believed the New Maiden to be rife with magic, wisdom, and power, in truth, Sabine had never been more ordinary.

Her followers were too busy clamoring for her attention to notice. The city had welcomed an influx of worshippers desperate to meet Sabine's iteration of the New Maiden. They intercepted her on the street, fell to their knees, begged for her blessing. Doubt bloomed like belladonna as Sabine received accolade after accolade. It was only a matter of time before the world realized she was a fraud.

Her family's arrival in the city square was a welcome relief. Katrynn, Artur, and their mother pushed their way to the front of the spectators. While she was under no illusion that the Queen of Velle had time to attend a sermon in the square, Sabine scanned the crowd for Elodie anyway.

The only Warnou present was the third daughter: Brianne. Sabine had not seen her since the girl had awoken from her strange sleep. Even though she'd returned to the realm of the living, Brianne still looked peaked, her skin waxy and her corn silk hair limp. Some of Sabine's own exhaustion was reflected in the eyes of the youngest Warnou. She wondered if Brianne, too, was haunted by the urgent warning she'd delivered to Sabine: *Your time will be short and the fall will be far.*

A few paces behind the princess was a much less desirable face: Tal's.

Their few interactions had left the New Maiden with little fondness for the Loyalist. Tal seemed a haughty, entitled boy whose easy relationship with the Queen of Velle set Sabine on edge. His eyes were always on Elodie, his lips always close to her ear, a gnat impossible to swat away. While she trusted the queen implicitly, Tal *was* pretty, as far as boys went. Sabine feared his words were as sweet as rotting fruit, that he might poison Elodie's affections away from her.

As though he could sense her scrutiny, Tal's green eyes met hers. A chill shot down the New Maiden's spine. His expression was coolly calculated, composed as a seasoned gambler. Sabine was the first to look away.

Her white-robed clergy lined the square's perimeter. The Royal Chaplain's purple sash glittered in the sunlight even as he scowled. His fingers twitched as though itching to ascend the makeshift pulpit and command the crowd himself. But his days of speaking on behalf of the New Maiden were long gone. Now Silas stepped forth to quiet the crowd and introduce Sabine.

They had practiced this sermon many times, Silas conducting Sabine like a sonata, reminding her when to breathe and where to pause dramatically. *Speak from the heart*, Silas reminded Sabine. *Her* heart. But every time Sabine reached inward for inspiration, she returned empty-handed. Yes, she had exorcised the darkness from her veins, but it had not left her joyful or free. She had instead fallen victim to the staggering weight of numbness. Adrift in the endless abyss of feeling nothing at all.

"I welcome you," Silas called warmly to the crowd. "As She does. I welcome Her, as you do." She gestured to her left. "The New Maiden."

Sabine ascended the steps. The new angle offered her a pleasing perspective: The crowd below her was united by hope. Sabine's trajectory from Harborside girl to reincarnated deity was proof that a person born to nothing could one day achieve greatness. She was proof that the New Maiden had kept Her promise to return, proof that goodness and righteousness prevailed amidst the uncertainties of life.

It did not matter if Sabine did not feel like the New Maiden. To them, she was.

That knowledge gave her the confidence to speak.

"Citizens of Velle," Sabine shouted, and the crowd roared in response, "friends from afar, I welcome you today, to this place where I was made, where you witnessed me call forth the darkness and then banish it. I am as She was—as She shall always be. The New Maiden's word"—Sabine paused as Silas cleared her throat pointedly, then adjusted—"*my* word is a light in that darkness. Trust in me, for my promises are always fulfilled. Follow me, for I will brave the first step down every path. Depend on me, for I am yours."

For hours after her remarks, Sabine was surrounded by a clamoring throng. None were willing to leave without a personal blessing from the New Maiden, and by the time the city's square had emptied, the sun hovered on the horizon. Pink and gold painted the sky as night crept nearer.

Sabine and Silas returned to Harborside in silence, save for the squawking of seabirds and the shouting of dockhands. The bishop was well attuned to the New Maiden's mood, never asking for more than Sabine could give. A rarity these days when everyone wanted something from her.

Harborside came alive when the stars began to wink down from above. Silas and Sabine walked the crowded cobblestone streets, past boisterous taverns and raucous gambling dens. Boarded-up buildings were plastered with flyers, the salt from the sea curling the corners of the parchment.

"A day of virtue, an evening of vice," the bishop noted solemnly, as they passed the open door of a gambling hall. Inside, Sabine spotted a familiar face, confounding in this context. Tal had exchanged his Loyalist reds for an ensemble of black. His hands were busy folding a piece of parchment.

His presence was unsettling. There was no reason for him to wander the seedy underbelly of Harborside, and certainly not without the protection offered by his Loyalist uniform. Sabine nearly called his name, but just as before, Tal's head jerked in her direction without prompting.

Their eyes met, and again, a chill slithered down Sabine's spine. Tal's mouth twisted into a nearly imperceptible frown. This time, he looked away first, furtively sliding the scrap of parchment into his pocket before vanishing into the crowd.

Sabine hardly noticed when they arrived at the front door of her family's apartment, so flummoxed was she by Tal's presence in her neighborhood.

"Well done today, Maiden," Silas said, gently untangling her from her reverie. "You shone as brightly as I expected."

"Thank you, Silas." Sabine offered the bishop a modest smile. It was quite the compliment, coming from someone who had been committed to the New Maiden's word longer than Sabine had been alive. Still, she was not entirely certain she deserved it.

She bid the bishop good night and pushed her way inside. She took no more than two steps before sinking to the floor with exhaustion, ready to sleep on the hard wood, no pillow or quilt required.

"All right there, Bet?" Her younger brother sounded amused.

"Fine, thanks, Artur," she mumbled, not bothering to open her eyes.

"Bet, get off the floor," Katrynn said. "If you're hungry, I made soup. It's mostly broth, but—"

"Sabine." It was the use of her real name that finally caused her to open her eyes. Her family was gathered around the table, expressions grim. Sabine sat up straight, exhaustion forgotten.

"What's the matter?"

"Why don't you come sit." Orla Anders patted the empty chair beside her.

"What's happened?" Sabine spun through endless horrible scenarios. "Is it Da?"

Artur produced a piece of parchment, folded several times over, nearly identical to the one Tal had pocketed. "Found this on a craps table in the Faceless Fox this afternoon." He passed the document over to his sister.

On the page was a penciled portrait of a moth, the insect's body bulbous like a maggot, its wings outstretched and spotted, antennae pointing up. *Why depend on Her*, the poster read, *when you could shine with Him?*

Sabine didn't need to wonder who *He* was. Sebastien. The Second Son, twisting words from the New Maiden's own sermon to mock her.

"The posters are all over," Artur continued, voice pained. "On building walls, at the bar, in the toilets, even."

In the hands of her least favorite Loyalist, too, if her suspicions were correct.

"He's coming," Sabine said flatly. It wasn't a question. The words

Brianne spoke in her incense-clouded bedroom floated again to the forefront of Sabine's mind. *He will hold the faithful in His iron grip, and Velle will fall at His feet.* "This isn't a warning." She swallowed thickly. "It's a promise."

The apartment was silent as a cemetery.

"I don't like this, Sabine," Orla Anders said. "Not one bit."

Sabine tried to smile, but her cheeks ached with the effort. There were no words of comfort to offer her mother.

"You should take this to the queen," Katrynn suggested. "Elodie will know what to do."

"No." The word was too loud amidst the fretful quiet of the tiny room. Her family frowned at her dismissal. "The queen has plenty on her plate," Sabine backtracked quickly. "She doesn't need another thing to worry about. Not until we have a better sense of the threat."

Her family's troubled expressions indicated they did not agree. But Sabine held fast. As the New Maiden, she could not allow herself to appear undermined already, not when Elodie had established herself as a generous, competent queen. Sabine wished to be a twin pillar, not a drain on the crown's resources. She was the head of the Church now. This was her problem, no one else's.

"I wonder why a moth." Sabine's mother frowned down at the page. "They're pests. Leave holes in all my best sweaters."

"Because they fly?" Artur suggested. "They can 'rise above'?"

Sabine stared down at the sketch, unease brewing in her stomach. She'd never paid much attention to the pesky insects fluttering uselessly in the dark, desperately seeking flames.

Understanding dawned on her. "It's because moths are drawn toward light." *The Second Son's* light.

It was a credo diametrically opposed to her own. Where the New Maiden urged her followers to uncover the brilliance within, the Second Son claimed He shone bright enough alone.

Sabine waited for the slippery voice in her ear to chime in with its usual nihilism. Instead, there was only silence. Its absence was a chasm.

Still, as Sabine refolded the parchment and tucked it into the pocket of her robe, she allowed herself the faintest sliver of relief. The poster's words held a familiar, cynical air, as though her darkness had expelled its judgment outward, onto posters hung in public spaces.

It was a dark comfort to know that the Second Son doubted Sabine almost as much as Sabine doubted herself.

2

The next day, Elodie rose before the sun. The hours when the sky still clung to midnight, evading the efforts of impending dawn, were the only time the Queen of Velle managed to find a moment's peace. As a child, Elodie had observed her mother's reign with scrutiny. Why, she had wondered, did Tera Warnou have no time for anything but her job?

The answer, Elodie had recently learned, was because the demands of the throne were all-consuming and never-ending. She entertained nobility in between slurps of soup, waved to babies on her way to sentencings, composed speeches while she reviewed bank statements and forecasts of export numbers.

There were so many demands that Elodie could not help but feel as though no one wanted the queen to actually accomplish anything. If she sourced labor or materials from artisans outside Velle's capital, the masons in the Manufacturing District stopped repairing the city's potholes. When she lowered the cost of grain to make food accessible to all economic strata, the accountants in the Commerce District had lectured her extensively about this disruption to Velle's currency, the kelber.

Even her breakfast was consequential. Marguerite, her lady-in-waiting, arrived every morning at six bells with a tray containing the same spread of fruit, nuts, and cheese.

If Elodie refused the fruit, she slighted the farmers of the Second Republic, whom Velle depended on for imports of citrus, berries, and greens. If she asked for ham instead of cheese, she insulted the dairy farmers of Vyen and offered undue recognition to the butchers of Lower Dale, which, according to the fine print of a decades-old treaty, was not allowed so long as she wished her army to have access to the road that led to the Fifth Republic.

Elodie had not expected absolute power and privilege to come with so many restrictions. The constant niceties and politicking left her exhausted, but there was very little time in a sovereign's itinerary for sleep.

Marguerite had just finished pouring her tea when there came a knock at the queen's chamber door. Elodie scowled, her time alone cut even shorter than usual. "Enter," she called, already irritated with the person on the other side.

"Oh, good," she said brightly, when she saw the subject of her ire. "Someone I don't have to pretend to be nice to."

Tal let out a good-natured laugh and settled himself on the settee opposite Elodie. He gestured to a cube of cheese. "May I?"

She nodded through a sip of tea. "Please. I can hardly stand the sight of it." She sighed, loud and long. "I never imagined it was possible to resent cheese."

"That's the price of power, Majesty," Tal said, shaking his head.

Elodie dipped a dried plum in honey, the sugar tense between her teeth. "Some days, I'm not certain it's worth the cost."

Tal considered this. "I think," he said finally, "that anything worth doing will always feel just a little bit like a sacrifice."

Elodie knew all too well what he meant. Once, she would have delighted in this image: Tal a decorated Loyalist, she the queen. Their closeness would have been a boon, not a burden. But that was before Brianne's warning had confirmed Tal's starry-eyed promises: The Second Son, whoever He was, would be the New Maiden's downfall.

Tal's devotion to this Second Son pitted him firmly against Sabine. Yet in order to disentangle His threat, Elodie had to pretend as though she didn't care, had to behave as though Tal's presence in her chambers was casual rather than curated.

The Loyalist nudged her foot with his. "What's on the agenda today, Majesty?"

Elodie reached for her teacup. "The usual. Opening an orphanage in the Arts District. Entertaining the nobility who control Velle's drinking water supply. Drafting a letter to the King of Vathi. Reading a letter from my accountant. Finding someone in this castle who can translate the letter from my accountant into something I actually understand."

Tal chuckled. "Rob was always good with numbers, wasn't he?"

Elodie's mood darkened at the mention of her brother. Ever since her coronation, Rob had been noticeably absent, locked in his room day and night, composing somber concertos that included heavy percussion and tolling bells. Elodie had tried to call on him, but he refused to speak to anyone who was not Tal, rolling his eyes at his sister's every inquiry.

"That boy is a thorn in my side." She leaned back against the couch.

"He's..." Tal looked thoughtful. "Going through something."

"And I'm not?"

Tal bit back a smile. "It's rather different, I think."

"Well, I wouldn't know," Elodie said dryly. "Because he won't speak to me, or answer any of my summonses. I don't even know if he's planning to show up for the orphanage opening, even though I invited him days ago and it will be difficult to explain to the parentless children why the prince couldn't be bothered to show up and bring them any toys!"

Tal flinched but recovered quickly. "Temper, Majesty."

Her face flushed. "Apologies," she said shortly. "You must find me most disagreeable."

"On the contrary." He straightened his shoulders, the gold chain around his neck glittering in the morning light. "There is nothing you could do to make me believe so. You are a wonder, Lo. Even when your cheeks bloom with rage."

Elodie squirmed beneath the force of his earnestness. Tal's feelings for her had always toed the line between friendship and flame. Her heart ached for what she could not offer him, and thus for years she erred on the side of suggesting hope, so that she would not have to watch him break.

Perhaps now, she might use that to her advantage.

"You flatter me," she said, reaching over to swat his knee. "I don't know what I'd do without you to keep me in line."

Surprise tiptoed across his face. He leaned forward, grinning. "Someone's got to."

"Pray tell, what might it take for me to convince that *someone* to wrangle Rob for me?" She looked up at him through her eyelashes. "I wouldn't ask, only you know he loves you more than he does me." She bit her lip. "Can't say I blame him."

Tal cleared his throat, ears reddening. "You know that I am always at your service, Lo."

She smiled through her unease. Her mother had touted manipulation as a queen's most tactical weapon. It was only right she should practice wielding it.

"Make sure he wears something green," she called after Tal. "If he won't act like a member of the family, the least he can do is dress in Warnou colors."

At seven bells, Cleo arrived with an armful of dresses, an exhausted-looking Brianne in tow. Elodie winced at the sight of her youngest sister. Brianne's cheeks had lost their rosiness, and dark bags had developed beneath her eyes.

"Bri, sit down." Cleo ushered the youngest Warnou onto a stool and started fussing with her hair. "El, I brought the dress you wore for Mother's birthday last year," she said through a mouthful of hairpins. "It's in our color, and the skirt is slim enough you'll have no trouble getting in and out of a carriage. You won't look foolish, nor too rich in the face of scarcity."

"Wonderful thinking, Cleo." Elodie was grateful for her middle sister's machinations. Cleo ensured that the queen always looked elegant and appropriate for events, and she never forgot a single name.

Elodie had just stepped into the gown in question when she was interrupted by another knock on the door. Marguerite hurried to open it, revealing a servant with a letter on a silver tray. While the serpent sigil pressed into the wax seal was unfamiliar, it nagged at some moribund memory. The queen opened the envelope to find handwriting that crept across the page like a spider. Half-dressed, Elodie sank into a chair, the floral perfume emanating from a bouquet of pink begonias turning her stomach as she read.

> *To Her Majesty the Queen of Velle (and my betrothed),*
>
> *Imagine my surprise, beloved, when your carriage arrived without you in it. I don't know if you think me foolish, or you believe me weak, but either assumption is made in error. I was promised your hand in marriage, and I intend to get what I am owed. It will be easier if you don't resist. Marry me of your own accord, and I'll let one of your sisters ascend the throne. Deny me once more, and I cannot guarantee I will be so gentle.*
>
> *Sincerely and lovingly yours,*
> *Edgar DeVos, Senator of the Sixth Republic*

It was, without a doubt, the most ridiculous missive the queen had ever laid eyes on.

"He cannot be serious." The sun was hardly in the sky and already Elodie was facing threats of racketeering. She had expected it to take longer, to prove herself a global threat.

"Ellie?" Brianne's eyes were wide as she watched her sister pace. "What is it?"

"That boy from Ethliglenn believes he is owed my hand in marriage."

"Tell him to jump in a lake," Cleo said, gesturing for Elodie to hand over the letter.

"With stones in his pockets," Brianne muttered.

Elodie's hands began to tremble. "This is unbelievable."

"What's unbelievable?" Tal had returned with Rob in tow.

"Edgar DeVos unkindly requests that I honor our engagement," Elodie sputtered. "Or else."

"What are you going to do?" he asked, as Cleo passed the letter to Rob.

"Ignore him," Elodie answered immediately. "If he thinks this will garner a reaction, he's an even bigger fool than I believed."

"You should respond to him," Rob said, addressing her directly for the first time in over a week. "He's hurt. Perhaps you should apologize."

"What could I possibly have to apologize for?" She turned toward Tal, who glanced deferentially at Elodie's brother. "Don't tell me you agree with Rob?"

"*I* certainly don't," Cleo said darkly.

"Nor me," Brianne confirmed.

Tal looked uncomfortable. "If you don't address this, Edgar might make your life difficult. He does nothing to veil his threats."

Elodie gritted her teeth. "The two of you must think me as weak as he does," she said finally. "I'm not going to roll over so he can bite at my underbelly. I am a Warnou woman. I *make* threats—I don't give in to them."

"I urge you to reconsider, Elodie," Rob said softly. "You're getting emotional, which can cloud your judgment."

"And I urge you to keep your opinions to yourself," Elodie snapped. Their lack of solidarity left her feeling exposed. She needed to finish getting dressed. "Everyone out. I've got an orphanage to christen and a country to run. I do not have time to humor hurt feelings." She swallowed the lump forming in her throat. "The

Queen of Velle will not be swayed by idle threats. Not from Edgar DeVos, and not from any of you." She scowled at the bewildered faces of her siblings and Tal. "All of you! Out!"

When at last Elodie was alone, she allowed herself exactly ten seconds of emotion. Then she used Edgar's letter to wipe away her tears and threw the offending message into the fire.

3

Sabine spent days poring over scripture, searching for anything that might help her understand the Second Son's threat. It had been nearly a week since her sermon in the city square, and thus far she had come up empty-handed. The *Book of the New Maiden* offered little insight into Sebastien's temperament. Ruti, one of the New Maiden's seven Favoreds, had focused her transcription so intently on Her word that the man who would become the Second Son was described only in errant adjectives.

There was little of Her character, either. The New Maiden might have been anyone, a faceless girl upon whom the world projected their need for guidance. That sort of belief—in what *could be* rather than what *was*—had always been difficult for Sabine to stomach.

She much preferred to focus on the present: the wooden pew beneath her, the scripture in her hands, the call of the seagulls muffled by the stained glass windows.

Harborside's house of worship was her favorite among Velle's chapels and undoubtedly the smallest. She craved its snug embrace each time her footsteps echoed in the airy churches of the other districts, where clergies and worshippers varied almost as much as the architecture. The Arts and Manufacturing Districts had embraced her handily, while those in the Garden and Commerce Districts had been more selective in their welcome. Sabine had not received a single invitation to the royal chapel since her ascension.

It was no matter. She much preferred the stoic company of Silas and the dependable grit of her neighborhood. She coveted the sighs of relief from dockworkers who ducked through the door to gain reprieve from the sun. She cherished the sparkle in the eyes of children as they wandered inside to gape at the colorful mural on the ceiling.

That was how faith was made. Through tiny comforts and moments of awe. Surely, Sabine told herself as the great wooden door opened with a *whoosh*, the Second Son knew nothing of community. He could not dismantle what He did not understand.

A trio of men entered the chapel, younger than her father, older than her brother. All three removed their hats to reveal sunburned cheeks and peeling noses, made all the more noticeable by their cheerful red pocket squares. Two slipped into an empty pew. One paused before the prayer candles, lips moving silently. Sabine peeled her gaze away to afford him a modicum of privacy.

"Maiden?" She had not heard the woman approach, so careful were her footsteps. "I do not mean to interrupt, I had only hoped..." Her eyes flickered to the confessional. "Have you the time?"

"Always." Sabine closed the *Book of the New Maiden* and tucked it carefully back beneath the pew. She led the way to the booth, ensuring the woman was settled before closing herself into the other side. Sabine traced the intricate divider between them, the craftsmanship impossibly delicate. The confessional booth was a sacred place. It was here that she could do true good as the New Maiden.

"Forgive me." Safely tucked away in the confessional, the woman's voice began to tremble. "It has been so long since my last confession, for until now I had nowhere to go." The woman's voice lilted like the sea, and she had the soft *r*'s of the neighborhood. This was Harborside, after all.

Sabine caught a whiff of smoke. Strange, that she would smell the strike of a match from the other side of the chapel.

"Not only did I steal herbs from my neighbor's garden," the woman continued with a reassuring obliviousness, "but I used them on my husband. I brewed a potion to keep him asleep so that I might have a few moments when his hands were not on me in anger."

Sabine clenched her fists until her nails left crescent moons in the meat of her palms. The litany of women who had come through pleading forgiveness for their pain, their emotions, and their wanting left her exhausted and devastated in equal measure. These women were hurt by cruel hands and judgmental tones, were embarrassed by their own ambition, were made to doubt themselves by those who feared their success. It was a suffering Sabine knew well, one she would not wish upon anyone.

"You need not apologize," Sabine said plainly, for the woman had begun to sniffle on the other side of the screen. "Indeed, it is your husband who should be begging forgiveness, for putting *you* in such a position."

22

"Oh, Maiden, no, I'm certain I deserved it," the woman said quickly.

"Do not grasp for meaning where there is none," Sabine began, but her thought was interrupted by pounding footsteps. Silas wrenched aside the curtain and pulled the New Maiden to her feet. Smoke slithered about her like a shroud.

The bishop's sleeve was pressed against her nose and mouth. Her eyes were wide with panic. She extricated the stunned woman in the confessional with similar swiftness, gesturing for them both to follow her to safety.

The altar was alight, a halo of flames encircling the effigy of the New Maiden that hung upon the back wall. The prayer candles had been overturned; wax oozed across the floor, held back by a dam of broken glass. An astringent scent rushed Sabine's sense. Upon closer inspection, she saw that the pews were soaked with barrel brew, the clear, noxious alcohol crafted in the hulls of disreputable merchant ships. Unless a person was courting death, the stuff was no good for drinking. It was, however, perfect for starting fires.

Once she confirmed that Silas and the woman had made it out, Sabine turned back.

The Harborside chapel had been her first achievement as the New Maiden. She had helped scrub the brick clean, had repaired the curtains, had painted the walls. She had made the house of worship a home.

Just as the New Maiden had watched the Lower Banks burn, so Sabine now witnessed the destruction in her own neighborhood. She kicked at the shattered shards of the prayer candles, eye catching on a blood-red kerchief. She had seen the color before, tucked into the coat pocket of the man who struck the match. It felt too bold a signal to be coincidence.

Sabine reached for it but was stopped by a firm hand on her shoulder. Everywhere she looked, Sabine saw red. The flames that devoured her chapel, the handkerchief on the floor, the uniform of the Loyalist who restrained her.

"Let me go." She squirmed in the soldier's grip, but the fingers only squeezed tighter.

"Does the New Maiden believe she can walk through fire?" It was his voice that stopped her flailing.

"What are you doing here?" Her suspicion was thick as tar.

"My job," Tal said dispassionately, guiding the New Maiden away from the hungry lick of the flames and releasing her into the hazy afternoon.

A crowd had gathered on the other side of the street to gape at the destruction.

"Aren't you going to do something?" Sabine shrieked. Several Loyalists stood among the motionless spectators. "If we make a line and pass buckets from the harbor, surely we can—"

"Sabine," Silas said solemnly, putting her hand on the girl's shoulder. "It's too late."

"No," Sabine said, irritated eyes watering from the smoke. She cursed the empty tears that painted her cheeks. They held no emotion, only inadequacy. The ink had barely dried on the hymnals, and now they were ashes. The pews had just been polished, and now they were dust.

Silas turned toward her, fear scrawled across her face. "Maiden, who would do this?"

Sabine knew the answer. But she wanted proof.

A quick scan of the surrounding area offered her exactly what she was looking for. A piece of parchment had been nailed to the door of the boarded-up tavern across the alley. Even from a distance, Sabine could make out the outline of an insect with spotted wings. She marched up to the building and tore the paper from its nail, crumpling the page in the process. This time, the Second Son's message was different, but no less pointed: *Fathers do not wish for daughters*, it read above the moth. *Instead, they pray for Sons.*

4

The New Maiden tracked ash into the Queen of Velle's quarters.

"You look like you walked through all twelve hells," Elodie said, glancing up from the sofa where she was considering a request for resources from the province of Prottle.

"Feels like it, too." Sabine flung herself onto the settee opposite, eyes fixed on the ceiling.

Elodie set down the correspondence and offered her full attention to the other girl. "There was a fire?" The sleeves of the New Maiden's purple silk vestment were singed, and she stank of smoke.

Sabine made a face. "What gave you that idea?"

Although the New Maiden's voice was steady, her distress was tangible in the way her left foot shook on its axis. Elodie squeezed in beside Sabine on the velvet cushion, placing a hand firmly on the other girl's knee. "Are you all right?"

The New Maiden stilled. "No." She fixed her gaze on the opposite wall, brown eyes empty. "It was the chapel, El. In Harborside."

Renovating the musty, padlocked structure had been their first initiative as Church and crown. Sabine had been the one to throw open the doors in welcome. As sunlight spilled upon the entryway, the New Maiden might have been made of gold, so brightly did she shine alongside the rewards of her first action.

"An accident?" The queen's voice was too hopeful. Its high-pitched waver made Elodie cringe.

"Arson," Sabine confirmed darkly.

Elodie forced her features to steady even as her pulse raced. "Surely not." More likely it had been a prayer candle blown over by the wind.

"They doused the sanctuary in barrel brew," Sabine insisted. "This was planned."

Elodie swore. Perhaps she had not taken Edgar's idle threat seriously enough. "Marguerite!"

Her lady-in-waiting appeared instantly. "Yes, Majesty?"

"Draw the New Maiden a bath." At Sabine's raised eyebrow, she added a belated "Please."

"Your privilege is astounding," Sabine sighed, rubbing her neck.

"And your neglect of your own basic necessities is tiresome," Elodie countered, using her fingers to work out a particularly pesky knot in the New Maiden's shoulder.

"The people cannot worship a figure they do not relate to or understand," Sabine said through a muffled groan of relief. The criticism held all the threat of a butter knife, but it sliced Elodie's fragile ego as though it were a sword.

"I suppose it is a good thing I do not wish for them to worship me, then," the queen said curtly, rising to her feet.

"Elodie, stop." Sabine was suddenly beside her, fingers twisting carefully into hers. She put a hand to the queen's cheek, her calloused fingers sending a thrill skittering down Elodie's spine. "You took a blow I had meant for myself."

Elodie leaned into the other girl's touch. "Aren't we a pair? That means your troubles are mine as well."

A delicate cough. Marguerite had reappeared in the doorway. "The bath is ready, Majesty."

Elodie led Sabine to the bedroom, where the tub sat behind a folding partition. The steaming water smelled of lavender. She brushed the New Maiden's smoke-stained robe from her shoulders with a soft *thump*. The simple wool dress beneath had been untouched by the flames.

"Is that all the help you're going to give me?" Sabine's brown eyes glittered.

The queen suppressed a smile. "Best never to be presumptuous." Sabine's fingers tightened around Elodie's wrist. That was answer enough.

As she unfastened the line of buttons on the back of Sabine's dress, Elodie marveled at the gentle arc of the other girl's spine. She brushed her lips across Sabine's shoulder blade, the protruding bone as delicate as a baby bird's wing.

When the dress, too, fell to the ground, Elodie's gasp caught in her throat. She was overwhelmed by the sight of Sabine's soft curves, wanted to commit her body to memory, to worship at the altar of her physical form. Sabine crossed her arms over her chest. "I'm feeling a bit exposed."

Elodie's tongue soured with dismay. "I thought you wanted me to stay."

"Not stay *dressed*." Her face split into a wicked grin.

Elodie shed her own gown, and together they sank into the bath, Sabine's back against the queen's chest. Elodie wrapped her arms tightly around the girl's middle, pulling her closer. Her scalp still carried the scent of smoke. It was lucky that the arson had not led to murder, that the New Maiden had emerged unscathed.

Sabine tapped her finger idly on the water's surface. The motion sent ripples all the way to their toes.

Every action had its consequence. The queen had not responded to the letter from Edgar DeVos—an undiplomatic action that may have stoked the boy's anger into a raging flame. Elodie was a fool if she did not draw the logical conclusion.

She cupped her hands into the bath to gather water and send it trickling down Sabine's head, a shoddy mimicry of the baptismal ritual used to induct clergy into the New Maiden's fold. The bathwater grew murky as she scrubbed the soot from Sabine. Elodie's mood darkened, too. Her plan to ignore Edgar was no longer possible, not if defending her pride put Sabine in harm's way.

Once the water ran clear through Sabine's hair, Marguerite brought towels and long dressing gowns. They settled at the foot of Elodie's bed, wet hair soaking the fabric around their shoulders.

"Can I ask you for something?" Sabine's gaze was fixed on the gold threaded quilt.

Elodie frowned at the pretense. "What's the use of being queen if I cannot help those I..." She paused, trying the word she meant on her tongue before she spoke it. But in the end, she cowered. "Care for?"

Sabine's breath hitched, a soft exhale that Elodie thought might be disappointment. Her stomach twisted regretfully, but the moment had passed.

"I need a safe place for my family to stay. This time, my enemies came for the church, but next time…" There was no need for her to finish.

It was so obvious a request that Elodie frowned. "The south wing is always available for guests."

"It isn't an imposition?"

Tera Warnou would have turned up her nose at the thought of Harborsiders wandering the halls of Castle Warnou. But Elodie did not hesitate. "I would do anything for you."

Sabine pressed her lips to Elodie's. The queen lost herself in the New Maiden's kiss. Let it wash away the soot and the grime that clung to her soul. When their embrace ended, she emerged anew. She sent Sabine with Marguerite to procure a coach that would collect her family. Then the queen finished getting dressed. She had business to attend to.

Elodie was intercepted three times on the way to her study. First by a doctor she had asked to examine Brianne. The youngest Warnou's vitals were sound, the woman insisted—she merely required rest. It was an odd assessment of a patient who had spent days suspended in sleep, but even as Elodie accepted the prognosis, she made plans to procure a second opinion. Next, she was stopped by the castle steward. Bale was old as sin and convinced that all the servants were pilfering the royal silverware. Elodie dismissed him easily with a mumbled excuse. Finally, outside her study door, the Queen of Velle was detained by Maxine.

The broad-shouldered Loyalist nearly barreled her over as she turned down the corridor. Elodie's face softened in apology until she registered with whom she had nearly collided.

"Hello, soldier." Elodie pursed her lips. The last time she'd shared air with Maxine, the Loyalist had bound her hands and locked her in the royal chapel.

Maxine was nothing if not disciplined. She offered Elodie a terse bow. "Majesty. Our meeting is fortuitous." She tossed her long braid over her shoulder. "I have something for you."

Elodie raised an eyebrow. "Is it an apology?"

"A letter came for you," Maxine continued, as though the queen had not spoken. She produced a thick envelope from her breast pocket and handed it over. "I'm not an errand boy, you know."

"I won't tip you, then." Elodie turned the envelope over, breath catching as she glimpsed its serpentine seal. "Actually"—she scowled up at the Loyalist—"here's a tip: If you don't apologize for participating in my detainment at the Church's request, I will remove you from your post. You do not want me as your enemy, Maxine."

Maxine's jaw clenched. "I apologize, Your Majesty," she finally managed, Elodie's threat decidedly greater than the blow to her pride. The guard had no way to know the true subject of Elodie's ire was the boy whose unsteady scrawl had spilled ink blots across the envelope in her hand.

"Very well." Elodie sighed. The outburst had offered her no relief. "You are dismissed. If you see Tal, send him to me."

"You seem to have forgiven *his* betrayal," Maxine muttered darkly as she turned away. It was not worth Elodie's energy to engage her further.

The moment she stepped through the door into her study, the queen tore open Edgar's letter with her teeth.

Elodie Dearest,

I fear my last correspondence failed to inspire you.
When I speak of marriage, it is much more than our
union. Indeed, I foresee the foundation of an empire:
Velle and the Sixth Republic united by land and love.
Perhaps your reluctance comes because you simply can-
not see my vision? I've enclosed a map illustrating my
tactical ambitions. Once our armies are united, we will
move westward until the continent is ours.

Elodie extracted the map and spread it on her desk. Edgar had used ink to darken the edges of both Velle and the Sixth Republic. Alone, they were separate stars, but Edgar had traced their borders to sketch a second country, this one a constellation of landmarks. The boy was an artist.

He was also completely mad if he believed the Sixth Republic and Velle had the resources to conquer the continent. His strategy was as sophisticated as a wooden sword.

If, however, the letter continued, *your silence stems*
from bitterness as I suspect, I will send word to the rest
of the Republics that my wife-to-be is most uncoopera-
tive. They—unlike you—recognize marriage as a vital
mode of political growth, and so they've agreed to help
bring you home where you belong. Unfortunately, they
will require payment for their troubles. Everything has
a cost. And so, should you refuse to align yourself with

me, I shall distribute Velle's land among them equally. If I cannot have my empire, at least I will have my wife.

Faithfully yours,
Edgar DeVos

Elodie did not need to reference Edgar's map to understand the implications of this far more realistic threat of invasion: The Republics surrounded Velle like a waxing crescent moon of overthrown monarchies. Her country was backed into a corner, its only escape the sea. If Edgar truly could wrangle the other five Republics, Velle's current military strategy would need to be dramatically reconfigured.

She penned a hasty letter to Rob's father, the highest-ranking general in Velle's army, requesting a meeting the following afternoon. Then Elodie Warnou lay down on the floor.

That was how Tal found her, nearly an hour later, Edgar's letter crumpled in her fist.

"Give that to me." He extracted the paper gently, frowning at Edgar's shoddy penmanship. His disapproval did not last long. At the letter's second line, Tal began to laugh.

"He's attempting a coup," he said, struggling to breathe through his mirth. "Edgar DeVos can hardly order his toy soldiers into formation, let alone a real army, yet he believes he could be an emperor. Oh, Lo, this is rich."

"I've written to General Garvey," she told him.

"I hardly think that's necessary." Tal chuckled, eyes still on Edgar's letter.

Elodie bristled at Tal's easy dismissal of her concerns. "The letter is already sent," she lied. "Don't tell Rob."

At any mention of his father, Elodie's already sensitive brother grew as delicate as spun sugar. Despite the general's best efforts, Rob refused to enlist. It was an especially sore subject considering that Cade, Rob's older half brother, had followed in their father's footsteps. Rob was the family's outlier, and he suffered for it.

"Of course." Tal finally put the letter down and extended a hand to help her off the floor. "I'm glad you did not marry Edgar DeVos," he said seriously, when they were face-to-face.

"Me too," Elodie said, unnerved by his closeness. She adjusted her skirt, taking a surreptitious step away.

"You deserve more than a fool."

"I do," Elodie agreed. Sabine was far better than anything she deserved. Theirs was the bond that could birth an empire. Theirs the partnership that could stage a coup. Where Edgar's threats were empty, the New Maiden's promises were a shield.

Elodie would do whatever it took to ensure theirs was the love that endured.

5

The Anders family were not prepared for the finery that awaited them in Castle Warnou.

Their quarters in the south wing were larger than the Harborside apartment five times over. Clothes tailored to their exact measurements had been hung in each bedroom, where the mattresses were almost obscene in their plumpness. Leather-bound books lined the shelves in the shared sitting room, crystal vases housed blooming bouquets of flowers, and on a glass end table sat a plate of pepper tarts with crust so intricate they might have been sculptures. For people who had spent so much of their lives wanting, it was an embarrassment of riches.

"Oh no, dear," Orla Anders insisted, shooing the chambermaid away from the hearth. "I can do that myself." She plucked the dustpan from the astonished girl's grip and began to sweep away the ashes.

"Oh, but your dress, marm," the young woman protested, eyes widened with fear.

Sabine's mother chuckled. "Nothing left of the skirt to ruin. They're all patches." Hunched in front of the fireplace, Orla might have been a castle employee, rather than a guest.

"Am I even allowed to sit on this?" Artur gestured to a couch, its fabric hand-embroidered with daffodils.

"Only after you've burned those pants," Katrynn teased. The eldest Anders sibling had already traded her hand-me-downs for a midnight-blue ball gown. She waltzed around the room. Sabine gave her a twirl, the skirt fanning out in a spectacular show. Katrynn clapped gleefully. "I think I'm going to like it here."

"Don't get too comfortable," Sabine said darkly. "I brought you here for protection, not frivolity. And you must promise not to steal anything." She looked pointedly at her brother, who had already begun casing the room, opening every drawer and peering behind every oil painting. Artur, now examining a silver letter opener with interest, let it clatter back onto the desktop.

"Trust no one," Katrynn said, practicing her curtsy. "Understood. Would you like me to take a vow of silence as well?"

Sabine rolled her eyes. "I'm only trying to protect you, Rynn."

"And you're very sweet for that, Bet." She gently tugged a strand of Sabine's brown hair. "But we're all right." She tapped her side. "Anders family rule number one."

Sabine laughed, despite herself. She could still recall her father, sitting at the kitchen table with his three children at his feet like ducks in a row. *Now, if you only listen to me once,* he'd said to their six wide eyes, *listen to me now. There's plenty in this world that will harm you. You can fight it, tooth and nail, but in the end, it's your gut that'll save you.* He'd tapped his left side, just as Katrynn had done. *Rule number one, my chickadees: Only the shrewd survive.*

Sabine's sister was right. Her family's intuition was blade-sharp. That discernment would be their saving grace.

Her relief was interrupted by a knock on the door. The chambermaid, still watching helplessly as Sabine's aging mother usurped her duties, hurried toward it. On the other side were the two younger Warnou sisters. Cleo carried a bouquet of blue flowers while Brianne clung to her sister's shadow.

"Hello." Cleo smiled brightly, stepping forward to press the flowers into Katrynn's arms. "We thought it only appropriate to check on the comfort of the castle's newest guests."

"Elodie asked us to look after you," Brianne whispered to Sabine conspiratorially. Warmth flooded Sabine's chest at having been so thoughtfully considered.

"How kind of you," Orla called from the floor.

"Mama." Sabine hurried over to help her mother rise to her feet. "Come and meet the princesses."

Introductions were exchanged. While Brianne hovered awkwardly near the door, Cleo and Katrynn bonded over complimenting each other's dress. Artur's ears burned red as he admired the middle Warnou sister. Orla cursed a new hole in her blouse.

"Can I help you locate something more suitable for dinner?" Cleo offered. "It tends to be a formal affair."

"Better get you changed, too, then," Katrynn said, eyes sweeping across Artur's grimy trousers.

Their tasks left Sabine alone with Brianne. Sabine approached the girl gently, as she would a wounded bird. "How are you feeling?"

"I'm afraid to fall asleep," Brianne admitted. The bags beneath her eyes confirmed it. "I'm afraid of what I might see. What I might learn about the Second Son."

Sabine put a hand on the princess's trembling shoulder. Her carelessness had played a significant role in Brianne's enchanted slumber. Had she not been so enthralled by Elodie, she would not have mixed up the vial that had sent Brianne to the strange realm of suspension. Now the girl was haunted by murdered third daughters, the ranks of whom she had only just evaded.

"He will not hurt you, Bri," Sabine said gently. "His threat was meant for me."

"But if I'd never been born, you'd be safe," Brianne insisted. "He wouldn't have known. You might have stayed hidden."

"If it wasn't me, it would have been someone else," Sabine said honestly. "This conspiracy looms larger than any one of us."

"I'm afraid," Brianne whispered.

"Me too," Sabine said placatingly. But the emotion rang false. Without her darkness, the self-preservation upon which she used to rely had dulled. Brianne's fear tugged at Sabine's heartstrings, but she found it difficult to conjure a similar sense of dread. She could not comprehend the gravity of the Second Son's threat. Could not fight what she was unable to see.

"I wish there was something I could do to help," Brianne said.

Sabine could not bear to let the young girl's worry fester. Brianne's position had been exploited time and again: by the Church, by her birth order, by even her father and eldest sister.

"Actually"—the New Maiden paused—"there *is* one thing you can do."

Now that her family was safely settled, it was time to consider the fire's other casualty. Silas was a bishop without a parish. Sabine needed the woman by her side. If Silas could influence and observe Chaplain René, a conniving man whose actions did not serve Her word, so much the better.

Brianne nodded urgently. "Anything."

The New Maiden grinned. "Tell me where to find the Royal Chaplain."

Sabine immediately regretted refusing Brianne's offer to accompany her. The castle was a labyrinth—crowded with winding staircases and long corridors that all looked the same. She had chanted the directions to herself like a sea shanty, yet despite her best efforts, she ended up facing a dead end. To her left was a broad door, cracked just enough to reveal a lone figure with a familiar silhouette inside a training room.

Tal sparred with an invisible partner, sword slicing through the empty air. He was a trained fighter: his feet nimble, his stature controlled. His motions were beautiful, a choreographed dance Sabine found she was able to follow: *step, slice, jab, turn*. As she thought it, Tal spun to the left and caught sight of her staring from the other side of the door. He stopped moving, the dance abruptly ending.

Tal's menacing gaze was unsettling enough for Sabine to break the silence.

"Are you following me?"

Tal chuckled humorlessly. "I believe it is *you*, Maiden, who interrupted *my* training." He gestured to his position in the center of the room.

"What did the air do to offend you?"

Tal sheathed his sword. "Never know when you'll need to battle the shadows." He shrugged. "Once, I was unable to protect myself. Now that I know how, I prefer to stay vigilant."

Sabine gaped at him. Tal moved about the world so easily in his Loyalist reds. His posture projected confidence, his easy arrogance implied entitlement. But in this moment—in this sentiment—they were the same. All Sabine's life she had warred against the shadows. Until now, she had never met anyone else who spoke so plainly about their own struggle.

"Shadows don't have swords, Tal."

"No, Maiden," he said, rubbing his right thumb across the sleeve of his left forearm surreptitiously. The memory of his pain was tangible, hinting at demons that still lurked beneath the surface. "They possess far more terrible ways to wound. But you already know that, don't you?"

There was a flutter of familiarity in his words. Tal had sounded just like her darkness, hissing yet seductive in his subtle taunting. She fought the urge to step toward him. To rekindle the insecurity she had once embraced. Instead, she cleared her throat, and the tension that had filled the room broke like a summer storm.

Tal fiddled with the gold chain around his neck. "What are you doing here, Sabine?"

"I'm staying in the castle indefinitely. I hope that won't be a problem?"

"Certainly not, Maiden." His smile was all teeth. "Any friend of

Elodie's is a friend of mine." Sabine thought it best not to correct him on the parameters of her relationship with the queen. "But I meant here, in the training room."

Her cheeks flushed. "Took a wrong turn. I'm looking for the chapel."

"Of course you are." Tal chuckled dryly. "Head back down the corridor and make a right. You'll come to a gray door whose handle sticks. Give it a good push and you'll find yourself in the courtyard. The chapel is just past the mausoleum." Sabine blinked at him. "I grew up here," he added. "I know my way around."

"Thank you." She nodded curtly. "I'll get out of your way before you decide to use me as target practice." She could feel Tal's eyes on her until she turned the corner.

Tal's directions were sound and soon Sabine found herself outside. Moonlight reflected off the fountain, painting the royal garden silver. Fronds sparkled with dew and the air held the fresh, round scent of life. Precisely as he'd said, the white marble mausoleum sat in the center of the expansive courtyard. Just beyond it, the church was equally opulent, with tall windows and gold leaf plating on every surface.

The New Maiden's footsteps echoed in the high-ceilinged sanctuary. Bergamot wafted down the aisle while tapers flickered in their sconces and shadows pooled beneath the pews. The room was empty, save for one man who knelt before the altar, head bent.

"Chaplain?" The man stiffened.

"The New Maiden herself." The Chaplain's voice rang out as he rose to his feet. "To what do I owe the pleasure?"

Sabine smiled serenely. "I have not found a moment to connect with you. But our meeting cannot be delayed any longer. Now that I am residing in the palace, the Royal Chaplain will become my right hand."

The holy man arched an eyebrow. "I did not think the New Maiden would ever leave Harborside."

"Nor I," Sabine said, truthfully. "But the decision was made for me. You heard about the church, I presume?" She parsed his expression for a hint of recognition.

While the Second Son's prophet had yet to reveal himself, Sabine had suspected the Chaplain the moment Brianne issued the third daughters' warning. René's actions during his daughter's incapacitation had been telling. He had ruled as Queen's Regent, had claimed to be Her voice, had not even tried to wake Brianne. It was clear the Chaplain did not serve the New Maiden. What remained to be seen was whether René followed the Second Son or was loyal only to himself.

"Yes," the Chaplain answered her probing blithely. "Pity."

"Your sincerity is noted," Sabine said sardonically.

"There will always be detractors," the Chaplain continued. "It's what you do with their doubt that makes a difference."

She folded her arms across her chest. "And what would you recommend?"

"Not to get too comfortable."

A moth with lace-thin wings hit the window with a nearly inaudible *thump* as it scrambled desperately toward the candlelight. Sabine pursed her lips at the subtle reminder of what—*who*—she was up against.

The Chaplain was studying her intently. "You've seen them, then."

"The posters? Yes." Sabine had not learned much of value from her father, but she knew it was important to never show an opponent her hand. "A fleeting threat. True believers will find no reason to stray."

"You are young," he said darkly, "and so naive. This is only the beginning." His eyes glimmered ruthlessly.

"You're right," Sabine agreed. "I have only just begun to make my mark. Things will change, and soon."

"Do not mistake emotions for strategy," the Chaplain warned. "Some believe they make a leader weak."

Sabine could not help but laugh. Her emotions were the reason she was in this position at all. "Those who truly believe in Her righteousness know I have nothing to prove."

"Are you accusing me of something, Maiden?" The Chaplain glowered down at her. "If so, please do speak your mind."

That was invitation enough for Sabine to air her suspicions. "You spent so many years devoted to the New Maiden. You were certainly invested as the father of the prophecy. Yet since I ascended, I've seen none of that self-same piety. Surely your faith is not so fickle?"

René's expression simmered with fury. "What you deem fickle, I call discerning."

"What I'm hearing," Sabine said, raising her eyebrows, "is that you worship the myth, not the Maiden. Your faith lies only in what you can control."

The Chaplain advanced on her, face reddening. "Do not think for a moment," he said, "that I could not control *you* if I wished." His breath was hot upon her cheek. "I was granted this role because of my discernment and my loyalty. I never favored the New Maiden. My life's work is in service of *Him*."

The spark of triumph in his eyes extinguished as his confession echoed in the eaves. Sabine's expression hardened. René could not remain in Her service. The truth was too damning. Judging from the venomous expression on the Chaplain's face, he knew it, too.

"I accept your resignation," Sabine said, ripping the aubergine sash from René's shoulder. "Effective immediately, you are dismissed as Velle's Royal Chaplain."

6

Velle had been at peace for most of Elodie's life, so she'd had little reason to frequent the War Room. As she entered the dark, polished space the next day, she admired the wooden walls, brass fixtures, and sprawling maps crafted by Cleo's father, a renowned cartographer. A wide table built from peich-nat trees sat in the center, the spiral wood grain a dizzying focal point of an already striking room.

Ten chairs were arranged around the table. Three were already occupied. At the head sat General Garvey, a gruff, mustached man of fifty. His red uniform boasted more gold than the royal coffers, and each time he moved, his medals clattered like the wind chimes Rob often used as percussion.

Despite her plea to Tal, Elodie's brother was there, too, seated as far from his father as the room allowed. His mouth was pressed in the tight pinch only the general seemed able to elicit from his son. The stern line of his lips further cemented at the sight of his older sister. Elodie had neglected to repair their relationship after she had used Sabine's tears to put Brianne to sleep. Their rapport was still jagged—a shattered mirror no longer reflecting the full picture.

Across the table from Rob sat Tal. In the presence of his former commander, his posture was impeccable, his spine stick-straight, his shoulders so still they could balance an egg. When at last he met Elodie's accusing eye, his expression was sheepish.

"Your Majesty." The general rose to his feet and offered her a stiff salute. "You were just a child the last time I set eyes upon you."

"General." Elodie gave the man a half curtsy before taking the seat beside him. She did not wish to speak of her childhood, to entertain frivolous memories of birthday parties and lingonberry tarts. "Thank you for answering my call."

"*You* called for him?" Rob's stony expression shattered at this perceived betrayal.

"Anything for Velle, Your Majesty," the general responded, ignoring his son's outburst. "My"—he cleared his throat, looking deeply uncomfortable—"condolences about your mother." His eyes swept across Rob before falling to rest decisively on the tabletop. "She was a fine woman. She would be so proud, seeing you strategize together now."

Regret clouded the air like incense, suffocating and difficult to dispel. Despite sharing the same physical space, Rob and his father were visibly divided, the general a solitary fortress of emotion whose walls had yet to be breached.

"How would you know?" The quiet righteousness of Rob's anger swirled about him like a cloak.

Elodie shot Tal an exasperated look. This sort of outburst was the reason she had wanted to keep Rob ignorant to his father's visit.

Tal rapped the table with his knuckles. "Perhaps we should begin?"

It was then that Cleo and Brianne burst into the room, Edgar's note in tow. Elodie spread the boy's maps on the table before her while her sisters claimed their seats.

The general frowned, not at the maps' ink-darkened borders, but at the presence of the two youngest Warnou children. "Is this really appropriate, Your Majesty?"

Cleo's and Brianne's expressions shuttered.

"They are my council just as much as Rob," Elodie explained. "Their attendance is my preference."

The general frowned at his son. "Most unusual." Although his expression remained troubled, he did not push further.

"I have called you here," Elodie said, drawing the room's attention back toward her, "because I have reason to believe we may soon face an invasion from the Republics."

"Nonsense." The general's tone was incredulous. "Velle has been at peace with the Republics since the inception of the First. I see no reason why that should change."

"The Sixth Republic has been sending me threats," Elodie explained, gesturing to Edgar's letter in the center of the table. "Edgar DeVos believes he is owed my hand in marriage. His intention is to unite our countries by matrimony and begin building an empire. Failing that, his contingency plan is to enlist the other five Republics to assist in physically claiming me."

She handed the missive to the general for review. He took in a single line before he began to chuckle. As he continued to read, his laughter grew. Tal nudged her foot beneath the table, as though to say *told you*.

Elodie bristled at their amusement.

"He's just having a bit of fun," the general finally said, tossing the letters to the center of the table. "Edgar is a fine young man with a sound mind. He has a flair for the dramatic, yes. But what boy doesn't when it comes to women?" Rob cleared his throat uncomfortably. "You hurt his feelings and so he has retaliated with a childish outburst. But your love life does not warrant military interference."

Elodie turned to Rob. "You said that I should take him seriously," she accused.

Her brother shrugged, avoiding eye contact with the queen and the general at all costs. "I just told you to apologize."

"But I didn't *do* anything," Elodie said through gritted teeth. "*He's* the one threatening *me*."

"Wars are not waged over bruised egos, Elodie," the general said, none too gently.

"'Your Majesty' will do." She was losing control, not only of the room but of her patience. "Tal?" She turned to the one other person with military experience.

"It's a waste of resources, Lo." Tal at least sounded apologetic. "Think of the soldiers you'd have to feed and clothe and arm."

"You all would have him take me, then?" Fury spewed from Elodie's tongue, hot and metallic and impossible to swallow. The night of Brianne's coronation, Edgar had cornered her in the garden. She could still smell the peich-nat on his breath, trace the pattern of the bruises his fingers had left around her wrist. "You would subject me to life as a hostage in the Sixth Republic?"

General Garvey, too, was losing his patience. "The Republics are complex governments, Majesty. They do not have time to cater to the whims of a boy obsessed with some silly girl who broke his heart."

With her last few ounces of composure, Elodie kept her voice measured. "We'll see how silly I appear when Edgar steals me from my bed. When this novice despot burns our castle to the ground with the help of his neighboring allies."

Rob stifled an eye roll. "Surely it won't come to that."

"No, it won't," Elodie snapped. "Because your father is going to send troops to patrol our border." She used the top of her palm to smack the table the way her mother had once done. The sound was resonant, and better, it did not hurt. "You will not let Edgar DeVos cross the line, General. That is an order, from your queen and commander." If her council was not willing to protect her, Elodie had no choice but to take her safety in her own hands.

The general sighed heavily, pinching the bridge of his nose. At last, he nodded. "As you wish." He got heavily to his feet, his medals tinkling as he adjusted the collar of his uniform. He turned to his son. "Robin, should you care to accompany me back to the front lines, there is always a place for you by your brother's side." The silence that ensued was louder, even, than the red blooming on Rob's cheeks.

"No, thank you, sir," he mumbled. "I have no interest in war."

"Most of us don't, son," the general said wearily. "But the world gives us no choice." He cast a rueful glance at Elodie.

"General." Elodie dipped her head in dismissal, folding and unfolding her hands upon the tabletop. "I look forward to your reports from the field. Take strength."

Using the final drops of her patience, Elodie waited for the door to close behind General Garvey before rounding on Tal and Rob. The two of them had been so useless as to be offensive.

"If this is how you treat your queen," Elodie spat, embarrassed by the general's dismissal of her fear, "I'll have you expelled from my council. Speak in my defense or not at all."

"El—"

"Lo—"

"Do not undermine me with pet names at a time like this." Rob opened his mouth, but Elodie held up a finger to stop him. "You do not know what it feels like to be preyed upon by a man who confidently intends to own you," she continued, "a boy who thinks he deserves you as his birthright. You have never needed to imagine what happens if he wins." The release of her anger left her cold. "Get out of my sight."

This time they obeyed, leaving Elodie alone with her sisters.

"Do you really think he'll come for you?" Brianne whispered.

"I don't know, Bri," Elodie admitted.

At this point, she had no choice but to take the threat seriously. More and more it seemed that being queen meant defending unfavorable opinions, fighting to convince others of a truth they could not—or would not—accept. As a monarch, she had expected to be met with collaboration and partnership. Instead, Elodie had never felt more alone. How had her mother lived like this for over twenty years? At this rate, Elodie might not survive a single season.

"Thank you for defending our presence." Cleo was picking at her cuticles.

"I always will, Cleo," Elodie said, looking at her sisters

mournfully. "You have my trust and you are my comfort. And so, I hope that when I ask you both to leave me now, you understand that it has nothing to do with either of you, and everything to do with me."

"We know, Ellie," Brianne said, almost reverently, as she got to her feet.

"Do not stew so long that you lose your tenderness," Cleo said, tapping Elodie on the nose.

That elicited a laugh from the queen. "What does that even mean?"

Cleo shrugged as she headed for the door. "Something Artur Anders said." Although her smile was placid, her eyes glittered mischievously. "I assume it has to do with meats, but what do I know of cookery."

Once alone, Elodie again resisted the urge to tear Edgar's letter into shreds. His slanting scrawl taunted her. She could not bear to look at the poisonous promises but knew better than to destroy the record of such a potent threat. She went searching for a hiding place, rattling the wooden panels and rifling through the sparse drawers.

She had nearly given up when she noticed a discoloration in the paneling where two walls met. The wood stain was a single shade too dark, the difference in color difficult to perceive where it rested near to the floor.

She squatted down, using her fingernails to peel back the wood, levering it until it gave. In the crevice sat a stack of letters tied up with string.

Alight with anticipation, Elodie opened the top letter to reveal words penned in her own mother's hand.

I have been a fool, Tera Warnou wrote, with no recipient indicated at the top of the letter, *waiting so long to write you. Without you, I have nowhere to turn. Without you, I have no one to trust. I pretend as though I am in control, but such delusions will not save me. I am constantly looking over my shoulder. Come back,* her mother wrote, *for a Warnou woman cannot rule alone.*

Elodie frowned. Although her mother had spent significant time raising Elodie to be a Queen's Regent, Tera Warnou's advisers had been discarded almost as frequently as her lovers. She had never trusted anyone the way she had Elodie. Strange, then, that she had committed her insecurities to writing, that she would detail the frustration that came from trying to balance life as a mother, a ruler, and a human being.

Even after scouring the entire stack of letters, Elodie was unable to identify their recipient. Still, Tera's words offered her eldest daughter comfort. Not once in her life had she found a crack in Tera Warnou's polished veneer. Thus, Elodie had held her rule to unmeetable standards, certain she was not strong enough to maintain her mother's legacy.

These letters told a different story, offering a record of a woman unmoored. Tera, too, had buckled beneath the weight of Velle's crown. Perhaps the two of them were not so different after all.

7

The bishop was not pleased by her promotion.

It was a perfect morning to deliver good news—brisk air carried the fresh scent of dew; crisp golden foliage crunched beneath their feet—but when Sabine presented Silas with the aubergine sash, the woman's face fell. The position of Royal Chaplain had only been vacant for two days, and already Sabine was losing control of her clergy.

"Sabine," Silas said carefully, peering past the New Maiden into the depths of the royal chapel, "what did you do?"

"I thought you would welcome this new responsibility." Sabine brushed imaginary dirt from her shoulder. "It's rather an important one, I'm told."

"There are many holy folk far more tenured than I," Silas said, sinking heavily into a pew. "Maiden, I have not earned the honor."

It did not seem so complicated. Where the New Maiden had Her Favoreds, so, too, should Sabine surround herself with those she trusted to ensure Her work was done. "Silas, you're the only one I am certain of. I need you by my side."

Silas frowned. "And what has become of René?"

"René holds other loyalties," Sabine said darkly.

The older woman stilled at the implication. "He is the moth?" It was the first time Silas had mentioned the posters.

"I cannot prove it," Sabine said. "But I have my suspicions."

Silas sighed wearily. "I suppose you had no choice. Still, you should have consulted me."

"Next time I find a wolf within my flock, Silas," Sabine said, offering the woman a hand, "you will be the first one I warn." She helped the new Royal Chaplain to her feet and led her toward the castle.

"Where are we going?" Silas's voice was tense as they ambled through the royal garden.

"To your quarters." Sabine plucked a pink camellia from a nearby shrub. "I know you are used to scarcity, so I hope you are not corrupted by Castle Warnou's opulence."

The Chaplain stopped walking. "Maiden, no," she said firmly. "I cannot accept."

"Nonsense." Sabine used the flower to wave away her protests. "Now do try and keep up. It's far too easy to get lost within these walls."

She led Silas through the innards of the castle, accustomed enough with her surroundings that she no longer questioned her instincts. The Chaplain's thin lips were pinched as she observed a smudged suit of armor, her wrinkles deepening as she frowned at the portraits hung in gilded frames. Finery, it seemed, made the holy woman uncomfortable.

Sabine hurried them up the stairs. She did not wish to offend Silas any further than she already had. In her haste, Sabine nearly collided headfirst with the queen.

"Oh, hello," Elodie said brightly as she steadied herself. She gave Sabine's hand a careful squeeze. The queen was dressed in an elaborate maroon gown accented with gold stitching. It boasted a train that required the oversight of two stewards.

"Majesty," piped up Marguerite, her lady-in-waiting, "if it pleases you, the ambassador was expecting us ten minutes ago."

"You're being far too polite, Marguerite," Cleo said from Elodie's other side. "El, you'd do well not to incite a political crisis over being tardy for tea."

"It's this dress," Elodie protested. "It is both oversized *and* too tight—tripping and suffocating me in equal measure."

"It's the only gown we have in Vathi colors," Cleo said, for what must have been the tenth time that morning based on the tension in her jaw.

"Well, it's flattering." Sabine's eyes followed the length of the dress's plunging neckline and the pale expanse of skin it exposed. A slither of wanting coiled in her belly. Elodie met her gaze with a similar hunger. Sabine's cheeks burned as bright as the queen's gown.

"Oh, now we're being terribly rude." Elodie had just noticed Silas, who, despite her towering height, had done her best to shrink back behind Sabine. "Who is your guest?"

"This is Silas," Sabine said, stepping aside. "Previously the bishop of Harborside's chapel."

"I was dismayed to hear about the fire," Elodie said. "Where are you stationed now?"

Sabine's heart skipped a beat. Although she had used Marguerite to secure Silas a room in the south wing, she had not actually informed Elodie of the change to the Church's leadership. It was not clear if their roles were intertwined enough to warrant an intimate level of consultation. But then, as she was the New Maiden, the Church was Sabine's purview. She had every right to make personnel changes the same way Elodie did with Velle's public servants.

"Silas has graciously accepted the role of Royal Chaplain," Sabine answered, relishing the flicker of pride that flashed across the queen's face. "Effective immediately."

"Welcome, Chaplain Silas," Elodie said, offering the woman an impressive curtsy. "I hope you'll be kinder to the Warnou family than your predecessor."

"It would be my honor," Silas returned Elodie's curtsy with surprising ease. Her eyes lingered on the queen.

"This has been lovely," Cleo said, looking perilously close to tears, "but we absolutely must go." She began to pull her sister down the corridor. Elodie turned over her shoulder to wave.

When they reached the Chaplain's quarters, Sabine addressed the woman plainly. "I know this is much to take in," she said, barreling past the Chaplain's protests, "but I would not ask if I did not have the need. You are good, and I require guidance. Please"—Sabine exhaled sharply—"have faith."

Without Silas by her side, Sabine could not keep the New Maiden's word afloat. Alone, she would drown from the effort.

"Of course, Maiden," the Chaplain said, solemnly. "Your will be done."

It wasn't. Three days later, Artur returned to the family's quarters, expression grim.

"Found this in the Manufacturing District," he said, producing a now familiar sheet of parchment. That cursed moth brought another new message, embittered words scrawled above and below the insect: *What She takes, He will return. What She replaces, He will reclaim.*

"There were others," Artur said, fussing with the collar of his fancy frock. "I took down as many as I could, but I didn't want anyone to notice me."

Sabine shook her head quickly. "No need to make yourself a target," she agreed. "I'd rather they only focus their attention on me." Orla Anders let out a soft hiccup that might have been a sob. Sabine put her hand on her mother's. "It's all right, Ma," she whispered softly. "They're only words."

But they weren't. The Second Son's threat had been swiftly exacted, as Sabine found later that day when she called on Silas in the royal chapel.

The candles were all extinguished, the hymnals closed, no incense lit. Silas knelt before the altar, lips moving soundlessly. She paused her prayer when the New Maiden approached.

"I have failed you," the Chaplain said, her usually impassive expression pained as she gestured to the frontmost pew. The dark washed wood was covered in squares of white fabric, shimmering like pearls in the daylight. The cloth was out of place, for the chapel's pews did not offer cushions.

"I don't understand."

"They're discarded vestments, Maiden," Silas said gravely. "Resignations across the country in protest of my appointment. There have been ten today already."

"Surely René was not so beloved?" Sabine offered the woman a lighthearted smile, which the Chaplain did not return.

"René was known," Silas said, tucking her short hair behind her ears. "They are"—she searched for the proper word—"*uncomfortable* with your choice."

"Why?"

"Maiden," Silas said softly, "not once in the history of Her Church has the position of Royal Chaplain been held by a woman."

Sabine blinked blankly. "But the Church *belongs* to a woman."

"Yet its terms of worship were created by a man," Silas corrected. "In Her memory. The clergy understand the Maiden as a figurehead, a silent artifact. You destroy that orderly illusion by having your own voice, by appointing yet another woman to the highest position in your Church."

"Am I to stay silent, then," Sabine challenged, "while others twist Her word for their own gain?"

The new Chaplain put a hand to her heart. "Maiden, I do not presume to tell you how to act. I only tell you what I know." She sighed wearily. "This upheaval is exactly what I was concerned about."

Sabine blinked at her. "You doubt my judgment, as they do?"

"Of course not, Maiden," Silas said, bowing her head reverently. Sabine was suspicious of such unflinching loyalty. Either Silas was indiscriminate to a fault, or worse, the Royal Chaplain did not trust Sabine with her truth.

Sabine now missed her darkness more than ever, craved the slippery sense of relief that washed over her when confronted with its candor. She was desperate for the emotion elicited from such sincerity. That space where her sadness had lived was now tormented with endless fog. Only once since its disappearance had she found anyone direct enough to incite that familiar feeling. Unfortunately, that person was one she did not particularly care for.

Soliciting reproach from a stranger was the sort of impulse her darkness would have instantly put to an end. Expecting a person to fill an emotional void was foolish. Dangerous, even. But without its voice in her ear, Sabine could not be bothered with self-preservation. And so, when she left the royal chapel, she did not retreat to her family's chambers. Instead, she headed for the training room in search of Tal.

The room was empty, save for the swords strapped to the walls. Silver blades glinted in the sunlight, leather handles stank of oil, wood gleamed with polish. The weapons were as beautiful as they were deadly, could carve right to the heart with one slip of a hand. Sabine observed them keenly, running a finger across the edge of a dagger. The blade sliced through the top layer of her skin but did not draw blood. She marveled at the cleanness of the cut.

"What are you doing?" Tal was leaning against the doorframe, watching her with amusement.

"Testing the blades," she said, as though the New Maiden had any business with swords.

"And?" Tal raised an eyebrow.

"They're perfect."

"Ought to be," he said, grabbing an axe from the wall. He sliced at the air like he himself was partially made of steel, wielded the axe like it was both craft and calling. "I sharpened them all myself."

"I didn't take you for the manual labor sort," Sabine said snidely. "Your boots are far too polished."

Tal smirked. "Did those myself, too." He returned the axe to the wall, trading it for a sleek sword. His hands were rough and calloused, nothing like the delicate digits of nobility. Now that she had located the first crack, Sabine could see the tiny traces of poverty in Tal's appearance. The collar of his coat had been repaired with thread a shade too light. The scuffs on the sole of his boots had been filled in with pitch. The lengths to which he had gone to disguise his shortcomings filled Sabine with an unexpected tenderness.

"You hide it well."

Tal cocked his head curiously. "What?"

"Your lineage."

"I am well-versed at keeping up appearances, Maiden," Tal said darkly. "Do you begrudge me for it?"

"On the contrary." Sabine discarded her cloak to reveal the patchwork dress beneath. It didn't feel right to constantly masquerade in the fine things provided by the palace. Not when so many still had nothing. "I am intimately acquainted with that reality."

"That's right," Tal said, sheathing his sword. "The New Maiden hails from Harborside. How could I forget?"

"I hope I never do," she said quietly. It was easy to get wrapped up in the niceties of the castle, how simple life was without the responsibility of survival. Yet an entire class of people lived in the palace only to serve, practically invisible. There was little difference in qualification for the role of queen and the role of scullery maid. Who held which came down to nothing more than luck.

"They'll never let you," Tal said, an edge to his voice. "No matter how desperately you wish to leave behind your old self, no matter how well you think you've blended in, there will always be a prying eye, a snide remark in the hall, a titter behind a hand. Anything that makes you different makes you a target. Elodie's mother tried to ban me from playing with her children, you know."

"I'm certain Elodie did not entertain such a command," Sabine said, thinking fondly of the queen's passion.

"That she did not." Tal laughed softly, a tenderness in his eye when the queen's name was spoken. "I was a nervous child, accident-prone, and frightened of the fire my blacksmith father used to forge." He pursed his lips. "I was not, according to my father, brave enough or clever enough to warrant the cost of keeping me fed. When your own family believes you're worth less than dust, you expect others to discard you just the same. But Elodie stomped right up to her mother and fought viciously to defend our friendship, even though at that point all I had ever done was sneak her sugar cubes from the stables. She used to suck on them while she thought, scrunching her eyebrows together."

He mimicked the expression, which made Sabine laugh outright.

"Elodie brings out the best in everyone," she said fondly.

"Indeed. Everyone loves her." His tone was bitter, as though he thought the queen ought to be his, alone, to admire.

Tal scoured the wall of weapons, selecting a small dagger. The handle was carved with intricate gold etching and set with a green stone. He crossed the room and pointed the dagger at her chest.

Sabine's breath caught in her throat. "What are you doing?" She knew how carefully Tal had sharpened those blades. He needed only to take a single step forward in order to plunge the dagger into her heart.

Tal spun the weapon in his hand so he could offer the handle to her. "You seemed so enamored by the weapons that I only wondered if you wished to hold one."

Pulse still racing, she closed her fingers around the hilt.

Tal made a soft clucking noise. "Not like that," he said, adjusting her grip. His touch was a spark of white-hot light. She jerked away as though she had been burned, sending the dagger clattering to the floor. Tal's eyes held hers. The hair on the back of Sabine's neck prickled at the intensity of his gaze.

It was nothing like the energy she felt when she touched Elodie. Nothing like the warm, toe-tingling comfort that the queen provided her. No, this was a searing pain. A branding. Sabine half expected to see the outline of his fingers on her own. But she was unmarked, the moment preserved only in the space between them.

Sabine looked away first. "I have to go."

Tal bent down to collect the weapon. "Next time, I'll teach you how to use it."

"Next time?" Sabine was surprised by the open invitation. She had expected Tal to find her tiresome. But judging by the curious expression on the boy's face, she was just as fascinating to Tal as he was to her.

"A soldier can never be too prepared, Sabine," Tal said, shrugging. "And by the look of those posters, your battle has only just begun."

It wasn't until she left the training room that Sabine was able to pinpoint the source of her unease. After their hands had touched—when Tal had fixed his unflinching gaze upon her—Sabine could have sworn that his green eyes had flashed gold.

Tal

By the time Tal arrived at the border, the stench of burning flesh had cleared from his nostrils. His grimace upon enlisting in Velle's Second Battalion came not from the commitment, but from the pain. His wounds had stopped their weeping, were clinging weakly to the weave of his shirt, but signing his name wrenched that tender flesh free, and his skin began to sob once more.

The gray-haired soldier who had taken Tal's signature frowned down at the boy before him. "Are you hurt, son?"

Tal was ashamed. To show pain was to admit weakness. He would never become a competent soldier if he was so quick to admit defeat.

"I'm fine." Tal shook his head. The motion set his back to screaming. He hissed.

"You're not," the man said, not unkindly, gesturing to the blood seeping through Tal's shirt. "You'll want to come with me."

The medical tent was barren, little more than a bedroll, a stool, and an assortment of tinctures and bandages. The soldier tended to Tal's wounds with the swift methodical means of a man who had seen it all. This comforted Tal, who had suffered much worse.

When the soldier used a cloth to apply a bright, acidic tincture to the wounds, Tal did not even flinch. For some reason, the man's expression grew unbearably sad.

"Who did this to you, son?"

Tal swallowed the emotion that crept up his throat. Cruel, that this man would call him son when it was Tal's own father who had written this rage across his skin, had pressed irons fresh from the fire into Tal's flesh. The brands were his father's way of reminding Tal that he did not belong to himself. He belonged first and foremost to the family.

"A stranger," Tal replied. The soldier was kind enough to allow Tal his lie.

"You are angry." It wasn't a question and therefore Tal saw no need to answer. "You are joining the ranks to ensure that none could ever harm you again."

It was divine, to be seen. To simply nod and be known.

"What if I told you there was another way?"

"To vengeance?"

"To power." The soldier's tone was reverent. "I see something in you, young man. An anger that will guide you. A likeness that will endear you to Him."

Tal would have done anything to secure a patriarch's praise and attention. And so he asked: "To whom?"

This was how he was introduced to the Second Son.

PART TWO

The Second Son's father had been a vicious leader. Under his reign, the Lower Banks were a muted, oppressive place. So when the New Maiden sank to her knees in the silt and wept, Sebastien flinched. He waited for his father's venomous voice to chastise the New Maiden for her weakness.

But his father was gone, and so no such cruelty came. Instead, the water returned. The earth began to sing. Sebastien observed the New Maiden with acute interest. Tears spilled down her face, yet no one struck her. She cried out with pain, yet no one silenced her. Rather than being punished for her emotions, she was rewarded for them.

He could not make sense of it. The last time he shed a tear, his father's hands had wrapped around his throat. If you cannot control yourself, you'll have to join her, *he had said, gesturing to the lifeless body of Sebastien's mother.*

So when the New Maiden playfully teased his stoicism, Sebastien did not laugh with her. Where the New Maiden was unburdened—filled with hope and light—he would never escape the darkness within. She was almost as cruel as his father, for making him wish that he could.

—Psalm of the Second Son

8

Delegates from Kirre, a small state in the southwestern region of the continent, were to dine with the queen at sunset. In the week since she'd met with General Garvey, Elodie had rehearsed her talking points about the overdue tariffs owed by the Kirrish chancellor in hopes that the coin could go directly toward funding the military's efforts. Yet today, when she ought to be putting the finishing touches on her plea, Elodie was preparing to take half a day's journey to the Highlands, Velle's most fertile acreage, where the entirety of the next season's crops had been drowned.

As she stormed through the corridors on her way to Rob's chambers, she reviewed for the tenth time the correspondence she'd received over breakfast. *The source of the flooding*, the Duke of Minvin had hastily penned, *is unknown as of yet*. But the water had swept all the flowering fruits from their branches, drowned the wheat, and waterlogged the corn. Everything the township was meant to be harvesting was instead drenched and rotting and, according to the duke, *emitted a very particular stench that will take at least a season to eradicate.*

Strange, he continued, *for it has not rained in several months. The only reserves of water nearby are the dams of the Second Republic just beyond the border. These dams have been carefully maintained for centuries. It makes little sense that they would spring a leak.*

But Elodie knew this had been no accident.

She burst into her brother's room without knocking. Rob's chambers were pristine, so meticulously tidy that the spines of his books were organized by color. It was a strange prism of light dancing around a room that was otherwise devoid of pigment—his bedspread, his furniture, his curtains were all decidedly dark. Stringed instruments hung on the walls like art. A lute leaned against the desk. A piano had been pushed into the corner, the afternoon light illuminating a thin layer of dust across the keys.

Rob was on the floor, surrounded by parchment and bottles of ink. A quill was tucked between his fingers, but instead of scribbling on paper, he was writing in the air. Opposite the prince was Tal, watching Rob speak with a reverence usually reserved for his interactions with Elodie.

"This is why," Rob was saying, his back to his sister, "the message must be clear. It is not about Him, so much as the possibility He provides. It's why I—"

Tal coughed pointedly, nudging his chin toward the queen.

At the sight of his sister, Rob fell silent. He swept the pages into a haphazard pile, which he stuffed beneath the sofa. "It's common courtesy to knock, you know," he said with a frown.

Elodie waved away his indignation. "Your father needs to see this." She waved the duke's correspondence in her brother's face.

Rob scanned the letter with a frown. "What does my father care about a flood?"

He was being purposely obtuse. "This has Edgar's name all over it," she said.

"It's not as though the Republics left a calling card," her brother replied, handing the note to Tal. "For all you know, this *was* an accident."

"And for all I know, you *are* an idiot," Elodie shot back.

Tal watched their exchange with amusement. "If this was Edgar's handiwork, don't you think you'd have another letter from him, trying to claim credit?" He raised an eyebrow. "He's not exactly subtle."

"He's baiting me," Elodie insisted.

Rob rolled his eyes. "Clearly it's working."

Tal's dismissal of her suspicions left Elodie exasperated. Her brother's snide remarks made her angry. Short of an invasion, she could not fathom what additional proof was required to align themselves with her. This meant that Rob's refusal was rooted solely in spite.

Unfortunately for her brother, Elodie Warnou was well-versed in pettiness.

"Just for that, you're coming with me to Minvin," Elodie told him.

Rob scoffed. "This is none of my concern."

"Acting like a petulant child does not relieve you of your princely duties," Elodie told him. "You are a member of Velle's royal family, and so when your people suffer tragedy, you must show up to support them. You may scowl in the coach all the way to the

Highlands, but the moment you step outside that carriage you will offer comfort to the farmers who have lost their livelihoods. Now get changed. You've got ink on your sleeve."

Rob looked at his sister as though he wished she were a bug he could squash beneath his boot. "Edgar only wants you because he does not know you," Rob said. "If he knew how cruel you were, he would abandon his correspondence and none of us would be in this ridiculous mess." He stomped off to his bedroom.

Elodie turned to Tal incredulously. "What is the matter with him?"

The Loyalist frowned. "You're being rather hard on him, Lo."

"For asking him to do his job?"

"For assuming this responsibility is one he wanted."

"Yes, well," Elodie said tersely, wounded that Tal would take her brother's side, "we don't always get what we want, now, do we?"

"*You* did." Tal fought back a smile. "So, that's not a particularly persuasive argument."

The ease of his banter was profoundly irritating. She reached for the letter still in Tal's grip, slicing her finger on the sharp edge of the page. The queen hissed as blood bloomed bright on her pale skin. She looked desperately around for something to clean it with.

"Here." Tal rummaged in his pocket. "Take my handkerchief."

Elodie shook her head. "It'll stain."

"Not this one," Tal laughed, offering up a square of fabric the same shade of red as her wound.

Just then, Rob reemerged in a doublet, looking furious. He stalked toward his chamber door. "Let's get on with it, then."

The queen, who had cleaned her paltry cut, tried to return the handkerchief, but Tal waved her away. "Keep it." He winked. "I've more where that came from."

In the stable yard, Elodie and Rob were intercepted by Cleo. "I've got this all scheduled out," she said, waving her siblings into the coach. The horses took off at a clip through the north gate. "This visit will move quickly," she continued, as they left the city behind. "Just a 'hello, so sorry for the damage, you can expect resources shortly, oh and isn't it wonderful that the queen was able to clear her very busy schedule to be here?' We'll be back in time to bathe before dinner."

Elodie rubbed her temples. "You make it sound easy."

"Because it is. You'll shake the Duke of Minvin's hand, offer a few compassionate frowns, and then we'll be on our way."

Elodie wrinkled her nose. "That feels a bit soulless."

The queen had witnessed Sabine's interactions with the New Maiden's followers. Each time she had made the moments significant and sincere. A few minutes with a duke in the Highlands could not compensate for an entire harvest's lost crops. Still, there was a vital reason why Elodie had ordered for a carriage, had even agreed to the grueling journey: to prove to her constituents that she cared for them more than the Republics could ever hurt them. These were the moments that defined a queen. The choices that cemented a legacy. When Elodie had accepted Velle's crown, she had committed to showing up, no matter how empty the gesture might seem.

"It's no more soulless than anything else the monarchy does," Rob brooded.

Elodie scoffed. "What is that supposed to mean?"

"I only mean that one cannot rule righteously," Rob continued. "Our system was set in place centuries ago as a way to oppress and subjugate. The House of Warnou is not inherently superior to any other family in Velle."

Cleo shifted uncomfortably in her seat. "Rob," she said gently, catching sight of Elodie's expression, but their brother continued, oblivious to his older sister's scrutiny.

"What gives a Warnou the right to rule over someone else?" Rob turned his inquisition toward Elodie. "Is the New Maiden's word even relevant in our current age? Just because Velle has always done things a certain way doesn't mean it must continue."

"What would you suggest the country do instead?" Elodie asked, clutching the carriage bench with white knuckles. She currently did not have the headspace to help her brother dismantle the monarchy.

"Oh, I do not presume to have the answers," Rob said with infuriating calm. "I have merely taken an interest in the theological. Naturally, it leads me to question everything."

"I thought the point of theology was faith," Elodie said dryly.

"On the contrary." Rob tapped his finger against his knee in a syncopated rhythm. "The point of theology is truth."

None of the Warnous had ever found much use for religion. They had been their mother's children, prioritizing crown before Church, and sometimes in spite of it. Yet it appeared that Rob had changed his tune.

Elodie examined her brother. The longer she spent ostracized from Rob, the more he began to feel like a stranger. The brother she had once known would never have gotten tangled up in such darkness. But this new Rob was changed enough that he might be unduly influenced. His desire to embrace a new order hinted at the threat of the Second Son.

After the tense carriage ride, it was almost a relief to slap on a smile and converse with the Duke of Minvin, a thin man with sun-soaked skin and kind eyes. The duke and his family were delighted to have the queen for tea, their smiles so wide it was difficult to believe that the entirety of their land had been destroyed.

"Apologies for the smell, Your Majesty," the duke said, his voice pinched. Elodie's eyes had begun to water. She buried her nose in her teacup, but the bitter herbs had not steeped long enough to suppress the stench.

"We won't have much to send to the storerooms," the duchess said apologetically. "Usually, we ship off ten tons of wheat and a thousand barrels of fruit, but those won't be available this year. Some of the root vegetables may have survived, and if we're lucky, the moisture will keep the soil strong. We'll know more in spring. Until then"—she grimaced—"I'm afraid there is little we can deliver from this harvest."

"Next year's lost, too," the duke added. "The seeds will take another season to sprout."

"I see." Elodie set her teacup down gently so they would not notice her hands shake. Without hard numbers and a review of their food stores, she could not say for certain how massive a loss this was, but the stitch in her side implied it was devastating. "Do you have a central square, or a gathering hall, perhaps? I'd like to say a few words to the township, if that's all right?"

The duchess's eyes widened. "It would be our honor. Richard!" She called forth a tiny boy of no more than six. "Go on and ring the bells!"

It took very little time to assemble the residents, as most were already in the fields sifting through the damage. Elodie stood atop a barrel, careful to breathe only through her mouth. Cleo looked worriedly up at her as though at any moment she might fall.

"Harvesters of Minvin," Elodie called, surveying the beleaguered expressions of the township's inhabitants. Many had scarves tied around their noses and mouths to suppress the smell. "I hope my presence here today offers comfort in response to this devastating tragedy. I urge you, do not fret, for with the support of the crown and prayers from the New Maiden, the Highlands and Velle will grow stronger than ever before. Your focus now should be on rebuilding, on helping the land recover. Come spring, the earth will be renewed. Velle will rise victorious," she shouted, fueled by the nods and applause from the crowd, "and our enemies will fall, poisoned at the root!"

Cleo dug her fingernails into the soft skin of Elodie's ankle. Too late, the queen realized her mistake. To the people of Minvin, this had been an accident, faulty dams that had all sprung leaks. Yet their queen had informed her people of a threat—an enemy that, until now, they had known nothing about.

"Did she say enemies?"

"Are we at war?"

"Should we be afraid?"

"You are not in danger," Elodie added, in hopes of tempering their reactions. She felt a tug on the hem of her dress.

"Time to go," Cleo said sharply while Rob chuckled softly beside her. "Wave goodbye, Elodie."

Elodie cursed her loose lips as she extracted herself from the clamoring crowd. This venture had been meant to curtail emotions, not exacerbate them. As the Warnou siblings returned to the carriage, to venture along the same roads they had traveled mere hours before, Elodie could not help but concede that in this round of their battle, Edgar had emerged victorious.

9

The pews of the royal chapel were empty save for Sabine. It had only been little more than a week since she had removed Chaplain René from his post, but already she could feel the punishing aftereffects. Mass attendance had dwindled by half. Even the altar children had abandoned their posts.

News from beyond the castle was not much better. The slew of resignations had left district churches without clergy. Sabine could only imagine the havoc the Second Son's prophet could wreak with all those empty pulpits. Especially if, as she suspected, His prophet had previously been a man of Her cloth.

The words of warning that Brianne brought back from her ghostly dream state echoed in Sabine's head as she lay prostrate on the unforgiving wooden bench: *He will hold the faithful in His iron grip.*

A profound pause, as she waited for the darkness to snipe at her, to tell her that fire could melt metal, if only she could locate a spark. When it did not come, Sabine felt a flutter of disappointment. Every time she waited with bated breath, praying she might hear that serpentine voice—her constant witness and companion—she was disappointed. Its absence left so much room for self-doubt.

She was the one who had retired René from his post and compelled the clergy to resign. Her embodiment of the New Maiden was not enough to help the devoted maintain their conviction. Instead, her presence seemed to repel them away from Her word, as though their faith had nothing to do with the New Maiden at all.

Worse, a flock in search of a new shepherd was primed to look upon a poster and find the Second Son. With a rebel congregation in want of a worship hall, what was stopping the prophet from claiming one of the New Maiden's sanctuaries for Himself?

Sabine sat up, knocking a hymnal to the floor with a dull *thump*. The swishing of bristles stilled.

"What is it?" Brianne leaned the broom against a pew and turned to the New Maiden, concern swimming in her blue eyes. In the absence of a clergy, the youngest Warnou had taken to lighting the chapel's prayer candles and sweeping the floors, dutifully maintaining the space in her work boots and trousers. The labor was hardly fit for a princess, but she didn't seem to mind.

"Can you call us a coach?" Sabine turned to the Chaplain, who was using a cloth to polish the windows. "Silas, I'll need my robe. We're going into the city."

The Chaplain frowned. "Whatever for?"

"I cannot sit idly by while the Second Son turns the tides against me," Sabine said. "We are going to remind Velle why its loyalty belongs to Her."

"This energy is curious," the Royal Chaplain mused, once Brianne had skittered away. "What has come over you?"

Sabine leveled her gaze. "Do you disapprove?"

"It depends," Silas said, studying her intently, "on what you intend to do with this newfound mettle."

"I intend to stand up for myself, Silas. To ensure that the districts' chapels remain in our possession."

"Very good, Maiden," the Royal Chaplain said, bowing her head slightly to hide her smile.

They began their tour in the Arts District, where the chapel was tended to by a young girl called Freya. The New Maiden's arrival left her aghast.

"I would have dusted!" she shrieked, wringing her hands apologetically. "I've been busy touching up paint."

On the far wall was a mural of the New Maiden and Her Favoreds, its colors eye-catching even from the farthest pew. It was obvious where Freya's brush had recently been—the rich, earthy browns of the New Maiden's hair, the corn silk of the halos that hung above the Favoreds' heads, the deep gold of Sebastien's eyes. Sabine shivered as she took in the Second Son. There was something eerily familiar in his stare, although she could not place it. No matter where Sabine stood in the church, Sebastien's eyes seemed to follow.

"Are you alone here?" Silas asked the girl, who looked to be about Cleo's age.

Freya shook her head. "My aunts run service. I haven't taken my vows yet."

"But you wish to?" Brianne asked.

"Oh yes." Freya took a shy step toward Sabine. "Sometimes I pretend my tears are magic," she confessed, brown eyes shining. "It makes me feel powerful instead of afraid."

The sentiment stole Sabine's breath. She had never imagined that her ability, which to her had been a burden, might offer another comfort.

"You *are* powerful, Freya," she said, pulling the girl into an embrace. "You cannot even fathom how strong you are."

Sunlight streamed through the window of the carriage as the group headed onward, hope bright on Sabine's tongue. She had been right to leave the safety of the royal chapel, to immerse herself in the outside world. But her optimism was extinguished when they entered the Manufacturing District, to find propaganda plastered to the doors of masonries, the wide-winged moth mocking her from all sides. The messages were ones she had seen before, but still, they made her ache—a finger pressed hard onto a bruise. The sun slipped ominously behind a cloud as they approached the house of worship.

The sanctuary had been stripped bare. The pews had been pried up from the floors, likely chopped into hobby wood for the artisans. The candelabras had been stolen, surely to be used for forging. The hymnals had been shredded, the leather covers stripped away, the paper left behind to litter the floor. The craftspeople were resourceful, at least, to reuse Her resources so intentionally.

After all, "She provides" could mean a number of things.

Shaken, the Maiden, the princess, and the Chaplain continued to the Garden District, the queendom's most affluent neighborhood. While the afternoon air was fresh, Sabine's stomach soured as she took in the posters pasted to tree trunks and shellacked to the front doors of the spindly stone church. The poster read:

Tears and feeble platitudes do not a savior make.

Faith belongs in stronger hands, to those who will not break.

The Second Son's messages were growing more pointed. More personal. If Sabine allowed the posters to affect her, she was giving the prophet exactly what He wanted. So instead, she turned her attention to the church doors. They were bolted shut. The silver padlock glittered mockingly in the afternoon light, so reminiscent of the chain that had kept Harborside's chapel closed for most of Sabine's life.

The New Maiden rattled the handles of the towering oak door, kicking at the wood furiously with the heel of her boot. Passersby stopped to whisper and stare openly at her distress.

The first time Sabine had set foot in the Garden District, she'd been a peasant out of place in the lavish apothecary shops. Now, despite the fact that she had arrived in a palace coach wearing hand-dyed silk and gold hairpins, she was still an intruder—a girl who did not belong. The chain on the chapel door only reinforced that truth.

Silas placed a hand on her arm. "Don't waste your energy."

"But Her people are barred. *I* am barred from my own house of worship." Sabine slipped out from beneath Silas's hand, unwilling to be soothed. "And for what? Because He is *jealous*?" She used a thumbnail to peel the poster off the chapel door in long curling strips. "He is poaching my followers, using *my* Church to do so."

"It's not such a loss, Sabine," Brianne said, chewing on her thumb. "These are the worst of the constituents anyway."

But it would be a tremendous loss if He lured them into His fold.

Bark flaked from the trees as she ripped posters from their nails, crumpling up the parchment and discarding them on the cobble-stones. She moved methodically down the street ripping down the sheets and shredding them into scraps that floated away on the wind. She was making a scene, but she did not care. The polka-dot wings of the moth winked at her in the wind.

Sabine's darkness would have hissed at her furiously, the way that Silas and Brianne called to her now, but she could hardly hear their voices, so focused was she on the deadening silence in her head. The quiet was consuming, echoing upon itself, over and over again. She was the New Maiden, a prophecy completed, but instead of possessing divine rights, Sabine was empty. She had even been stripped of her shadow.

Tearing down traces of the Second Son was the only thing that allowed Sabine to feel anything at all. And so she continued, ignoring the citizens who had paused their errands to watch as the New Maiden wreaked havoc on the city's wealthiest district.

This outburst was the opposite of what she had intended do. Sabine had meant to reclaim, not to destroy. But she would not stop—could not stop, it seemed—until Silas strong-armed her into the carriage, until Brianne called for the driver to take them back to the castle, until she was alone in the stable yard with bloody fingernails and a ringing in her ears. In that moment, all she wanted was to find the one person who could reach her the way her dark-ness once had.

She did not have to go far. Sabine had taken no more than a single step before Tal strode out from the stables, hand on the hilt of his sword. He looked her up and down. "What happened to *you*?"

Sabine gritted her teeth. "That obvious?"

"Afraid so." He waved a hand vaguely at her expression, which nearly made her laugh. For so long, her emotions had not been visible on her face. Instead, they had been scrawled across her skin, coursing through her veins. It was almost a relief to have her feelings present themselves more overtly, in a way that made others comfortable enough to engage in turn.

"Well, don't worry," she said, sniffing. "I won't weep in your company. Some find that offensive." She bristled again at the thought of the posters' pointed jabs.

"The *Book of the New Maiden* testifies that She was emotional, too."

"You don't strike me as a follower." The truth slipped out far too easily.

"My mother was." Sabine was surprised Tal trusted her enough to refer to his mother in the past tense. "My older brother drowned in a lake when I was two," he continued. "Afterward, church was the only time I saw her smile."

The New Maiden's heart ached, but she did not offer him condolences. Instead, she extended sympathy in the form of her own truth. "My father is a gambler. We nearly lost our apartment ten times over. But Her word made me believe there would always be a place for me. Offered me hope that I could be more than what I was born into."

"Fitting," Tal said, eyes sweeping over her, "considering."

The silkiness of his tone left her smarting. She could not believe how easily he had coaxed forth the contents of her heart. This was not what she had intended their relationship to become. She was so used to being guarded.

The rumble of a carriage interrupted their delicate moment. The stable boys pushed past them to unlatch the horses. From inside the coach emerged a beleaguered-looking Cleo, a sullen Rob, and a sour-faced Elodie.

The queen appeared startled to see the two of them together, but her surprise passed quickly. "The Kirrish delegates arrive in two hours," she said, words that meant practically nothing to Sabine. "Both of you will dine with us tonight. Velle needs to put its best foot forward, and we won't be able to do so without you present."

Sabine and Tal exchanged a look. It was not entirely clear which *you* the queen meant.

"As you wish, Majesty," Tal said, offering her a sweeping bow.

Unwilling to be outdone, Sabine swept into a curtsy. "Of course, Your Majesty."

"Enough with the formalities." Elodie sighed wearily. "Just don't be late."

"Sorry," Cleo mouthed over her shoulder. "Difficult day. But please," she added before hurrying after her sister, "do *not* be late."

"Wouldn't dare," Sabine said, but the royal cohort had already gone.

"I hate these delegate dinners," Tal muttered. "They're full of the most odious people, the kind who size you up in a single glance." Sabine's stomach fluttered with nerves. She had already spent the afternoon being gawked at. She was not certain she could handle being on display yet again. "It usually helps if you don't make your entrance alone," Tal said gently. "We could arrive together, if you like?"

Sabine considered the proposal and found no downside. Tal was conventionally handsome and a known friend to the crown. He would be a perfect shield for any judgment that might befall her. "All right, then."

He looked surprised but pleased. "All right, then," he echoed. "I'll see you tonight."

It was only after Sabine had enlisted Katrynn's help to ready her for the night's event, envisioning Tal's nod of approval and Elodie's dazed expression, that Sabine realized she was not entirely certain which one of them she was dressing for.

10

Delegate dinners at Castle Warnou were notoriously ostentatious events. This evening, the linens were the cobalt blue of the Kirrish coat of arms and the silverware had been swapped out with cutlery that shone gold. Tables were arranged in the center of the ballroom's polished floor in a U shape, the better to see, the worse to hear.

Many an accidental enemy had been created this way, most notably the delegate from Upper Tyne who thought that the delegate from Lower Tyne had inquired: "May I lie with your wife?" instead of "May I borrow your knife?"

A different table arrangement might have prevented such misunderstandings, but subterfuge was an essential part of courtly politicking. The Kirrish delegates were only nominally important, children to placate with shiny objects. Elodie's true audience tonight was Velle's nobility.

Before the country learned of Edgar's threats and the tarnished harvest, Elodie needed to ensure that public opinion was firmly on her side. Tera Warnou had taught her daughter that if she wanted to shape the narrative, she needed to start with those who held the most influence in her court.

To prime her guests for gossip, Elodie had arranged for servants to hover in the doorways, holding trays of bubbly nut wine. Glasses were pressed into the hands of the delegates and nobility as they entered. Peich-nat went down far too easily. In a matter of seconds, Elodie's own glass was nearly empty. She'd intended to take a single sip to calm her nerves but had absentmindedly continued to drink and was now inauspiciously light-headed as she greeted the guest of honor.

"Chancellor Wilden." Elodie's skirt swished softly against the polished floor as she offered the man a half curtsy. She still wasn't used to the extra weight of the crown on her head. "It is a pleasure to enjoy your company tonight."

The chancellor, a portly man close to her father's age, inclined his head politely. "The pleasure is all ours, Majesty." He clinked his glass with hers, then took a sip of the carbonated liquid. He grimaced. "Not my taste," he grumbled. "Don't suppose you have any plum brandy?"

Elodie fought the urge to roll her eyes. Not five minutes into the proceedings and the man was already insulting her. "Alas," she said, smiling so wide it hurt, "I don't suppose we do. Unless your delegation brought us a bottle as an offering?"

She knew they had not.

The chancellor wandered away with a mumbled excuse, discarding his glass on an empty tray. Elodie shook her head, hoping the bubbles in her brain might settle. Tonight, she desperately needed to keep her combative instincts at bay.

The Kirrish delegates huddled in the far corner, no doubt gossiping about her aperitif. The more permanent fixtures in Velle's court were chatting among themselves, fawning over the Duchess of the Upper Banks, who was dressed in a shimmering silk set that made her look like a spider's web. Near the door stood Cleo, resplendent in a yellow gown, her dark hair pinned in an elegant bouffant. On her arm, inexplicably, was Artur Anders, looking uncomfortable in a cravat. It was the first time Elodie had seen Sabine's brother in trousers that actually fit. The queen glided toward them.

"Artur," she said, not bothering to hide her surprise. His name had not been included on the seating chart. "How unexpected."

Artur turned to Cleo, looking panicked. "I thought you said—"

"It's fine," she interrupted, putting a hand on his arm placatingly. "Brianne told me Sabine had a difficult day," Cleo told Elodie, as though this was a natural thing for her to know. "I thought a familiar face might help make this event easier for her. Court dinners are not for the weakhearted."

"She has work to do tonight," Elodie said sharply, trying not to let on exactly how stressed she felt. "If the New Maiden dazzles the court, she may begin to command favor beyond Velle's borders. I would not parade Sabine around without purpose."

Cleo looked wounded. "I was only trying to help."

Elodie sighed, very nearly running a hand through her hair, which would have disturbed the constellation of pins Marguerite had meticulously assembled. "I know, Cleo. I'm sorry, just...no more surprises tonight, all right?"

Cleo cleared her throat pointedly, eyes fixed on the door behind Elodie. "In that case, I'd advise not to look behind you."

Elodie turned to watch Sabine enter the ballroom, a vision in white. The bodice of her gown was fitted closely to her form, and Elodie's eyes followed every one of the New Maiden's gentle curves. She clutched her wineglass with both hands. There was little left for her to imagine. The skirts fanned out, layers of tulle spilling from the soft swoop of Sabine's waist. When she moved, it appeared the girl was walking on a cloud.

But the true surprise came when Elodie tore her eyes away from Sabine to take in the person beside her. Tal was outfitted in black, fingers decorated with silver rings, a gold chain glinting around his neck. There was a softness in his eyes that Elodie had not seen since they were children, a gentleness in his step. Sabine did not shy away from him. In fact, if Elodie had not known better, Tal and Sabine might have appeared a couple.

Half a step behind the pair was Rob, donning a purple doublet and looking cross. Elodie's mood matched her brother's. Tal and Sabine's closeness discomfited her. Tal's allegiance to the Second Son was in direct opposition to Sabine's role as the New Maiden. Yet because Elodie had not warned Sabine of Tal's rebel alliance, he had managed to infiltrate the New Maiden's trust more easily than Elodie could have ever imagined.

Pressing her empty glass into Cleo's hands, Elodie hurried to intercept the group near the doorway. She plucked another flute of peich-nat from an errant tray and wondered at the pair of them, at Sabine's ethereal beauty and Tal's carefully indifferent expression. She wondered what they talked about.

"Majesty." Sabine conducted her skirts into an impressive

curtsy. "Thank you for the invitation. I hope that I've dressed adequately for the occasion?" Her brown eyes held Elodie's, sending a warm flush up her spine. The heat lingered in her cheeks.

"Very much so," Elodie managed, her gaze tracing the jut of Sabine's collarbone. "I find your appearance here tonight to be extraordinarily pleasing." Rob coughed, the disruption righting Elodie's attention. "Tal." She pinched the black fabric of his uniform, which lent his skin a pallor that was not apparent in the red of his Loyalist garb.

"I hope my appearance is no less pleasing to Her Majesty?" Tal asked with amusement. His green eyes held Elodie's, offering none of the warmth she had found in Sabine's.

"I am delighted to welcome you both." She smiled beatifically before taking a long swig of her wine. "A word, Tal?" She slipped her arm through his and pulled him toward a shadowy corner. She needed to remove the New Maiden from Tal's orbit. But if she confessed Tal's loyalties to Sabine, the New Maiden might accuse her of aligning with the enemy.

"You look stunning this evening, Lo," Tal breathed, but the compliment bounced right off her.

"What are you doing?" Her whisper sparked like hot coals.

Tal looked flummoxed. "You invited me here."

"Not at my *dinner*," Elodie said through gritted teeth, keeping a smile stuck to her face for any onlookers. Indeed, several sets of eyes were fixed plainly on the pair. "I mean with the New Maiden."

Tal shook his head slightly, as though her answer was not what he had expected. "I am not *with* her," he said, his lips quirking up with pleasure. "Although I must admit your jealousy is most flattering." Elodie clenched her jaw even tighter. "No, I am simply offering a sympathetic ear. I fear the pressure of the posters may be getting to her." Amusement twinkled in his green eyes, as though they shared an intimate joke.

"What posters?"

Tal might as well be speaking in tongues for how little Elodie understood him. He behaved as though he had a relationship with Sabine, as though *he* were the New Maiden's confidant, not Elodie. Yet Sabine had been suspicious of Tal the moment they'd met. Tal had been plotting the New Maiden's demise before Sabine had even revealed herself as the deity's true manifestation. They could not— were seemingly *destined* not to—get along. Still, there was an ease between them. Elodie took another sip of wine, hoping to drown out the jealousy blooming in her gut.

Before Tal could answer, the dinner bell chimed. Elodie took her seat at the center of the table, her family fanning out beside her: Cleo to her left, next to Artur, beside Sabine; Rob to her right, next to Tal. The other long tables held Kirrish delegates and Velle's courtiers. So many forks were included in each place setting that there was nearly an arm's length between every guest.

Elodie hardly tasted the first course, so troubled was her mood. But as the meal progressed, sauces were spooned from tureens onto roasted birds; charred vegetables dripped with butter and herbs. Her tension dissipated as her stomach filled and she sobered up. While she ate, Elodie monitored the various attempts at conversation. Nearly everyone was yelling, competing with the long tables, the wide place settings, and the clinking of cutlery as they dined.

Elodie turned toward her brother. "How is your food?"

Rob glowered at her. "There's nothing wrong with my mood,"

he shouted, falling victim to a classically absurd misunderstanding. "Even if there was, that does not concern you."

Elodie sighed. "I was only asking about your meal," she said as Rob turned away. She could not understand what had possessed her brother. Elodie watched him throw a disgruntled look at Sabine. It was unclear if her brother's distaste for the New Maiden had to do with her status, or the person upon whose arm she had arrived.

On the other side of the table, the Anders siblings were faring slightly better. While Sabine had first appeared nervous, having Artur by her side seemed to have loosened her tongue. As the meal progressed, she had shifted from timid to excitable, and finally, friendly. The New Maiden looked on enthusiastically as a Kirrish woman told an exuberant story, occasionally flittering her eyes toward Elodie, the Maiden's gaze so earnest and wanting it left Elodie feeling exposed.

By the time the dishes had been cleared and tea had been poured for the guests, Elodie was ready to address the thorny topic of debts owed. She summoned the Kirrish chancellor to sit in Cleo's now abandoned chair—the princess had gone to ensure dessert was being plated appropriately—and leveled with him.

"Had you incurred this level of debt under Velle's previous regime, my mother would have already sent a battalion to break down your doors," Elodie said coolly, hands folded beneath her chin. The chancellor choked on his tea. "Now, I'm not going to do that," she continued. "I'll give you grace to settle your scores. I know you're a man of honor."

"Oh, I am," he said, leaning back and draping an arm around

the shoulders of her chair. "I'm glad to see that a girl as lovely as you possesses brains as well as beauty."

Rage circled her like a housefly, impossible to ignore. It was the same snide dismissal she had faced at the hands of Edgar.

"Would you like to know a secret?" Elodie waggled a finger to draw the chancellor closer to her. He had a speck of roasted bird stuck to his whiskers. "My strategy would be the same if I had the head of a horse, and the First Battalion would answer my call just the same."

The chancellor's eyes widened as Elodie pushed back her chair. "If you do not pay what you owe by the next full moon," she continued, "my army will mobilize to settle the balance. We will strip your houses, brick by brick, send your children to our front lines and our factories until we have recouped our due." She tossed her soiled napkin on the chancellor's lap, smoothing the forest green velvet of her skirt. "Understood?"

The chancellor's face turned red. "Majesty, you are out of line."

"And you are out of touch," she snapped, glancing over her shoulder to ensure she had been loud enough to allow the courtiers to hang on her every word. She needed whispers to spread that Velle's monarch would stop at nothing to ensure her country received its due. "You may consider this your final warning."

She rose to her feet, righteous adrenaline making her feel warmer than all the wine in the world. Across the room, Sabine leaned against the wall, watching Artur delight Cleo and a group of courtiers with sleight of hand tricks. Elodie joined them, settling into the space beside Sabine. The queen dropped her hand so that it rested beside the New Maiden's, their fingers almost touching. Sparks shot up Elodie's arm. This almost nearness wasn't enough.

She could not shake the swirling uncertainty surrounding Tal and Sabine's relationship. She needed to understand where she fit in. *If* she fit in.

The Queen of Velle issued one final instruction that night, whispered into the curve of the New Maiden's ear. Elodie delighted in the shiver her words incited, the goose bumps that appeared on Sabine's pale skin in their wake. Now there was nothing to do but wait and hope that her invitation would be accepted.

11

Sabine waited until her sister fell asleep before slipping out of the bed they shared. In a palace this size, the New Maiden could have requested her own mattress, but Katrynn's presence was a soothing reminder of the life she'd once spent tucked beneath blankets, sharing space with her sadness. Without her magic or her darkness, Sabine felt as hollow as footsteps in an empty chapel. A choir that sang only the harmony line.

This was why she did her best to ensure she was never alone. In the mornings and the evenings, she had her family—her mother, Katrynn, and Artur. During the day, she clung to Silas and Brianne. Only occasionally did she allow herself to stray from their safe haven.

Sabine had not intended to suffuse her emotional void with Tal, but he was the closest approximation to her old ghosts that she had found thus far. His sharp, wry words took root in the most vulnerable corners of her heart, making her blood rush and her skin prickle.

But even he was not enough, and he certainly couldn't compensate for Elodie's recent absence. Tonight, Sabine would find comfort in the queen.

She shrugged on a dressing gown. It was silky and entirely useless against the cold of the corridors, but she wanted to look nice. Or as nice as anyone could look in the vacant hour between the moon and the sun.

Sabine stuck to the shadows of the south wing. She did not wish to incite gossip, and whispers of the New Maiden on her way to the queen's bedroom would spread through the palace faster than a plague through harbor rats. When she reached the western staircase, she quickened her step, as though momentum could render her invisible.

Sabine arrived at Elodie's door unscathed. Even though she had been issued an invitation for this midnight tryst, she knocked gently. The door flew open. Elodie's eyes were hopeful, her cheeks flushed. "You came."

Sabine tucked a lock of pale hair behind the queen's ear. "I cannot fathom a world where you ask for me and I do not obey."

She swept Elodie into a kiss, pressing her backward into the room so the door could shut behind them. A swell of wanting rose in her chest. Their bodies pressed together so tightly not even sand could have sifted between them.

"I'm sorry we didn't speak much tonight," Elodie murmured. The queen's hands were tangled in Sabine's hair, her teeth tugging at her bottom lip as they stumbled toward the bed. "But lady above, you looked incredible."

Sabine answered her with action. Her interior life was cluttered with so many words she thought she might burst. There was a war within—a battlefield of fears and desires, nihilism and hope. For once, Sabine wanted to give in to her feelings without having to examine them. The desperation with which Elodie kissed her back implied the queen felt the same.

Sabine reached for the ribbon that held her dressing gown closed. Elodie's fingers tightly cupped the base of her skull, holding her in place. Sabine began to feel as though if Elodie let go, she would melt down into wax, a puddle at the queen's feet.

Elodie let out a low moan as Sabine tenderly bit the soft skin of her neck. Her breathing slowed even as her heart raced. A different kind of power thrummed through Sabine. The ability to make someone feel good—feel desired, feel seen—was a magic all its own.

"Is this okay?" The queen's voice was husky. Sabine shivered even as she nodded. Elodie pressed her down onto the mattress, softer even than the one in her room.

The first time Sabine slept beside Elodie Warnou, she had been terrified lest even their pinky fingers touch. Now, she pulled the queen closer, drew herself into the depths of this winsome, wonderful girl. She would gladly drown in Elodie's salt, would draw her water into her lungs. A wave of pleasure crashed over her, soaking her to the bone. She gasped as she returned to the surface.

Still working to settle her pulse, she turned her attention to Elodie, whose jaw, even now, was clenched. She wanted to make the girl forget herself, forget the way the world conspired against her, against *them*. For someone like Elodie, who was always tasked to remember, Sabine wanted to be the one who briefly, exquisitely, made her forget.

"Are you all right?" She made sure that Elodie's inner feelings agreed with her outward reactions.

Elodie answered with a kiss, pulling her closer, somehow, ever closer. Sabine sank into it. The nearness fueled her and moved her forward. She reveled in the way Elodie's body moved beneath her fingers. The way Elodie lost herself, found herself, then lost herself again, all because of Sabine.

When at last they were exhausted, their thighs slick, their fingers sore, their lips bruised, they did not speak but merely lay side by side, staring at the shadows that danced across the ceiling.

A twinge of sadness pulsed beside Sabine's heart. Next to Elodie, Sabine was safe. Here she was seen for exactly who she was: She could speak without words and share more than just her emotions. Yet a heaviness hung in the air, as though there would be something to grieve when the morning dawned. This moment was only evanescently theirs as they lay tangled in the dark.

The longer she stayed between the four posts of the bed, the more certain Sabine was that this restless, tentative thread between them could be severed. Elodie turned to look at her, gray eyes drooping with exhaustion as she brushed a thumb across the New Maiden's cheek. Sabine interlaced her fingers with Elodie's and squeezed.

"You'd tell me, wouldn't you," the queen mumbled, words lazy and long with exhaustion, "if something was the matter? If you needed my help?"

"Of course," Sabine whispered guiltily. She would not trouble Elodie with propaganda and threats penned in ink. She could not let the queen know how quickly Sabine had lost the faith of her clergy, how incompetently she peddled the New Maiden's word. Sabine was so tenuously in power that she could not share her weakness, certainly not with such a successful monarch.

Elodie's lips curled into a gentle smile. "Good." She nuzzled her nose into the curve of Sabine's neck. Her breathing slowed.

Sabine sighed softly, willing her brain to quiet. The lie was worthy. The two of them were owed this sacred moment of peace. The silence would not last, but it ought to be observed. And so Sabine held tight to Elodie, fingers intertwined, as she drifted off to sleep.

12

Sabine was snoring softly when Elodie woke. The New Maiden was curled up on the very edge of the mattress—a girl only used to sharing a bed with a sibling. Her expression was peaceful in slumber, her dark hair swept across the silk pillowcase, her breathing steady. The queen rolled closer, pressing her cheek to the other girl's bare shoulder, relishing the warmth that radiated from her body. It was a delightful contrast to the crisp, cool sheets beneath the New Maiden's bare skin.

She remained in bed far longer than she should have, wrapped around Sabine while she slept. It was only when the clock struck six bells that Elodie realized how far behind schedule she had allowed herself to fall. Cleo would come by for tea at any moment. As she hurriedly disentangled herself, the New Maiden sighed sweetly.

"I hoped we might never have to get up," she said, sounding forlorn. "Yours is the most comfortable bed I've ever slept in."

"You're welcome to it any time," Elodie said, and despite the flir-tatious nature of the comment, she truly meant it. Greeting the day with someone by her side made the unknown feel more manage-able. "But right now, I need you to get dressed."

Sabine grimaced, holding up her dressing gown. "I only brought this."

Elodie's eyes went wide. "Absolutely not. You'll borrow some-thing of mine for the walk back to your rooms. Here." She offered Sabine the dress she had worn the day before, an unfussy, long-sleeved gown the color of the morning sky. "This will look beautiful with your eyes."

Sabine struggled with the buttons, but once she had squeezed into the gown it flattered her greatly. The New Maiden gave a small twirl. "Perfect," Elodie said, stepping into a dress of deep violet. "I could get used to mornings like this."

Sabine planted a kiss on Elodie's cheek and smoothed the tail of the queen's braid. "Me too."

They had only just settled themselves in the sitting room when Cleo arrived. Her eyes swept across the table—absent a breakfast tray—then snagged on the sleeve of Sabine's dress. Her lips quirked up with amusement as she recognized the gown. To the queen's intense relief, Cleo merely greeted Sabine with a bright smile and settled herself on the chair opposite the sofa.

Marguerite bustled in with the breakfast tray and was pouring tea when there came another knock on the door. Elodie stiffened, her good mood souring the moment she was presented a letter with the dread-inducing serpentine seal.

"Not again," she pleaded, but her prayers were for naught.

"What is it?" True concern painted the New Maiden's face. Her open expression offered Elodie a safe place to shatter.

But the queen could not bear to speak the truth aloud. Despite Edgar's threats, she would never be a man's wife. Would not cower to the whims of an aspiring emperor. The eldest Warnou possessed a mind and a heart and a soul, but all of that was seemingly lost on this boy with vindictive eyes. Elodie would not share this burden with Sabine. Edgar was not worthy of tormenting both of them. Every word devoted to this obsessive, broken boy only served to make him loom larger in her mind. And so the queen held her tongue.

"It's nothing." Elodie laughed, her smile pained. "Just another administrative headache I don't wish to bore you with. In fact," she said, too brightly, desperate for the New Maiden to leave before those gentle eyes coaxed the truth from her lips, "you probably ought to be going anyway."

Sabine looked wounded.

"My duties are extraordinarily tedious," Elodie clarified quickly. "If you don't take your leave, these contract negotiations will turn you comatose, and then I become the villain who has prevented the New Maiden from doing her good work."

Sabine's mouth twisted into a wry smile. "Fine. But you're not rid of me forever."

"Thank goodness for that," the queen said, squeezing the other girl's hand gently. Her smile fell the moment Sabine exited the room.

"Why didn't you tell her?" Cleo frowned, but Elodie was too consumed by the letter's contents to respond.

I wonder, Elodie Warnou, Edgar had written, *what is required of me to earn your confidence? I thought the flood would be enough to turn the tides (pun most certainly intended). But it seems you require more proof of my influence before you agree to take your place by my side.*

You told me once, the letter continued, *that you had no time for seasoning stews because you were too consumed with strategy. In this way, we are perfectly matched. I have thus taken the necessary steps to show you my tactical mind at play.*

The Republics have agreed to pause all imports to Velle, effective immediately. On the enclosed map you will see the alterations made to the transcontinental trade agreements. None will do business with you, for fear of our collective retaliation.

I do not wish for you to starve, my wilted flower. I only wish for you to understand how seriously I value your hand in marriage.

Elodie scowled at Edgar's words. The boy behaved as though he were playing a parlor game, moving pieces about the board with no regard for the very real lives he was affecting. What he saw as a strategy to gain Elodie's attention, she saw as a crisis with devastating implications.

First the drowned harvest had ruined most of Velle's own stores. Now an embargo had been enacted when they needed access to the Republics' bounty most. Elodie had been planning to spend ample coin in order to import enough grain, cheese, and smoked meats to last the country through winter. This change to the agreements meant her people were going to starve.

"What about the Jvin Channel?" Cleo asked, after she'd reviewed Edgar's harbinger of doom. Despite the abject horror of their circumstances, Elodie was proud that her middle sister was thinking tactically. She had jumped to the same potential solution as the queen. "Merchant ships could circumvent the mainland and head for the harbor."

But Elodie shook her head. "It's nearing winter. The water has already started to freeze. Ships won't be able to clear the pass until spring."

Cleo looked crestfallen. "What are we going to do?"

"We need to get ahead of it as best we can." Winter was coming, yes, but Velle had some reserves. Elodie needed to start by getting an accurate understanding of their existing food supply.

She called for Marguerite to ready a coach to the Commerce District.

"Will you summon Rob, too?" Cleo asked Elodie's handmaid, ignoring her sister's furious glare. "This is far greater than your silly feud," her middle sister insisted. "You need help."

"I'm fine," Elodie protested, but her assertion came out sounding pained.

Cleo extracted a pile of parchment from her pocket and dropped it on the table. "Not according to these."

They were the letters Elodie had found in the War Room.

"Cleo," Elodie spluttered. "You can't just go snooping around in my things. As head of state, I am privy to very sensitive information now."

"Then you should find better hiding places." Cleo shrugged. "So? Are these for Tal or for Sabine?" When Elodie did not speak, Cleo sighed and sat back on the sofa. "It's all right. You can trust me, you know."

"I didn't pen those letters."

Cleo frowned. "No? Who else would be this desperate for help?"

Elodie pursed her lips. "Ouch," she said dryly. "But why do you even care who wrote them or what they're for?"

Cleo picked at a loose thread on her skirt. "I'm worried about you. All this nonsense from Edgar and the Republics is taking its toll. I can see it is. You deserve more experienced advisers than your younger siblings."

Elodie sighed, wishing again she could speak directly to their late mother. If Queen Tera had found trusted allies and confidants, perhaps, with the right consultant, there was yet hope for Elodie to worm her way out of this predicament.

But she would never hear her mother's voice again. All that was left of Tera Warnou were memories—and these letters made it clear there was much about her mother that Elodie had not known. Those truths about Tera remained only in the minds of those who had loved her most.

Elodie could have kicked herself. There *was* a resource she had yet to exhaust. Someone who had known her mother intimately, but whose loyalty belonged staunchly to Elodie.

I am not only your queen, Elodie wrote hastily, to Duke Antony Wilde of Upper Dale, *but also your daughter. And so, when I beg you to join me for tea, it is not a simple request, but a royal decree. I am eager to see you soon.* She signed her name with a flourish and sealed the note with the family's fleur-de-lis seal.

She felt lighter as she handed Marguerite the letter to send. Silly, too, that she had not reached out sooner. It wasn't as though Elodie forgot she had a father; it was simply that he had never been relevant to her royal ambitions. He was content up in the hills with his farm and his animals. Elodie could not imagine a duller fate. Still, he always brought her comfort, and perhaps more urgently, he could bring her information. Her father had known Tera before she was queen—had loved her not because of her power and ambition, but in spite of it. If anyone was still keeping Tera Warnou's secrets, it would be him.

Elodie spent the ride to the Commerce District grim-faced yet determined. She maintained that resolve all the way to the treasury, up the steps to the accountant's office, even as she sat between Cleo and Rob on hard-backed wooden chairs, listening to a sharp-jawed man rattle off figures.

"Your stores are lower than usual for this time of year," the accountant said, leaning back in his upholstered seat, pointing to a large deduction a few weeks prior, "due to your recent pricing adjustments. A most"—he coughed pointedly—"*interesting* initiative that allowed for discounted access to wares."

Elodie resented his efforts to shame her for a policy that had allowed her constituents affordable food. Still, the numbers illustrated an inescapable truth. Yesterday's feasting had ensured tomorrow's famine. She would need to enforce strict rationing if her people were to make it through the winter.

It was not until the Warnou siblings arrived at the granaries, where a kind older man unlocked several padlocks and rolled open the door, that Elodie wholly shattered. Less than half the gigantic storeroom had been utilized.

The man gestured to the empty space. "That's where we will store the harvest from Minvin."

Guilt shuddered in the queen's stomach. She had not yet made public the unusable state of the Highlands' harvest.

"But only *this* storeroom," she insisted, quickly. "Surely there isn't so much empty space to be filled in the others?"

"There is, milady," the man said, looking apologetic. "We diversify our stores in case of pests or spoils. That way, if something goes awry, the country won't have to subsist on nothing but rutabaga for an entire season." He chuckled softly, which only stood to further sour Elodie's mood.

"Thank you, sir." She offered the man a sweeping curtsy. "This tour has been most informative."

The queen managed to maintain her composure until she was safely inside the coach. Then Elodie burst into tears. Without access to imported goods, the country faced impossible odds. If she did not act drastically, Velle would starve.

"Maybe I should accept Edgar's proposal," Elodie said, once her tears had dried. At least that way she'd have control over the trade routes.

Cleo looked horrified. "Ellie, you can't."

"I see no other way out of this." It pained her greatly to admit defeat.

"You are appealing to the wrong person, Elodie," Rob said softly, eyes fixed on the passing scenery. "If you were willing to pledge fealty to the Republics, you could eliminate the threat of Edgar once and for all."

Elodie frowned. Although her brother's voice was casual, it was clear this was a proposal he had put quite a lot of thought into. "And how would I do that?"

"The best way to get the Republics on your side," Rob said, gesturing out the carriage window to a piece of parchment stuck to a lamppost, "is to align yourself with their greater power."

Elodie pressed her face to the glass and scrutinized the poster, which boasted an unsightly moth and ink-splattered words: *Faith belongs in stronger hands, to those who will not break.* Elodie had not noticed them on the ride into the city for they had blurred into the background of her fears. But now that Rob had directed her attention, she saw them everywhere.

Elodie squinted at the spotted moth. "What do they mean?"

"Are you not familiar with the Republics' religion?" her brother asked.

"I am not," she said tersely. Tera Warnou had always kept a strict separation between theology and the throne.

Rob shook his head derisively. "You have been so distracted by the crown that you have failed to see what was right in front of you."

His bravado irked her. "Please, speak plainly."

"The Republics do not worship the New Maiden," Rob told his sister, pressing a hand to the carriage window. "They were founded on the word of the Second Son."

13

Sabine spent the morning stalking the hallways of the castle, a wounded animal searching for refuge. The warm, blissful glow of Elodie's attention and affections had been snuffed out by her swift dismissal. The queen's ask had been entirely reasonable. Still, it made Sabine feel as though she were a child who needed minding. Out of place and in the way.

She fiddled with the unfamiliar neckline of Elodie's borrowed dress, the gown straining uncomfortably beneath her arms. She had hoped her time with Elodie would be healing, but instead a harsh truth came to light: If Sabine relied on other people to fill her emotional well, she would always be depleted the moment she was left alone. The absence of her darkness made it impossible to navigate loneliness, left her chasing something just beyond her control. If Sabine was ever to regain authority over her emotions, she needed to find new ways of centering herself.

She thought she'd start with some food. But the moment she turned the corner, she ran headlong into another distraction.

"Don't tell me," Tal said, at the sight of Sabine's glum expression. "Too much peich-nat last night?"

Sabine shook her head, toying with the cuffs of the gown's long sleeves. "Difficult day." She had no desire to share with him the specifics.

"Already?" His lips quirked up in amusement. "The servants haven't even cleared away the breakfast trays yet."

Sabine was in no mood for his teasing. Any other time, this reminder of her darkness might be welcomed. Today, it hurt.

"I'm sorry." Tal abandoned his mocking tone as quickly as it had appeared, almost as though he could read her mind. "Whenever I'm in a foul mood, it always helps to stab something." He looked at the New Maiden curiously. "Want to try it?"

In that moment, what Sabine truly wanted was companionship. And so she told him yes.

Back in the now familiar training room, Sabine chose the dagger with the inset stone from its place on the wall, adjusting her grip the way Tal had shown her. The floorboards yielded beneath her feet like the docks in her neighborhood, albeit without the harbor's creaks and moans. She sliced at the air in front of her half-heartedly, certain she looked ridiculous.

"You won't feel better if there's no power behind it," Tal said. He had ignored the sword strapped to his waist, opting instead for a twin blade to Sabine's. He brandished the dagger wildly. "Make it mean something. Use this as an opportunity to grapple with your demons." He darted forward and back, impossibly light on his feet. It was clear he had done this hundreds of times.

"You have a lot of demons, I take it?"

"Yes." Sabine had asked the question in jest, but Tal's response held no levity.

"I'm sorry," she mumbled. "I didn't mean—"

"Don't be." Tal waved away her apology. "You are haunted, too."

"I..."

"It's all right, Sabine," Tal said, tossing the dagger over his shoulder and catching it behind his back. "You don't need to pretend. I see you."

"Do you?" The New Maiden could not keep the amusement from her voice.

"Don't you feel it?" Tal asked, as he returned the dagger to the wall. "This thread between us?" He unsheathed his sword, slicing at the air in the shape of an X.

She knew the strangeness he spoke of. In Tal she found comfort where it shouldn't be. Despite their competition for Elodie's attention, Tal's presence was certain as stone, his words soothing as the sea. She had not realized he felt the same.

Unnerved by his line of questioning, Sabine tightened her grip on the dagger. She cried out in pain as the blade sliced the thin web of skin between thumb and pointer finger. The weapon clattered to the ground as Sabine searched the pockets of Elodie's gown for a makeshift bandage. She emerged with a handkerchief, a square of red fabric the same shade as the one amidst the ashes of Harborside's ruined chapel.

Her blood ran cold. What reason could the queen have for possessing such a thing? It was not the Warnou color, nor did it look particularly well loved. But before she could truly panic, Tal used his sword to snatch the fabric from her hand.

"Where did you get this?" Tal looked just as betrayed as Sabine felt.

"It's Elodie's."

Perhaps it was not that the queen didn't trust the New Maiden. Perhaps she was actively working against her.

"I know it's Elodie's," Tal said, voice strangled. "*I* gave it to her. I'm asking why *you* have it."

Sabine suddenly recalled that Tal had been in Harborside just after the fire. Watching as the flames devoured her sanctuary.

Distrust made her cruel. "I'm wearing Elodie's dress. I borrowed it this morning."

Tal's face twisted as he pieced together the implication. When at last he understood, the soldier went unbearably still. Then he strode forward and knocked a shield from the wall. It clattered loudly against the ground, continuing to rattle until he stilled it with the sole of his boot. "But you're no one," he said breathlessly, expression pained. "How can she love *you*?"

Tal's feelings for the queen had always been obvious. Sabine had not intended to use her relationship with Elodie to hurt him, but then, it seemed, they both had secrets they were keeping from each other.

One by one, pieces of the armory were ripped from the walls and thrown to the floor. But Sabine paid no attention to the noise. Instead, she focused on Tal's face. His expression was contorted as though he were being scolded. Throughout his phantom berating, his eyes were empty, glittering gold instead of green. And then all at once, as though a match had burned out, Tal and his green eyes returned.

Sabine realized she was looking in a mirror. Tal, too, was

plagued with a darkness—harassed, questioned, and criticized by the intruder in his own mind. A force so powerful it could belong only to someone who had drawn from the same well of resentment for hundreds of years: the Second Son.

"It's you," she whispered.

"I tried to tell you." He sounded almost apologetic. "But you are too trusting to perceive the truth." He ran a hand through his dark hair. "That was Her problem, too."

Sabine's skin prickled. "What do you know of the New Maiden, Tal?"

"More than I wish to," he said. "I see Her in you, in that thread that connects us. It's a shame, really."

"What is?"

Tal took a step toward her. "That our story must end this way."

Sabine moved backward in sudden terror. "What do you want from me?"

Tal sighed. "It is not about what *I* want, Sabine. Surely you understand." He unsheathed his sword, holding it lazily by his side.

Sabine glanced desperately across the room, where her dagger lay abandoned, the blade streaked with her blood. She took a step toward it, but Tal used his sword to stop her.

"We were not meant to be enemies," he said, moving forward so that she was forced to retreat. "A series of unhappy accidents has simply put us in this perilous position."

Her heart sank as she realized she had been backed into a corner. "There's no need to hurt me, Tal."

"I like you, Sabine," Tal said softly as she shrank against the wall. "I truly do. But my allegiance belongs to Him, and the Second Son's goal has always been to eliminate the New Maiden."

Sabine watched him approach as though through smoke, her vision and her hearing dulled. She understood rationally that she was in immediate danger. But it was difficult to react in kind, to search for a trace of power she knew had long abandoned her.

"It's funny, really," Tal said, once he was close enough for her to smell his soap. "The world seeks from you salvation, but you can't even be bothered to save yourself."

That taunt was just enough darkness to drive away the fog.

Sabine lunged, slashing at the soldier's face, the nubs of her fingernails leaving long red streaks along his cheeks. She kicked at his shins and pulled on his hair, trying desperately to duck beneath his arm and flee.

At such close range, Tal could not find purchase with his sword. He sent it clattering to the ground and had just managed to wrap one hand around Sabine's throat when their scuffle was interrupted by a yelp. A boy about Artur's age stared uncertainly at them, and the shield he clutched crashed to the floor. The sound took Tal by surprise. That lapse in his focus gave Sabine the briefest moment to extract herself from his grip.

"Trap her!" Tal shouted, but the boy was too slow.

Sabine fled, heart pounding in her throat. Blood rushed to her head, making her steps uncertain. She focused only on putting one foot in front of the other, on leaving behind Tal's wicked green eyes and his bone-chilling smile. She did not stop until she was safely outside the confines of the castle, until she had ducked behind a wilting rosebush, gasping to pull the autumn air into her burning lungs.

Once, she'd felt a tentative kinship toward Tal. Now she knew the truth: They were bound by fate. With Tal as His vessel, the

Second Son was a true, tangible threat, one whose desire for vengeance was exacerbated by the prophet's love for Elodie Warnou.

There was no more pretending. The Second Son wanted the New Maiden eliminated, and Tal would stop at nothing to ensure His will was done.

14

lodie was accosted by her youngest sister the moment she disembarked from the coach.

"Not now, Bri." The queen had spent the entire ride back from the bank digesting the implications of the Republics' faith. Her head ached something terrible.

Brianne flung herself in front of the queen, barring the path forward. "You need to come with me," she said sternly. "*Now.*"

The youngest Warnou had been spending all her time with Sabine and the new chaplain, so it was no surprise to Elodie that Brianne led her through the waning garden and toward the church.

"Bri," Elodie said, a bit more pressingly. "I really don't have time for..." But all protest paused the moment she stepped inside and saw Sabine. The New Maiden was curled up in a pew, her eyes dull. Her hands were folded, blood caked beneath her fingernails, wrists bruised. Her whole body shook, her teeth chattering like she'd been caught in a winter storm. Katrynn and the new Royal Chaplain hovered in the back of the chapel, looking concerned.

"We found her like this," Katrynn said, the moment she saw the queen. "She won't say a word."

"We thought she might talk to you, Majesty." The Royal Chaplain's eyes were grave.

Elodie knelt beside Sabine. She wanted to hold the New Maiden's hand in hers but refrained. She would wait for Sabine to tell her if she wished to be touched. "Sabine." She whispered the New Maiden's name like a prayer. "What happened to you?"

Sabine had not moved when Elodie entered the room, nor when her sister or Silas spoke. It was only at the sound of the queen's voice that she stirred. "I . . ." It sounded as though she had been crying, but her face was dry.

"It's all right." Elodie placed a hand on the wooden pew. "You can tell me."

"Tal . . . ," Sabine began again. That one syllable nearly shattered the queen.

"What did he do to you?"

Sabine reached for Elodie. Her fingers curled around the queen's so tightly it was almost painful. "It's him." When met with Elodie's mystified expression, she tried again. "Tal is the prophet of the Second Son."

Elodie's stomach dropped out from underneath her. She had grown so distracted by Rob's theological musings that she had ignored the most obvious suspect. Tal was unmoored and military minded, used to following orders without question. He understood that in order to defeat an enemy, he needed to understand them first. And so he had forged a relationship, and Sabine—lovely, compassionate Sabine—had taken the bait. Elodie had refused to believe her oldest friend was capable of such deceit, which meant she was at fault. Just as much as Tal.

"That bastard," she said fiercely, her fury tenfold knowing His word guided the predatory Republics, too.

Sabine blinked at her with surprise. "You believe me?"

It broke Elodie's heart that she had harbored any doubt. "Of course I do." The queen sat back on her heels, looking up at Katrynn, Silas, and Brianne. "I'm going to confront him."

"You can't."

Elodie frowned at the New Maiden. "Yes, I can. I do what I wish."

But Sabine shook her head. "Elodie, he's dangerous." She swallowed thickly. The motion drew the queen's gaze to the New Maiden's neck, which was dappled with bruises. "He threatened my life in the training room. I managed to get away, but if he sees me again, I don't know that I'll be so lucky."

Elodie leapt to her feet. "I'll kill him," she said, anger rising so quickly it threatened to knock her off balance. "I'll banish him, I'll lock him in the dungeon to rot."

"You can't protect me from him." Sabine's voice was so quiet Elodie hardly heard it over the ringing in her ears. She had nearly lost Sabine, all because she was too frightened, too *weak*, to see the truth.

"Tal is only the vessel. If we eliminate him, the Second Son will move on to someone else, the same way that if I die, the New Maiden would choose another third daughter. No," Sabine said, shaking her head resolutely. "The Second Son intends to finish off the New Maiden and we need to learn *how*. I am in danger, yes, but so is She."

Elodie wondered at the other girl's loyalty to the New Maiden.

The queen would sacrifice the deity in a second if it meant she could save Sabine.

"We need to use your ties to Tal to get ahead of Him," Sabine continued. "You should go to your friend and let him tell you his side of the story."

Elodie felt sick at the idea of facing Tal after his fingers had left marks upon Sabine.

Katrynn clucked her tongue. "That won't do. If Elodie sidles up prodding for information, he'll grow suspicious. Deceitful men are always defensive."

The chapel was silent as the five women considered this.

"I know what makes him weak," Sabine finally said, looking miserable. "Tal needs to believe that we have ended our relationship. That your heart might one day belong to him instead."

Elodie blanched. This was so far from any strategy she could imagine. "What?"

"You were the catalyst for our argument," Sabine said sheepishly. "His jealousy was his undoing. If you have forsaken me, he'll be much more likely to trust you."

"But I don't—"

"It's probably best to orchestrate a public performance," Katrynn interrupted. "Something loud and messy enough that news spreads quickly through the palace and Tal hears about it from someone other than Elodie. That will feel more authentic."

"And I'll have to leave to uphold the optics," Sabine added grimly. "Although I won't be sorry to put some distance between myself and Tal."

Elodie bit her lip. Sabine would be safer that way. Still, the idea of the other girl on her own made Elodie anxious. She had been unable to protect the New Maiden from the Second Son's manipulations while residing under the same roof. What misfortune might befall her out in the world alone?

"I'll come with you," Katrynn declared.

"No," Sabine said. "Please." She turned to Elodie. "Let my family remain."

"It's not up for negotiation," Katrynn said darkly. "Ma and Artur can stay here, but where you go, I go."

"Me too," Brianne chimed in.

Elodie turned to her youngest sister, surprised. "Bri, are you sure?"

Brianne nodded emphatically. "I'm a third daughter. My place is with the New Maiden."

"All right," Elodie said. But there was nothing right about their situation. If she had discovered Tal's spiritual allegiance, if she had been less distracted by Edgar's threats, perhaps the other women in her life would be safe.

Brianne frowned curiously. "Where would you stage this quarrel to ensure an audience?"

"The corridor outside the south wing library," Katrynn answered immediately, much to Elodie's surprise. "I was having tea with the Duchess of the Upper Banks when two Loyalist guards stood there talking about the Duke of Arlington's second family in the Third Republic." The Duke of Arlington was a self-important man who was always late to deliver his taxes. Now the queen knew why. "His wife hadn't the faintest idea until she found out with the rest of us over tea." Sabine's sister grimaced. "But that's not the best part."

"There's a best part?" It seemed the Royal Chaplain had very little patience for gossip.

121

"The best part is that when I went to tell Ma, she already knew."

"How?" the Royal Chaplain asked, seemingly despite herself.

"She takes tea with the servants," Katrynn explained. "She's more comfortable there."

"And the servants' quarters are beneath the south wing?" Brianne ventured.

"Exactly!" Katrynn beamed. "Ma and I heard the same story at the same time."

Understanding dawned on the New Maiden's face. "The gossip will be dispersed by both servants and nobility. No one will be able to escape the rumors."

It was a decent plan, but Elodie didn't like it one bit. There were too many moving pieces. Too many unknowable parts. But the entire proposal hinged on her participation and subsequent execution. She owed Sabine that, at the very least.

"Fine," she agreed, against her better judgment. She helped Sabine carefully to her feet. The other girl still looked shaken, fragile as a hatchling. "I'm frightened," Elodie said. She put a hand to the New Maiden's cheek.

Sabine nuzzled into her palm, her brown eyes endless pools of light. "Me too."

"Promise you'll be safe?"

Sabine's grim laugh was not a satisfactory answer, but it seemed all the New Maiden had left to give.

"We need to move quickly," Katrynn instructed. "Bet, I'll accompany you to the south wing. Elodie, count to fifty before you follow."

The queen nodded, heart sinking like a stone. She pressed a swift kiss to the New Maiden's lips, as delicate as the flittering of butterfly wings.

On her way out the door, Sabine paused before the Royal Chaplain. "You've been quiet, Silas. Do you disapprove?"

"I know not what to say, Maiden," the older woman admitted softly. "I know not how to advise. I can only pledge to you my fealty and pray for your safety. I will protect your house of worship with all that I have."

Sabine offered the woman a true smile, dipping her head as though in swift prayer before letting Katrynn lead her from the chapel. The Royal Chaplain excused herself, heading for the small office behind the pulpit. This left only Elodie and Brianne. The queen examined the youngest Warnou outright. Where once Elodie would have described her sister as flighty and eager to please, Brianne now seemed stoic and measured, as though her days asleep had drained some of the vibrancy from her soul.

Her sister seemed to have been irrevocably altered, and Elodie was at fault. It struck her then, as she took in Brianne's quiet defiance and deep consideration, that she had never actually apologized for what she had done. With the future so uncertain, Elodie could not allow this fracture to remain between them, no matter the cost to her pride.

"Brianne." Elodie did not know what to say. The words *I'm sorry* felt empty in the wake of using her sibling as a pawn in a power struggle.

"Don't use my full name," Brianne said, wrinkling her nose. "You sound like Mother."

Elodie smiled softly. "You look like Mother. She used to wrinkle her nose just like that whenever she read correspondence from the treasury. It was always bad news."

"I didn't know that." Brianne's eyes were faraway. As she sank down onto a pew, Elodie was struck again by how small her sister was. She had endured so much in her thirteen years and had been alone for the brunt of it. Elodie had been lucky enough to receive the lion's share of her mother's time and attention. It seemed only fair to offer some of those stories to her siblings who had not been granted that same gift.

"She'd also emit this tiny sigh whenever your father left her chambers," Elodie continued, "just like"—she blew a small puff of air out from between her lips, emitting a muffled whistle—"that. Once, he addressed the noise and asked her if she was all right. She blamed it on her pet bird."

Brianne frowned. "Mother had a pet bird?"

Elodie grinned wryly. "She did not."

The room sparkled with Brianne's laughter. That brief glimmer of joy felt bigger than an apology. But Elodie still needed to say the words.

"I'm sorry, Bri." She cleared her throat, uncomfortable. "For what I did to you. It was wrong to put you at such risk. I can't begin to tell you—" Brianne held up a hand to cut her off.

"It's not all right," she said, shaking her head. "What you did."

"I know," Elodie said immediately.

"You could have killed me," Brianne said accusingly.

"I know," Elodie echoed.

"Did you really desire to be queen so badly?"

"No," Elodie whispered. She wanted desperately to reach for her sister's hand, but this moment was not intended for her comfort. This moment belonged to Brianne alone.

"I won't hold on to it," the youngest Warnou said. "I can't. I have too much to carry already." She stretched her arms toward the ceiling. "So thank you for the apology. I guess."

Elodie nodded. She felt almost relieved not to be forgiven. "You're welcome."

"Don't ever do it again," Brianne said, warningly.

Elodie crossed her heart with her right hand. "Never. I swear it."

"Good." Brianne sat back in the pew, foot jiggling with restless energy.

"Good." Elodie matched her pose, watching her sister in her peripheral vision. Brianne did not look happier, but her sadness seemed lighter, somehow. "I should go."

"Be careful, Ellie."

"You too, Bri." Elodie squeezed her sister's shoulder. "I'll see you soon."

The afternoon sun cast spindles of light across the browning hedges of the royal garden. The rosebushes had shed everything but their thorns, the brambles ready to snag an unsuspecting cloak. Elodie felt as sharp as those prickly plants, hated that she would have to make nice with Tal after he had targeted Sabine. But the New Maiden was right. Ingratiating herself with the prophet was the best way to keep Sabine safe.

Inside the castle, empty hallways incited fear that their spectacle might be for naught. But as she turned the corridor to the south wing, voices rang out from behind the many guest room doors. Elodie praised Katrynn for her sharp and devious mind.

One hand pressed to the smooth stone of the palace walls, the queen steeled herself for what came next. She called forth the grim, unyielding expression her mother wore when enforcing controversial decisions, and fit that look upon her own face. She exhaled her guilt and suffocating doubt, then strode toward the library where Sabine and her sister were stationed.

She called the name of the New Maiden, her voice hard and cold. Even though Sabine had been expecting her, she jumped. The fear in her eyes looked uncomfortably real.

Sabine swept into a considered curtsy. "Majesty. To what do I owe the pleasure?"

"You know why I am here," Elodie said chillily. "I heard about the incident in the training room."

"You did?" Sabine's eyes widened. "Then perhaps you can understand—"

"There is nothing to understand." Elodie's voice was merciless enough that Sabine flinched. There was movement behind several of the doors. One opened a crack, although none of them were brave enough to show their face. People were listening, then.

"You attacked a good soldier in a fit of madness." She tried to swallow her revulsion at using Sabine's darkness against her. "Endangering the life of a Loyalist is crime enough, but Tal is my oldest friend. Anyone who would treat him in such a way betrays not only her country but the heart of her queen."

"Elodie, I—"

"You may address me as *Your Majesty*," Elodie said coldly. Now several members of the nobility stepped out from behind their doors to stare openly. "I cannot indulge unrest within the palace, and thus, you have lost the privilege of my protection. Now pack your belongings and begone."

Sabine's eyes swam with tears. "Surely you don't mean that," she protested. "You wouldn't—"

Elodie wanted to run to her. Instead, she folded her arms across her chest. "Do not dare tell me what I will or won't do."

Sabine sank to her knees and began to weep. More and more

courtiers appeared, whispers building as they gawked at the New Maiden's misfortune. The louder Sabine sobbed, the worse Elodie felt. She knew the emotion was artificial, that her own cruel words had only been props in a production. Still, she could not shake the inherent horror that came from denying a woman the truth.

Elodie prayed the New Maiden had faith in the contents of her heart. Then she turned on her heel and headed for her study. There was nothing to do now but wait and hope the castle's inhabitants were as loose-lipped as Katrynn had led her to believe. If all went according to plan, Elodie would soon receive a visit from the prophet of the Second Son.

Tal

Tal was used to being hurt by those he loved: his father, whose calloused hands seemed made to inflict suffering; his mother, whose silence was proof her loyalty did not belong to her son; Elodie, who prioritized country above romance and thus did not return his devotions.

The front lines were a place to heal and grow in more ways than one. The Second Son offered Tal the satisfaction of being seen. He witnessed the boy's pain, the serpentine shadow that slithered through his bloodstream, squeezing the air from his lungs. Rather than chastising his inadequacy, the Second Son taught Tal how to tame his emotion. Where once the shadow sank its fangs into Tal's heart, darkening his mood and injecting him with paranoia, now Tal could suck the poison from his wounds and turn that venom into anger.

Tal's anguish became rage. His pain became power.

Made comfortable by the weight of a weapon in his hand, Tal wielded His word easily. He extracted dormant anger from his compatriots and filled the empty space with His teachings. Tal converted ten men, then fifty. Soon the medical tent grew too small to fit His followers.

"You have done well, my son," said Ludwig, the gray-haired soldier who had tended to his wounds and to his soul. "But it is time for you to go."

Tal's blood ran cold. "Have I displeased Him?"

"On the contrary." Ludwig smiled. "You have proved yourself essential. Your impact will be greater on the front lines of His battle than it ever could be here in the training camps. Take this"—he handed Tal a knapsack that contained discharge papers, a thin gold chain, and an unfamiliar uniform—"and take Him." He handed Tal a small glass vial. Inside was a single black berry.

Puzzled, Tal held the vial to the light.

"The better to know Him," Ludwig said. "May He guide your every step."

Tal smashed the berry between his teeth. A trickle of juice dribbled down his chin. A shadow flitted across his vision. A voice flickered to life inside his head.

In this way, the prophet was made.

When Tal returned to Velle, he did not do so alone. He carried with him the Second Son.

PART THREE

The Second Son was the only Favored impervious to the New Maiden's word. While the others melted like wax around Her wick, Sebastien alone remained untouched. His heart was guarded, the barrier impenetrable by tender words alone. This only made Her more invested in him.

Just as Sebastien's vision had foretold, the two grew inseparable. The New Maiden vowed to become acquainted with every piece of his soul, the better to reach him. They were so entangled it was sometimes difficult to remember where one stopped and the other began. Their minds met, their fingers intertwined, even their hearts beat in time. But one obstacle remained between them.

It was the New Maiden who first addressed the unspeakable.

"Let me unburden you, Seb," She whispered. "Let me hold the darkness for you so that I may know you fully."

Sebastien refused, for he did not wish to subject Her to such horrors. But She would not relent, and eventually he agreed. The Second Son offered the New Maiden his darkness, and then finally he was free.

—Psalm of the Second Son

15

Sabine had once dreamed of the freedom to weep without consequence, had coveted the thought of tears spilling heedlessly from her face, pooling at her feet, unbottled and uncontrolled. But as she wept in the south wing before an audience of courtiers, Elodie's call for her banishment still ringing in her ears, Sabine could not help but think that without her magic, crying was an empty gesture, a waste of energy. Worst of all, it offered her no release.

"Bet." Katrynn helped Sabine to her feet, her voice firm. "Bet, it's time to go."

The whispering had already begun, talk of the New Maiden's volatility fluttering about like a bird trapped indoors. Sabine wished it were so simple. She had only just begun to understand her emotions when she had ascended as the New Maiden. Then everything changed. Without the darkness, she could not connect her heart with her actions, could not identify the murky emotions that now guided her. They held none of the clarity of her darkness, offered no glimpse of its sharp tongue, refused to slither around her heart or slip beneath her skin. Her current emotions merely clung to her, dulling her senses and clouding her vision.

"You should all be ashamed of yourselves," Katrynn called to the onlookers as she guided her sister past their hungry eyes. "Have you nothing more valuable to do than spread gossip of the New Maiden's missteps?"

Not one observer seemed the least bit chagrined as the sisters hurried toward the Anders family's quarters.

"Well, that was the turnout we wished for, wasn't it?" Katrynn asked quietly as she pushed open the door.

To the sisters' surprise, their mother was there, as though she had been standing with her ear pressed against the wood, the better to hear. Artur was thrashing about the bedroom.

"What's going on?" Katrynn frowned at the chaos.

"We heard everything," Artur said, poking his head into the sitting room, his expression sour. "Clearly, you're not welcome here, and our family sticks together. So we're packing."

"He's right, love." Orla Anders pulled her younger daughter into an embrace. "I know you cared for her, and we appreciate the hospitality, but no one should speak to you that way. We won't stand for it."

Sabine used her sleeve to wipe away the tears still streaked across her cheeks. "You believe me banished, then?"

Her mother frowned. "Bet, she made that impossibly clear. She really was rather cruel."

"That's good." Sabine cleared her throat. "It means we were convincing."

134

Orla blinked at her bewilderedly. "Whatever do you mean?"

"It was an act." She waved for Artur to join them in the sitting room. "The Second Son's prophet has revealed himself, and Elodie agreed to keep an eye on him."

"By banishing you?" Her mother sounded skeptical.

"By proving her loyalty to him." Sabine pursed her lips. "To Tal."

Her brother's face darkened. "He keeps trying to get me to come to his inane meetings. 'Just hear Him out,' he said. But I always said no." He turned to his sister, eyes wide and earnest. "You have to believe me. I want nothing to do with his miserable cult."

"You must go to that meeting," she insisted, excitement rising in her chest. "Find out what he's preaching. Flying fish, Artur!" She clapped her hands together as she swore. "This is exactly what I need to understand His word—to infiltrate enemy lines."

"Are you sure?" Artur looked uncomfortable. "There is a wickedness about him and the others."

"I'm certain," Sabine insisted. "Just keep your wits about you. Tell the queen where you are going and fill her in on all the details."

"Tell Cleo, too," Katrynn added, winking at Artur, "so she can keep track of your whereabouts." His face bloomed a beautiful pink.

"I don't like this, Bet," her mother said, shaking her head. "We were supposed to be safe here."

"*You* are safe here," Sabine insisted. "I need you to swear to me that you will stay put. I am relying on you and Artur to be my eyes and ears in the palace."

Her mother was tearing up. "Sabine, you're just a child."

"I'm not." The New Maiden shook her head sadly. "Not since I learned the truth of my birth order. Not since I embraced what—and *who*—I am."

"Oh, Bet." Her mother's voice came out choked. "This is why Genevar worked so hard to keep my secret. *Your* secret."

Sabine owed much to the old woman who resided in the First Church. Genevar, the Archivist, had kept meticulous records of the children born to Velle, had protected Sabine from befalling the fate of the third daughters before her.

The Archivist had been the one to tell Sabine that she was Velle's highest deity, born to the salt of Harborside. Genevar had even shared with Sabine the original *Book of the New Maiden*. The ancient pages were filled with cramped handwriting and smudged ink, words recorded by one of the New Maiden's Favoreds, Ruti. In the corner of her mind, Sabine could almost picture a second book, this one with a blue leather cover, containing words written by the New Maiden Herself. Not Her scripture—Her journal. *Do you ever feel a stirring within?* Genevar had asked Sabine as she flipped through its pages. *Does power run through your veins?*

Sabine could have kicked herself. All this time, private reflections written by the New Maiden had been sitting, waiting in the depths of the First Church's Archives. She'd been so busy fretting over the Second Son's threat when she could have been studying confessions penned by the New Maiden. Perhaps within those pages she would learn about Sebastien, of their enmity and their love, and find a way to snip the strange thread that connected her to Tal.

"That's it," Sabine whispered, getting to her feet.

"What is?" Katrynn eyed her curiously.

"Sanctuary," the New Maiden said, finding comfort in the word. She got to her feet. "Let's find Brianne. I know where we can go."

The late autumn air took on the threat of winter as Sabine, Brianne, and Katrynn followed the path to the First Church. The chapel was small and unassuming, its white stone dingy amidst the dying leaves of amber and brown. Brianne heaved the door open with a low grunt, the hinges howling like the wind. The room was deserted, save for an owl slumbering in the rafters. A single prayer candle was lit. Its flame sent shadows dancing across the white-washed walls.

"Who goes there?" The Archivist's voice was harsh.

She stepped out from the shadows. "It's Sabine."

The old woman reached out a gnarled hand. Sabine rushed to clasp it. "What are you doing here?"

"I missed you," she answered honestly. Genevar and the First Church had been a port in Sabine's storm.

"And?" The Archivist leaned heavily on her cane, a small smile playing about her lips.

"And we need your help," Sabine admitted, introducing the Archivist to her sister and Brianne.

"Maiden." Genevar bowed her head reverently. "I would bend my knees if I thought they would survive it. As ever, it is my gift to serve you however I may."

Although Sabine had grown accustomed to being addressed by the moniker, it felt unearned coming from the Archivist's mouth. Genevar had been the one to reveal Sabine's place in the prophecy. But just as quickly as Sabine had embraced her darkness and its magic, they had escaped her. While her family, the Warnou sisters, and Silas continued to believe in her despite the absence of her power, the Second Son's cruel words and His swift annexation of her clergy had left Sabine feeling entirely unworthy.

"Do you really believe I am Her?"

If the Archivist was worth her weight in salt—and, as a Harborside native, she surely was—Genevar would speak the truth.

The Archivist frowned. "There is faith involved, certainly, but I am a daughter of Ruti, and we do not doubt what has been seen with our own eyes. I know what you can do."

"So you do leave the depths of the Archives on occasion?" Sabine had hoped that the old woman did not spend all her days in the dark.

Genevar's mouth quirked up into a mischievous grin. "I saw you call forth the shadows. Then I saw you let in the light."

But her conviction set Sabine spiraling. If the Archivist believed only in what she could see, then the absence of Sabine's magic would forcibly dislodge her faith in the New Maiden.

"This bothers you." The old woman studied Sabine's guarded expression. "Why?"

"Because," Sabine whispered, unable to stop herself. Genevar had already protected her life's most fearsome secret once. Sabine had to trust that she would remain faithful now. "Whatever magic I had once has run dry. I am just a girl from Harborside, tasked with an impossible fight."

"Nothing is impossible, Sabine, so long as you are equipped with the right information," the Archivist said. "You've come here for assistance. So tell me what you seek."

"I had hoped you might allow me to look upon the New Maiden's journal." Sabine squeezed her hands into fists to stop her fingers from shaking. Now that she stood in the chapel, she feared that she was misremembering, that no such document existed, and she would be forced to leave the Archives empty-handed. "I thought it might offer me insight into the person, the human, behind Her word."

"Certainly, Maiden," Genevar said, pointing them toward the circular staircase. "Please, follow me below."

The old woman led the way to the Archives. The first step plunged them into sharp, suffocating cold, unforgiving all the way down. Once they reached the ground, Genevar lit the lanterns one by one. Brianne's eyes widened as she took in their surroundings.

"There are so many words here," the youngest Warnou gasped.

Genevar chuckled at her enthusiasm. "Indeed, Princess. This is a room of secrets, and I am the keeper of them all."

Brianne looked awestruck, but Katrynn shivered. "Too much responsibility."

Genevar met her eyes. "At times it can feel onerous. But at others," she said, crossing the room to her large desk where she located a small bound book, "it is the most wonderful gift. A magic all my own."

She offered the journal to Sabine. The New Maiden wavered before accepting it. She stood there a moment, one hand atop the book, the other beneath it, as though she could ingest its contents without ever cracking its cover. She was frightened by the potential of such a document. She had no idea what she might find within its pages.

"Girls," the Archivist called to Brianne and Katrynn, "let me show you the script of the New Maiden's first sermon." She led them to a long shelf, just far enough from where Sabine stood that they were no longer in her sight. That semblance of privacy gave her the courage to peel back the first thin page and study the careful handwriting of the girl whose soul she had inherited.

I thought that what I wanted was power, the New Maiden had written, *when what I really wanted was love. I misunderstood the way the two can be seen, felt, and redeemed. They cannot coexist, not really, not ever. Now the world sits in the palm of my hand, and I have never felt more alone. I watch people fall at my feet, worship at the altar of my word, and yet to them I am an idol, not a person. I am nothing but what I can offer them, and I do not know what that means for the girl I used to be. How do I reconcile what was and what is? How can I get what I wanted, instead of what I have been given?*

Sabine gasped softly, heart fluttering. It was almost like having her darkness back, comforting in its needling, the way it wormed directly into the unguarded corners of her heart and settled like a sigh.

Genevar peered around a shelf. "Maiden, are you all right?"

Sabine nodded, mutely. She didn't know how to explain that the New Maiden's words read like sentiments she could have penned herself. It was uncanny, to see her own fear and insecurity scrawled across the page in a hand that belonged to another. She had expected the New Maiden to be an infallible figure, but on the page, she was a flesh and blood girl, the same as Sabine.

"Maiden, forgive me if I overstep," Genevar said gently, as she, Brianne, and Katrynn emerged from the stacks, "but your sister has told me of your recent plight. Is there anything that I can do to assist you?"

"I know not what the Second Son wants," Sabine said. "And so I cannot comprehend Him."

Genevar scowled. "Bad enough history had to suffer Him once. Twice is twice too much."

Sabine was so startled that she very nearly laughed. The Second Son was a figure shrouded in such mystery that it was a comfort to hear Him discussed so casually. "What do you know of Him?"

The Archivist's expression was far away. "Sebastien was the younger child of the Lower Banks' leader, destined for nothing. Second sons have no right to inheritance, after all."

So he'd had nothing to lose by abandoning his family, and everything to gain by aligning himself with power.

"In the *Book of the New Maiden*," Genevar continued, "he is said to fight Her word tooth and nail, but at the end of Her life, he was the one who founded the Church."

"So he could murder third daughters without consequence," Brianne said darkly.

"But why would She designate him as a Favored if he was so quick to question Her?" Katrynn asked the Archivist. "Surely if he was so terrible, She would have exiled him before he betrayed Her?"

"Oh, I'm certain their enmity was played up for dramatic effect," Genevar said. "If there was no tension in the *Book of the New Maiden*, no drama, it would be difficult to ensure readership. Her word is good, but word is not always enough. Platitudes without passion cannot stand the test of time."

Sabine was intimately acquainted with that truth. She clutched the New Maiden's writings tightly to her chest. The journal might help with understanding the dynamic between the New Maiden and Sebastien, but words would do nothing to bring her powers back.

"We may never truly know what occurred between them,"

Genevar said. "But within that book I believe you will find some of the answers that you seek."

"Do you think that will be enough to conquer the Second Son's darkness?" Sabine cleared her throat, her voice coming out hoarse. "Without Her magic, I cannot see how to defeat Him."

"Then we must resource your faith." The Archivist spoke as though it was all so simple. As though Sabine's fear was for naught.

"How?" the New Maiden whispered.

"By going back to where it all began," Genevar said, "to the place where Her magic first emerged, and where Her word was scribed." Sabine leaned forward, curiosity piqued. "At last, Sabine," the Archivist said, smiling true and wide, "we must travel to the Lower Banks."

16

Gossip moved quickly about the castle, easily taking on a life of its own. On the walk back to her chambers, Elodie was cornered by no fewer than five nobles inquiring if the New Maiden had killed a man. Another six wanted to know if Elodie and Tal were to be wed. Somehow, all eleven knew for certain that Sabine had been banished from the palace.

They each approached the queen with such eagerness, whispering theatrically as though they shared some scandalous secret. But Elodie had not delighted in her cruelty. The chilliness with which she had dismissed Sabine had left her own heart aching, and that coldness seeped straight into her bones.

After the theatrics of the afternoon, the queen wanted nothing more than to shut herself up in her bedroom, pull closed all the curtains, and wallow in complete darkness. So, when a frantic Marguerite located her in the east wing and informed her there was a visitor in her sitting room, Elodie wanted to scream. Instead, she steeled herself for yet another indignity. But the moment she opened her chamber door, all fluster was forgotten.

"Father!" She flung herself upon him violently, nearly knocking the poor man to the ground. Duke Antony Wilde steadied himself, wrapping his only daughter into a giant hug. It was then that Elodie gave in to her most elemental, childish needs and began to sob.

"Oh dear," said the duke, as her tears ran a river down his doublet. "I thought you might be happy to see me, but I certainly didn't expect you to be moved to tears. This is quite an honor."

Elodie laughed, wanting to hit him and hug him closer in equal measure. She settled for the latter. When she had finally managed to compose herself, she gestured for her father to sit, wiping away her tears with the heels of her hands.

"I almost hesitate to ask, but as your father I must inquire"—he grimaced, as though he already knew the answer—"are you...all right?" After the emotional events of the day, Elodie surely looked a fright.

"I most certainly am not," she said, gratefully accepting the teacup Marguerite placed in her hands before leaving the room. "I've never been more exhausted or afraid. I have no idea who I can trust, and people are only nice to me in hopes that I'll eventually do something to benefit them." She took a sip of tea, letting the floral liquid linger on her tongue.

"It is isolating, being queen," her father agreed, surveying the many bite-size cakes laid out before them, "but at least you're rewarded in miniature pastries."

Elodie laughed, despite herself. "Try the lemon." She gestured to a curd-filled ladyfinger. Her father took a bite, gasping in delight.

"Seems to be the monarchy's only benefit," she confirmed. "Unfettered access to tiny cakes."

"My dear, I don't know how you do it." Her father stirred cream into his tea. "Court politics overwhelm me. It's why I live so far from the city."

"And how do the farmers feel about the newly enforced rations?" she asked, clenching her jaw in anticipation of more terrible news.

"Oh, they're absolutely spitting with anger," her father said blithely. "They grow the food, and so think they should not have to bend to the whims of the crown. But all of them have clandestine crops they don't pay taxes on, so they don't really have a leg to stand on when it comes to ethics."

"I don't think you're meant to tell me that," Elodie said, trying not to laugh.

Her father considered this. "I never know what I should and shouldn't say. I can barely balance a grain ledger, let alone political machinations. It always surprised me how your mother managed to be so many places at once—somehow, she was able to prioritize her allegiances, build relationships abroad, rule, strategize, *and* raise you all."

Elodie snorted. While her mother had been an excellent monarch, she had been a terrible mother.

"Well, she kept up the illusion of maternal instinct at any rate," her father said, shrugging. "You likely got more of her time than any of your siblings, if I had to guess."

That was certainly true. Tera Warnou had been very particular about imbuing her first daughter with her knowledge. "I've wondered about that. Mother knew so much, not only about being queen, but also what it took to be the queen's right hand. She had me training to be an adviser my whole life, even though, were it not for her untimely death, Brianne would not have taken the throne until she was of age."

"That isn't so surprising, is it?" Her father reached for a sponge cake. "Tera was a third daughter, which put her third in line for the throne. An advisory role was the closest to the crown she ever thought she'd get. A set of strange, dark circumstances is the only reason that your mother ever ruled. I suppose she wanted her daughters to be prepared in case of something equally sinister."

Elodie put her teacup delicately down on its saucer. She did not want her shaking hands to give away exactly how desperate she was for the information that lay behind the door her father had just unlocked.

"What happened to my aunts?"

Tera Warnou had been notoriously tight-lipped about her two elder sisters. Elodie had learned from a very young age not to mention them, as her mother would close herself off in her study, leaving Elodie out in the corridor, alone. The one time she had pressed Bale, the elderly steward, for information about the deceased queens, he had gone pale as a ghost and promptly fled. That night, Elodie had received a swift, precise slap from her mother, the pain making it explicitly clear that Elodie's loyalty belonged to the living Warnou women, not the dead ones.

Her father sighed, putting down a half-eaten jelly roll. "I wasn't here then, so what I've heard is secondhand. I had taken a position as a tutor on an estate in Upper Tyne, instructing some ghastly relative thirteen degrees removed from the throne. While your mother and I corresponded frequently, I knew only what she told me: that they were gone within a month of each other. One took her own life; the other drowned. It was terrible, both for the country and for your mother. But she rallied, best she could. Took that grief and channeled it into something productive: securing Velle's future as the geopolitical backbone of the continent. No thanks to her sisters, mind you."

Elodie frowned. "What do you mean?"

"Aurielle and Ursula were not the most civically minded. They traded away bushels of vegetables to ensure that the finest silks were imported faster. They put a moratorium on education, let the Church have its way so long as the tithes were paid. Your mother spent half her reign trying to undo their work."

Elodie took a bite of cake to give herself a moment to spin up a segue. "Strange, isn't it, that mother didn't have an adviser?"

Her father squinted at her. "Is it?"

"This was a poor attempt at a leading question," Elodie admitted. "I found something of hers recently. A stack of letters. Trouble is, I can't for the life of me figure out who she was writing to." She pulled the missives from their hiding place beneath the table. "You knew her for so long and spent so much of your lives entwined, I just assumed, if anyone would know, it would be you."

"And here I thought you missed your precious father." He chuckled, reaching into his pocket to retrieve his spectacles. "Let me see." His eyes swept across the page. The longer he read, the harder he frowned.

"What?" He held up a hand, eyes scanning the page. "What?" Elodie repeated. Her father was very quiet, refusing to meet her eyes. "Father?"

"Elodie." But the humor in his voice wavered. Finally, he returned her gaze. "She wouldn't want me to tell you."

Triumph sparked in her chest even as she outwardly pouted. "Why not?" Her instincts had been correct. Her father knew the truth. Now she simply needed to coax it out of him.

"She made me promise never to tell her children. It feels wrong to break that promise, even now." He looked very sorry indeed. Still, his clear conscience would do his daughter no good.

"My mother died an untimely death," Elodie said flatly, "and I am tasked with upholding her legacy, which she loved more than any of her children." Her father pursed his lips, considering. "But I am failing. My mother is not here to tell me what to do, and while she prepared me to advise, she did *not* prepare me to rule."

Elodie looked at her father with mournful eyes. "I'm slipping. My people are starving because a petulant boy cannot accept that I will not marry him. The Republics have banded together, their alliance forming an army three times the size of my own. I need someone strategic to help me navigate these decisions. Lady above, Dad, I need an *adult*. Someone who understands what my mother would have done and how she would have prevailed. Who understands how tenuous and terrible this responsibility truly is."

Elodie slid from the settee onto the floor at her father's feet. The Queen of Velle was not too proud to plead, especially with someone historically powerless in the face of her vulnerability. A single tear ran down her cheek. "Please."

That did it. "Very well," her father said quickly, waving Elodie away with his handkerchief. "You're right. Your mother is gone, and she took many secrets with her. This one can be a gift for you." He chuckled darkly. "Nicely done, by the way, appealing to my tender sensibilities." His humor faded as he cleared his throat, looking uncomfortable. "Your mother had a third sister."

Elodie sat, stunned. She had envisioned an ally one continent over. Perhaps an admiral who provided intel from the sea. What she had not expected was a secret sister.

"Rowan was younger than your mother," her father continued. "They were thick as thieves, like you and Cleo. Did everything together. When Tera took the crown, she assumed that Rowan would stay by her side. Instead, the fourth sister fled. Tera didn't know where she'd gone. Hence the unsent letters." He gestured to the pile. "Something happened between them. Your mother never told me, and when I pressed, she urged me to stop asking. To swear I'd never speak of her again." He sighed. "There are far too many mysteries buried beneath the Warnou family tree."

But Elodie could not empathize with her father's remorse. Instead, she radiated with excitement. Somewhere in the world existed a person who had known her mother from birth, knew her intimately as only a sister could. Someone who could read her mother's words and understand the intent behind them. Someone who would be able to offer Elodie the guidance she so desperately needed.

"Thank you," she told her father. "Truly. My mother would thank you, too, if she could."

"I don't know where Rowan is, mind you," he said, still frowning. "Or if she's even still alive. And I cannot guarantee that you'll like what you learn if you do find her."

But Elodie would not let this potential discomfort keep her from the truth. Whatever had wedged a divide between Rowan and Tera was surely worth uncovering.

Elodie was visited by her own younger sister only moments after the duke had departed. Cleo barged into the queen's chambers without so much as a knock.

"What did you do?" the middle Warnou demanded, intercepting her sister, who had risen to draw herself a well-deserved bath. "Why would you banish Sabine?"

"You heard," Elodie said dully.

"Yes I heard," Cleo said incredulously. "The whole castle has heard. The only thing I can't figure out is *why?*"

"I take it you did not hear about her attack on Tal?"

Cleo frowned. "I just assumed he had it coming."

Elodie sighed. "I'm certain he did."

"Then why—?"

"Cleo..." Elodie raised her eyebrows, waiting for her savvy sister to put the pieces together.

"Oh." Cleo pursed her lips. "It was a ruse."

"And a half-decent one at that," Elodie added, "considering you fell for it."

"I would have realized eventually," Cleo sighed, sinking into a velvet chair. "Can I have this cake?" She gestured to the final lemon finger.

The queen nodded her permission. "Anything else you'd like to berate me for?"

Cleo did not speak until she had finished her pastry. "Oh. Artur asked me to give you this." She held out a folded piece of parchment. It was not sealed.

Elodie frowned as she flipped the paper open. It contained only a handful of words. *The Whispering Willow. Iron District. Tomorrow.*

Six bells. The queen turned the note over, hoping to locate further context on the back. She found nothing.

"What does this mean?"

Cleo shrugged. "I haven't the faintest idea." She paused. "Want me to find out?"

"If you wish," Elodie said. "But if you do, don't come back for at least an hour. I've had a terrible day and I wish to take a bath." Her shoulders were so tense that she could hardly lift them. Her neck was littered with knots.

"Certainly, sister," Cleo said, before disappearing as quickly as she'd come.

Elodie closed her eyes. The rhythmic sounds of Marguerite preparing the bath very nearly lulled her to sleep. Just as she sensed her lady-in-waiting's reappearance in the room, there came yet another knock on her door.

"Whoever it is, turn them away," Elodie said firmly. The water would stay warm for only a handful of minutes. But before Marguerite had time even to cross the room, Tal flung the door open and strode inside. His lip was split, and his cheeks boasted bright red scrapes. Otherwise, he looked unharmed.

"I just heard," the Loyalist said, kneeling on the carpet at Elodie's feet. "I cannot thank you enough for taking my side."

"It's nothing." Elodie hoped her careful expression belied her discomfort. "When I heard about the senseless attack, it was not even a question." She swallowed her disgust and put a hand to his cheek. "You look a fright."

Tal chuckled softly, leaning into her touch. "It doesn't hurt so much, now."

Elodie worried her lip between her teeth. This tender side of Tal had been the foundation of their friendship. She'd first met the blacksmith's boy in the stables when they were eight. After delivering a package of newly forged horseshoes, Tal hung around to feed sugar cubes to the animals. Elodie, preparing for a riding lesson, had found him in her horse's stall, whispering to Lula, her spotted mare. His cheeks flushed pink when he noticed the princess, hastily rolling down his sleeves to hide his bruises and burns.

This one's my favorite, Tal had declared, patting her horse's speckled rump affectionately.

She's mine, Elodie had told him, not wanting Lula to like anyone more than her. *I picked her because of her spots. They make her special.*

Tal had blinked at her with his green eyes. *I wish I was special.*

Elodie had never met anyone else who had expressed this sentiment aloud. For eight years, she had believed herself to be the only person ever to feel less than. The only person who ever cursed her existence or regretted her station.

She skipped her afternoon riding lesson that day, instead sharing stories with Tal while sucking on sugar cubes, laughing through their sticky lips. It was a wonder, to be understood. To escape the insurmountable isolation that came with being Tera Warnou's daughter. To avoid the crushing disappointment that came from knowing she would never be queen.

She saw that tender boy again now. The glimpse of Tal as he had once been only served to discomfit her more, knowing what malevolence he now contained.

"Do I have your loyalty, Lo?" Tal closed his eyes, his cheek still resting in Elodie's hand.

The question caught her off guard. "Of course you do," she lied.

"I must admit," Tal said, voice lazy and low, "there were many moments when I questioned your allegiance."

"It pains me that I ever gave you reason to doubt," Elodie said, the sentiment far emptier than when she had offered it to Sabine.

Tal fluttered his eyes open, his smile unbearably soft. "It is a welcome change, knowing the New Maiden no longer resides under this roof. Her madness was unnerving, I feared for my life." He shuddered theatrically, rising from the floor to join the queen on the couch. Elodie suppressed the urge to roll her eyes. "Now that I know you are truly on His side, He can recruit more openly."

"More posters?" Elodie asked. Tal looked pleased that she'd noticed the Second Son's tactics.

"We've begun meeting with potential followers around the city," he said. "Identifying those daring enough to suck the poisons from their wounds." He grinned. "We have a gathering tomorrow. Oh, Lo, you can't imagine the energy that fills the room. There is something so powerful about the moment He is accepted into their hearts."

"Don't leave me to imagine it, then," Elodie insisted, skin prickling with excitement. "Take me with you."

"Not yet." The two words knocked the wind out of her. "Your presence will only serve as a distraction, when they should be focused on communing with His word."

Elodie nodded placidly. Pushing Tal further would only make him suspicious. But she was not discouraged by his tight lips. She slid a hand into her pocket and wrapped her fingers around the scrap of parchment. Sabine was wise and her brother no less cunning. She was certain Artur Anders had supplied Cleo with the address of the very meeting where Tal would convert new followers to the word of the Second Son. "Whatever serves Him best."

"It is nice to hear you speak of Him," Tal said, nudging her shoulder gently. "I can't tell you what it means to me."

She offered him a weak smile. "Anything for you."

But Elodie was already plotting her next betrayal. She could not wait. She would not wonder. Tomorrow, she would don a disguise and sneak into the city, where she would learn everything she could about the Second Son.

17

The road to the Lower Banks wove south down the coast, the ocean waves lapping cozily against the shoreline, a reminder that wherever Sabine traveled, the sea was the same. This was the farthest she had ever been from Harborside, but the salt air that floated through the carriage window settled her anxious stomach.

Trees grew in strange, spindly directions, larger than anything even in the Garden District. Some trunks were ashy and burnt, others deep brown and full of flaky bark. The leaves spun and shifted in the wind, floating slowly down to litter the shoreline.

On the bench opposite Sabine, Katrynn and Brianne chatted quietly. The carriage jostled, sending Genevar's shoulder into Sabine's sternum. She squeezed her eyes shut, processing the pain.

"You've got the right idea," the Archivist said. "It's rather late. Might rest my eyes. I recommend you girls do the same."

She was snoring softly in seconds. Sabine, who had never known sleep to come so easily, didn't bother to try. Instead, as the conversation between Katrynn and Brianne finally tapered off into silence, the rhythm of the coach lulling them both to sleep, Sabine pulled the New Maiden's journal from where it rested against her hip.

The book was soothing beneath her fingers, the leather as soft as Elodie's sheets. Already, Sabine missed Velle's queen, craved their easy connection and the girl's tender touch. It hurt to leave, but in order to take on Tal, Sabine needed the ability to harness the New Maiden's full power. She would find that magic only by venturing to the Lower Banks.

She leaned her head against the window, reveling in the comfort of the cool glass against her skin. The landscape blurred in her peripheral vision as she flipped through a handful of pages, past musings about destruction and the concept of home, pausing on a passage that detailed Her relationship with Petra and Hera.

The sisters are loyal in both heart and help, the New Maiden had written, *in ways that I do not deserve. When first our leader turned away, plotting his venture to the world beyond, that voice within me—that guiding light—set to screaming. I knew I could not go, though I did not know why. Now, I understand its message. I had work to do.*

The sisters could have gone. Should *have gone. Yet when I turned to Petra, her hand wrapped carefully in mine, she had only to meet my eyes for me to know. "You're staying." It wasn't a question, but then, Petra has never questioned me. While I may not deserve her steadfast devotion, I am grateful for it. And wherever Petra goes, Hera follows. Three is a powerful number.*

Three makes a beginning.

The carriage jerked as they barreled through a rut in the road. Katrynn readjusted her cheek on the top of Brianne's head. The thirteen-year-old was slumped against Katrynn's shoulder, her breathing steady and slow. The two of them were just as dedicated to Sabine as the pair of Favored sisters had been to the New Maiden.

It is strange, the way love changes, slowly, then all at once. There was a time when Hera grasped at our skirts, showing up with little treasures, trying to sneak into our good graces. Now she never tries, she only does. She tends the fire, boils water, takes first watch without being asked.

She has turned her trinkets into offerings, has left so many on the hearth that we had to move the cooking fire. The stones are now littered with dried petals and gnarled sticks, tiny clay cups of wine.

"For you," she says, each time she adds to the collection. What she feels for me is no longer love alone. It's devotion.

Petra, too, has changed. Once my equal, the balance has been thrown. Her admiration frightens me, for it is unearned. There is no reason I should be the one to shape our new world from these ashes. I am simply a girl who refused to leave home. Who held enough emotion inside her to weep a thousand tears. I do not feel different than I used to be. It is only the response of others that has altered.

Sabine glanced up at Katrynn, who was snoring softly. Like Petra, her sister had changed. When Sabine had struggled with her sadness alone in their Harborside apartment, Katrynn had not always been so kind. But now that her emotionality held some greater purpose, she had the full deference of her patently ungovernable older sister. Sabine had done nothing new to earn that adoration. But then, was faith *earned*? She was not so sure.

Where the sisters offer me consistent comfort, the New Maiden had continued, *he is instrumental to my growth.*

Sabine's breath hitched. This could be only one person—the final member of the Lower Banks' strange quartet. Sebastien.

He questions me so intimately it treads close to invasiveness, yet there is something about him that will not leave me be, a curious pull that unmoors me and bids me to answer.

We were not meant to be enemies, Tal had told Sabine in the training room. The New Maiden's words seemed to imply the same. She had written of Sebastien favorably, captured the strange, tangible draw Sabine had felt toward Tal, who harbored within him the spirit of the Second Son. The two of them were tangled in an intricate web woven by their forebearers.

"Where did your goodness come from?" he asks, gold eyes white in the firelight. *"What does it feel like when you weep?"*

Sebastien tries so desperately to hide his pain, but it radiates from him. Each time he searches for a crack in my foundation, he exposes his own impossible hurts.

To him, I think I began as a convenient savior, a pertinent escape from a terrible situation. But the more time we spend together, the more profoundly I understand his heart, the more I truly wish to offer him salvation.

Sabine had known that the Maiden had risen to power at seventeen, the same age she was now. But seeing Her life laid out in Her own hand was the first time she truly understood: The New Maiden was not just a portrait hung above an altar. The girl who had brought back the water to the Lower Banks—who had promised good for generations, who had the power to heal and hope—had been human once, was a person with a heart and a soul. She had felt and feared, just like Sabine.

It was the closest she had ever felt to Her.

Sabine continued to read until the road thinned, the coach creaking with every bump. When her traveling companions began to wake, she slipped the New Maiden's journal back into her pocket.

They were deposited in a tiny port town, the entire village composed of fewer buildings than lined Harborside's main thoroughfare. They were directed toward the docks, where they found Skyr, a middle-aged man with ruddy cheeks and a large smile, who would ferry them to their final destination. At mention of the Lower Banks, he brightened.

"They'll be glad for fresh faces."

His boat was more of a small dinghy, which swayed at the hint of a whisper. As they crossed the water to a peninsula, he asked about their business in the Banks. They all looked to Sabine, who shook her head slightly. There was an easiness to anonymity, something she was no longer privy to in Velle.

"A pilgrimage, of sorts," she finally said.

Skyr's smile showcased a small gap in his front teeth. "Used to be plenty of those. Do you know that this was the site of the New Maiden's first miracle?"

"I do," Sabine said, reveling in the simplicity of it all. "I suppose I just wanted to see it for myself."

When the boat hit shore, Sabine let the others disembark first. She did not want to rush. As she stepped foot in the Lower Banks for the first time, something within her shuddered and sparked.

She stumbled. Brianne and Katrynn hurried to help, but Sabine waved them away. She was not weakened, nor was she in pain. She was moved by the power in the sand and the silt. By the rush of the water and the breeze on her tongue. There was magic everywhere, ancient and bright.

Sabine sank to her knees, and the Lower Banks embraced her.

The New Maiden was finally home.

18

Elodie's hair posed a problem.

Instead of sleeping, the Queen of Velle had spent the night fretting, unwilling to close her eyes for fear she would doze off and miss the Second Son's early morning gathering. As the final, fragile hours of night gave way to dawn, she scrutinized her appearance. Her attire was nothing like her usual flowing skirts and corset tops—her pants were perfectly tailored, her crisp shirt was buttoned all the way up to her chin—but her unmissable starlight hair still threatened to give her away. If Elodie stepped foot outside the walls of Castle Warnou looking like this, she would be instantly recognized.

She could not afford to be caught. Which was why, when a bleary-eyed Cleo burst into her older sister's chambers without knocking, Elodie was combing ash through her hair.

Cleo did not bother to hide her horror. "What in our lady's name are you doing?"

Elodie fumbled, streaking dirt across her cheek. "Do you ever knock?"

"Not when my sister, not to mention my queen, is nearing a breakdown."

Despite their height difference, Elodie shrank beneath her shorter sister's gaze. "I need a disguise," she admitted, slumping onto her bed.

"For what?" Cleo countered, stifling a yawn.

"I don't believe for an instant that you don't already know," Elodie said, tersely. "Why else would you call on me this early? More to the point, Artur Anders has been wrapped around your little finger for days."

Cleo fought back a grin. She held out her hand for the stubs of charred wood, which Elodie handed over reluctantly. "Start with your hair up. Less ground to cover."

Elodie made a face. "I hate wearing my hair up."

Cleo shook her head. "Oh, Ellie, it frightens me sometimes, how inept you are at deceit. Come here."

Elodie's sister twisted her hair up into a bun and began to methodically coat her white strands with the charred wood. The bun was so tight that it turned Elodie's taut features even more severe. The dirt on her hair changed her coloring.

"You're good at this," she told her sister begrudgingly.

Cleo made a soft noise. "I know."

Elodie snorted. "Humble, too."

"I'm a middle child," Cleo said disdainfully. "I don't have time for humility."

When, finally, Elodie's transformation was complete, Cleo squeezed her sister's hand. "Be careful," she pleaded. "Everything is spiraling so quickly out of control."

Elodie pulled her middle sister into a fierce embrace. "I promise."

"And a Warnou woman always keeps her promise," Cleo finished for her. "If you're not back by lunch, I'm sending out a search party."

Elodie rolled her eyes lovingly. "Don't act like you haven't already asked Artur to spy on me."

Cleo's feigned outrage melted off her face almost instantly. "He'll be"—she gestured vaguely—"around. Just in case."

The queen kept her head down as she hurried through the corridors. Billowing steam made it easy for her to pass unnoticed through the already bustling kitchens, her footsteps covered by the percussive chopping of knives. She wove past scullery maids and ducked into the pantry, where she heaved away a giant bushel of potatoes to reveal a trapdoor. She scrambled down the rope ladder, straining to shut the hatch behind her before descending into darkness.

Water sloshed loudly underfoot as Elodie slogged through the sewers. She pressed a handkerchief to her nose, grateful for her boots. The first time Tal had revealed this route to her, her silk slippers had become so soiled she had no choice but to burn them. It was not lost on her the way their roles were now reversed: Elodie sneaking through the sewers, while Tal strode confidently through Castle Warnou's front doors.

Elodie took two left turns and one right before reaching the cold metal of a ladder. She climbed carefully, fumbling in the dark for the handle to push the trapdoor open.

She emerged amidst the lush greenery of the Garden District. In the shadows of the early hour, the flora took on a life of its own, far more sinister than the gentle swaying of leaves in the afternoon breeze. Stems and tendrils curled, creeping up trellises and columns like spiders or snakes, but the most offensive insect was the moth plastered on the posters with the words *He is the light in the dark.* Beneath the moth there was an address, the one toward which Elodie was headed. Where before the messages had been ominous but vague, now they left no doubt.

On the other side of the bridge, the air was thin and metallic. The Iron District strained at its edges, the dregs of the night sky darker, the stragglers on the street rowdier. It seemed that Elodie was not the only attendee who had chosen to forgo sleep entirely. Almost every building she passed boasted the moth insignia, a creeping devotional to the word of the Second Son.

Elodie fell into step behind a gaggle of young men freshly dressed in tailored coats. Other than their hair, which was shorn short, she might have been one of them. She stuck close to their group as they followed the road to the tavern where the prophet of the Second Son would hold court.

The queue to enter the Whispering Willow moved quickly. The queen tensed at the sight of the red-clad Loyalists guarding the doors. She was a fool to have come here. Some trousers and a charred stick were not disguise enough to avoid recognition. But the guard, whose name was Mott, did not look at her face. His eyes moved immediately to her coat.

"Stop right there!" The guard put out a hand to bar her entry. Elodie froze, fear icing her veins. "Is this your first meeting?"

The queen nodded mutely, eyes wide. Mott exchanged a look with the man beside him.

"Welcome, stranger," the second guard said, producing a blood-red kerchief that he tucked into Elodie's front coat pocket. "He accepts you into His fold."

Now that she knew to look, she noticed the fabric everywhere. It was displayed in pockets, tied around wrists, used to pull back long hair. The handkerchiefs were just as much a uniform as the Loyalists' coats, ensuring that those who followed the Second Son were easily identifiable to one another.

She had seen this color before, the day Tal had offered up his own handkerchief for her paper cut. *I've more where that came from*, he had said. Elodie cursed her oblivion yet again. The signs had all been there; she had simply been unwilling to see them.

She offered a mumbled thank-you to the guard, hurrying inside the tavern before she could think better of it.

The Whispering Willow was unassuming, all foggy windows and dark wood. It smelled of sweat and stone fruit, the pungent sweet-sour scent making Elodie gag. Immediately it was clear that the crowd was not exclusively composed of locals—voices rang out loudly in the packed room, a cacophony of minutely different inflections and accents; clothing ranged from the standard cut of trousers and boots preferred by the nobility to the coveralls of merchants and the aprons of artisans.

A shout of laughter echoed from a corner. Tal and Rob were tucked into a booth, surrounded by a crowd of admirers. Elodie ducked behind a tall woman in a wide-brimmed hat and found herself moving inadvertently toward the bar, a fish trapped in a strong current. She could not believe so many were willing to gather before work, carefully slotting this meeting into the events of their day.

As she shifted her weight from foot to foot, she tried to observe snippets of conversation, but the voices that bounced about the room were disorienting and distracting.

". . . been starving lately, can't believe that cow had the audacity to redistribute rations."

". . . heard the New Maiden murdered a man with a dagger."

"No, not murdered, I heard that she was kissing the queen."

"I'm certain that stubborn girl is good for more than kissing."

The vile words shocked Elodie like a bucket of cold water dumped over her head. She was not often privy to the opinions of her subjects, but if these were the things spoken about her, she found that perhaps her ignorance was appropriate.

People continued to pour into the tavern. Someone elbowed Elodie roughly in the chest, sending her stumbling into the person in front of her. But there were so many bodies squeezed into the room that they could not even turn to confront her.

It was almost a relief to watch Tal wave people closer to his makeshift pulpit in order to offer those in the back the suggestion of space. The scrapes on his cheeks had begun to scab, making his injuries look far worse than they actually were.

"Welcome, friends," the prophet called. "We are all equals in this room. There is no front or back, no better or worse. That you chose to convene this morning is the first step. And for that, He thanks you." Tal paused, putting a finger to his lips. "Some of you are here because you already believe. Some of you, though"—his eyes wandered lazily, the silence gaining power the longer he held it—"are here begrudgingly. Dismissively. With hesitation in your hearts. But mark my words." Tal spread his arms wide and tilted his face to the ceiling. "By the time the sun has settled in the sky, there will be no doubt."

Tal clapped his hands, and the tavern plunged into darkness.

A hush overtook the crowded room like a hand clasped over an unsuspecting mouth. Then Tal clapped again, and the candlelight returned.

"Do you see?" He was close to laughter, his lips spread wide with pure joy. "Do you see how simple it is to turn light to dark and back again?" He ran a hand through his hair in a purposeful tousle, his eyes shining bright. "This is the power the New Maiden claims. But it is nothing He cannot do. In fact, He is the one who first originated that power."

A murmur ran through the crowd.

"That is what She does not wish for you to know," Tal continued, voice hushed. "That power that She claims? It was stolen from Him. But where He was strong enough to hold it, She was too fragile to contain it. The power twisted and corrupted Her. In the end, it defeated Her. Is that what you wish for the world? Will you put your faith in a girl too weak to save Herself?"

The murmurs grew to mutterings.

"This second coming of the New Maiden has already led Velle toward ruin," Tal continued. "Our neighborhood churches have been padlocked and burned to the ground. Our stores of food depleted. Our harvests were drowned, our access to imports cut off. Tell me, who has failed to protect us?"

Elodie felt the blood drain from her face. Tal was using his access to *her* intelligence—secrets told to him in confidence—to turn the crowd against Sabine.

"The world ran well before the New Maiden reappeared," Tal shouted above the crowd's rising jeers. "Our country was strong. We were free to invest our faith where it belonged. But now there is shame associated with dissent. A willingness to look past the truth in favor of what has always been. Is it not righteous, to question everything? Is it not just, to hold our gods to higher standards?"

Tal's words ignited the crowd like a dribble of alcohol introduced to a match. Assent rang around the room, burning bright. But he was not finished.

"I tried to reason with Her," Tal continued. "I approached Her calmly and plainly. But when She learned who I was, that I carry the word of the man She stole Her power from, the New Maiden threw Herself upon me like a rabid dog." He gestured to the wounds on his face, and the crowd began to boo. "She tore out my hair and drew blood from my skin. She would stop at nothing to silence me from speaking the truth."

All Elodie saw was red. The red of the Loyalists' uniform, the red of the kerchiefs tucked into lapels, the red of the anger blazing behind Tal's eyes. The prophet was twisting the facts, had repainted the scene to befit his own narrative. He was lying to her people and turning them toward a false agenda.

"The Second Son knows the danger of emotion," Tal said, his voice eerily calm. "He understands that stillness is strength. He recognizes your pain but will not waste your time with tears. Instead, he will fight for you. But first…" Tal grinned as the crowd leaned forward. He had them right where he wanted them. "You must let His light in so that Hers might finally be extinguished."

19

The light in the Lower Banks was not impeded by towering ships or teetering apartments. Instead, it cascaded dreamily across the lush green of the tall grasses, reflected the crisp blue water of the banks, and glittered gold against the minerals in the clay-colored silt.

It was the most beautiful place Sabine had ever been.

The land held untapped energy, a humming, wandering vibration that thrummed all the way to her fingertips. When Sabine smiled, she could feel its buzzing in her lips.

That morning, she woke before the others, left them slumbering in the spacious tent provided by the attendants. Pilgrimages to the Lower Banks were common enough that guest accommodations were not only available but well-kept. Their group fit comfortably in a circular tent, which contained cots with clean linens and a small jug of water available to freshen up. Sabine had been easily lulled to sleep the night before by the sound of the water and Genevar's gentle snoring.

Now she walked along the shore with bare feet, the cold sand tickling her toes. She inhaled, deeper than she ever had before. The influx of salt air set her brain reeling. The New Maiden had wandered this coast. She had dug Her fingers into the silt of this sand, had wept the tears that revitalized the banks. Here, She had summoned the power to save Her home when it needed Her most.

"Maiden?" A tentative voice, soft like a well-worn quilt, interrupted her musings. It was a white-robed attendant, one of the guides who inhabited the peninsula. The attendant was about her mother's age, with eyes that held the same kind creases in the corners from smiling. The attendant offered Sabine a pastry, a dense, seeded loaf crusted with pepper and caraway. "I thought you might be hungry, from such a long journey."

Sabine accepted the food gratefully. The group had arrived after supper, and the initial glow of walking in her predecessor's footsteps faded with every growl of her stomach. She tore off a giant bite, reveling in the crunch of the seeds. Her sigh of contentment made the attendant grin.

Sabine was thankful the local hosts were so inviting. They were the most steadfast protectors of the New Maiden's legacy. They had every right to be defensive of Her second coming, to compare Sabine to the savior they knew. Instead, they were honored to welcome her into their home.

Probably because the Second Son had not yet poisoned Her followers so far south.

Sabine waited for her darkness to chime in. Instead, she was forced to think the foul thought all by herself. She hated that the memory of the voice that had once offered her comfort was now conflated with Tal's taunting lilt.

The attendant pressed another pastry into Sabine's palm before sidling off. Sabine tucked away her spoils and had only just settled herself on the sand when she was joined by the youngest Warnou sibling.

"Good morning." Brianne's head blocked the sun so that rays cascaded around her like a halo, making her glow.

"Sleep well?"

"No." Brianne plopped down on the sand beside Sabine with a heavy sigh. "Genevar snores." She pulled a sour face. "But it's not just that. I've been thinking, and I want to be useful."

Sabine frowned. "You're already useful. Your presence alone is a help." It wasn't strictly true, but if it made Brianne feel better, that was surely good enough.

The youngest Warnou raised her eyebrows. "I was born a princess, Maiden. I can detect a liar when I hear one."

Sabine snickered. "You sound like Elodie."

Something like pride flashed in Brianne's eyes. "If I were Elodie, you'd be letting me help you."

"Very well." Sabine chuckled at Brianne's boldness. She had not always possessed such sure-footedness. Now that the youngest Warnou was no longer the prophecied Third Daughter, she seemed more certain of herself and her place in the world. Sabine envied that. "How about you help me figure out what I am meant to find here? How I might go about reigniting Her magic?"

Brianne clapped her hands together, looking vexed. "Did you always have magic?"

"Yes, and no. I was ten when I finally could identify it," Sabine said.

During those early years, the darkness had never held Sabine captive. Instead, *she* had clutched it tightly in hopes of eking out an ounce of magic, enough to pay rent or her father's debts. The darkness had initially been a fleeting presence, but always something she could control.

The first time the darkness had fully trapped her beneath its spell—keeping her veins inky black and her mind full of whispers—was the night of Brianne's coronation. It had come alive to contest the other girl's very public appointment as the queen and New Maiden. Had taken on an agency of its own so that Sabine would emerge victorious.

"And what do you feel like without it?"

"Empty." She glanced at the rushing riverbanks, imagining the soil dusty and dry. "Endlessly and impossibly dull."

"You don't appear that way to me," Brianne said, "if that's any consolation."

It was, if just barely. Sabine sighed. "I thought that by coming here . . . I thought I would instantly know what to do."

"The truth is hardly ever as simple as that." The young girl was much wiser than Sabine had given her credit for.

But things *had* been simple for Sabine, once. The darkness had told her what to think, who to trust, how to survive. Without that clear guidance, Sabine was ill-equipped to exist, let alone lead. Worse, she wished desperately for its return, wanted to revel in its familiar, punishing timbre. It was strange, to lose something that had once been such an integral part of her existence. Every morning that she woke to find her mind fully her own felt like reopening an old wound.

"It sounds like something's missing," Brianne said softly. Sabine sat up straighter, feeling exposed. "If the Lower Banks are where the New Maiden came into Her power, surely it can be the place where you return to yours. We just need to find a way to replenish you."

The youngest Warnou got to her feet and began to pace. "You've *seen* the water. That's the most obvious. Perhaps you need to drink it?" She frowned down at Sabine. "Although you ought to be careful, drinking the Maiden's tears." She chuckled darkly.

"I wet my lips last night when I freshened up."

"And?"

Sabine shook her head. "Nothing."

"The New Maiden dug her hands into the dirt and became one with the earth," Brianne said, paraphrasing a verse from Her book. "Do you feel anything move beneath you?"

Sabine held up a fist and let the soil trickle down her wrist. The earth murmured to her softly, but it held none of the force of true magic. "Still nothing."

Brianne sighed, sinking back down onto the sand. "What else is there? We've tried both the salt and the silt. Could there have been a sacred site? A place they gathered to worship?"

Water sloshed against the banks as the two girls sat in silence. According to the New Maiden's journal, Hera once left offerings on the hearth. But that did not feel sacred. At least not until it sparked the memory of a story Sabine had heard with Elodie, tucked away in a tavern where they ate pie and drank wine. The storyteller had spoken of the miracles Ruti returned to discover: the water running, the crops growing, the fire moved.

"'Where once there had been a hearth, sat an altar.'"

Brianne looked perplexed. "What are you talking about?"

Sabine leapt to her feet. "Her Favoreds built an altar." She made her way toward the center of camp, Brianne at her heels. She scanned the land, past tents and smiling attendants, laundry hung out to dry, and strips of meat laid out to smoke. "Surely something remains of it."

"Remains of what?" Katrynn emerged from their tent, hair mussed artfully, sleep crusting her eyes. She yawned, long and loud.

"The answer," Sabine said, heart pounding. If she could locate the altar and produce a worthy offering, surely that would be enough to reignite her power. "The way to bring my magic back."

By the time Genevar emerged from their tent to greet the day, Sabine, Katrynn, and Brianne were knee-deep in the dirt.

"What in Her name are you doing?" The Archivist looked inquisitively at the earth piled up around them.

Brianne leaned on her shovel, using her wrist to wipe a strand of hair out of her eyes. "Searching for the New Maiden's shrine. The attendants said it once sat in the center of the camp."

"Ah, yes." Genevar nodded. "The New Maiden first emerged from flames, and so Her altar would also come from the hearth." She eyed their haphazard hole. "I don't know what you expect to find, though. That was centuries ago; the stone and clay long shattered. This is why the written word is superior to any item made by humankind," she added sagely. "It is far less fragile."

"But not always as concrete." Sabine thought of how easy it was to hold an object, to see all sides of it, to test its weight, to *know* it so fully that its memory remained ingrained regardless of time or distance. Sabine had never been as successful with words.

"I think the New Maiden's word *is* rather concrete," Genevar argued, her eyes on Katrynn, who sifted methodically through the piles of dirt turned over by Brianne. "She was about community, about the betterment of others through equal access to resources. That is where Her power truly lies. Not in the promise of a better world, but in its realization."

A lump formed in Sabine's throat. Distilled so simply, the New Maiden's beliefs were the same as her own. But where Sabine had only longed for change, the New Maiden had *done* it.

Sabine took a break from digging to join Katrynn in her sifting. It was relaxing work, the rhythm of their hands matching the soft sloshing of water against the banks. Soon they had a small pile of stones, twigs, and shattered clay. As Brianne began to dig deeper, the dirt grew colder, wriggling earthworms sliding out from within the soil.

They paused their search for a meal of hand pies filled with roasted root vegetables and a tangy orange spice. From time to time, one of the attendants would join the search, uncovering a smooth river stone or a petrified rodent skull. They would place their findings in the pile beside Sabine, like some ritual of sacrifice, before wandering away, another white-robed attendant coming to take the previous one's place.

This was how Sabine came to know the people of the Lower Banks. Most had been here all their lives, born on the small stretch of land made famous by the Maiden's first miracle. They all had a relative who had been a follower of the New Maiden; one girl was even a descendant of Her Favored Beck. All were kind, quiet folk—kinesthetic thinkers who were quick to smile.

By the time the sun began to set, Brianne had blisters on her palms, the center of the encampment had been overturned two-fold, and the pile of unearthed sticks, stones, and bones was the size of a sleeping child. But there was still no sign of an altar.

Sabine wiped the sweat from her brow. Her cheeks were flushed; the skin of her nose was surely burned. But the exhaustion she felt was surface level, in her body, not her soul. A tired that could be repaired with food and rest in preparation to start again.

"Tomorrow, then," she said, hoping to soothe the beleaguered expressions of Katrynn and Brianne. Genevar had long abandoned them to shy away from the harsh sun. "We'll resume our work tomorrow."

Her companions nodded gratefully, stumbling toward the fire where the locals were doling out stew. Sabine stayed behind to survey their work. The hole was precarious, but then she supposed that digging up the past was never tidy. Sabine only hoped that communing with the Lower Banks, getting to know the New Maiden and Her word, would be enough fuel for the storm that was brewing.

She did not move until the sun sank firmly below the shoreline and the air turned cold enough to make her shiver. One of the attendants, a girl about her own age with a long red braid, brought her a steaming bowl of stew. After Sabine had filled her belly and helped the attendant do the washing, she slipped into bed, listening to the sound of the water lapping against the banks.

Sabine slept soundly all the way through the night.

20

Tal's sermon followed Elodie all the way back to the castle, his impassioned words circling her like a bird of prey. While the queen spent all her energy attempting to protect her people from Edgar's threats, Tal had been snipping the stitches of her delicate work, inciting in the hearts of her populace the exact panic and fear she had been trying to prevent.

Worst of all, he had used Elodie's failures to blame the New Maiden for every poor decision the queen herself had made. Tal had twisted Elodie's trust into a blade, then plunged it into her back.

When finally she arrived home, exhausted and furious, she could not bear to attend to her royal duties. Instead, Elodie retreated to her chambers, instructed Marguerite to ensure no one disturbed her, and buried herself beneath the down feather duvet draped across her bed. She could not face the day now that she had heard the Second Son's threat straight from His prophet's mouth. Her anxiety sent her into a fitful sleep where she dreamed of being suffocated by a snake, awaking in the early evening covered in sweat. Elodie kicked off the comforter and covered her head with a pile of pillows.

When next she woke, the sun was soft in the sky, the morning naked and new. The uncertain outline of her younger sister hovered above her.

"Lady above, Cleo," Elodie said, clutching her pillow to her chest, "you gave me a fright."

"I was worried about you," Cleo sniffed, pulling back the curtains to let the light in. "Had to strong-arm my way past Marguerite to get in. I'm glad you're safe."

Elodie rolled over. "Told you I'd be all right." But the words were bitter on her tongue. She wasn't all right, not after the scene she had witnessed in the Whispering Willow. The shouting and sweat clung to her even now.

"You don't look well," Cleo said, sniffing. "Nor do you smell it. I'll have Marguerite draw you a bath."

She wandered off to find the queen's handmaid, returning a moment later with a silver tray and a grimace. "Letter for you," Cleo said, looking just as nervous as her sister felt.

With trepidation, Elodie rose to retrieve the letter. She turned the envelope over and was flooded with relief when she found it sealed with a sword rather than a snake. It was only correspondence from General Garvey and his troops at the border. But the queen's solace was short-lived.

Your Majesty, wrote the general in a shaky hand, *our numbers are dwindling at an insurmountable rate.*

Elodie frowned. Velle's army was a commanding presence, one of the country's biggest assets and most important resources. Only a disaster of the highest magnitude could have wiped out all of their patrolling troops.

Our soldiers are not dying, the letter continued, *but they have been converted by zealots from the Republics. These soldiers have defected, crossing the border to join an army of a different kind.*

It was just as Rob had told her: The Republics worshipped the Second Son. But what Elodie had not considered was that while Edgar had distracted Velle's crown with his grand gestures and ineptitude, a more compelling poison had been brewing among its people.

My recommendation now, the general had written, *is to abandon this operation. For without an army, I have nothing to command.*

Elodie sank down onto the bench at the foot of her bed. Without the threat of physical altercation, Velle could not intimidate the Republics into reassessing their embargo. Alone, there was no way to save her people from starvation.

But the Second Son—already a figure of influence in the Republics—could. If Elodie pledged her loyalty to Him, perhaps He would assist. She would be forced to betray Sabine, but surely the New Maiden would understand that Elodie had only done what was necessary for the good of her people.

She would go to Tal, would beg him to ingratiate her with the Second Son, and soon the threat of Edgar and the Republics would be forgotten.

The queen got to her feet. But she had taken only a few steps when she remembered: Tal had already witnessed Edgar DeVos's every correspondence. He had even dismissed Elodie's fears as unfounded.

As the voice of the Second Son, Tal could have stopped Edgar with a single word. He could have lifted the Republics' embargo in seconds. Instead, Tal had let Elodie worry herself sick. He had offered her empty encouragement while he pulled the strings from the other side.

"Where are you going?" Cleo was looking at the queen with concern. "El, sit back down. The bath is almost ready."

But Elodie was too consumed with betrayal. Velle's daily hardships were directly connected to the campaign to discredit the New Maiden. And Tal, the person she'd once trusted most in the world, had used the queen as a pawn. "I'll be right back."

"Ellie!"

The queen ignored the curious looks she received as she stormed through the castle's corridors to the Loyalists' quarters. The space in the west wing was small—one long hallway with doors tucked tightly side by side, like soldiers on the front lines. A thick must of sweat and leather permeated everything, making her gag.

"Are you lost?"

The queen turned to locate the owner of the bitter voice. Maxine had abandoned her braid, her long hair falling like a wave down her back. While her hair was different, the guard wore her usual disaffected expression.

"I'm busy, Maxine," Elodie said, battling the urge to sigh. "Where's Tal?"

Maxine rolled her eyes. "I imagine he is busy, too."

"Oh, bite a blade, Maxine," Elodie snapped, unable to hide her irritation. "I know you have no love for me, but if you care at all about your country, you will tell me which room is his."

The guard pursed her lips. "You cannot ask me to pick between my country and my comrades. It is an impossible choice."

The queen sighed. "Very well. If anyone complains about the extraordinary lengths I am about to go to, I will tell them it is entirely your fault."

Maxine frowned. "I don't underst—"

Elodie began flinging open doors, much to the horror of those inside. Grumbles and shouts filled the hallway as she passed half-dressed, half-awake guards in search of the boy who had betrayed her.

"Tal!" She pounded on the doors that were locked, screaming the prophet's name. Her hurt was a fresh wound, the adrenaline stronger than the pain. "Show yourself!"

Guards had gathered in the corridor to watch the queen's outburst. Once she had reached the end of the hall, the final door opened mid-knock.

"Lo, what are you—" Elodie's momentum sent her fist crashing into Tal's face. "Elodie," Tal yelped, blood spurting from his nose. "What in His name has gotten into you?"

The queen's knuckles ached from the awkward angle of impact. She felt none of the thrill of violence, only deep, impossible sorrow.

"I should ask you the same thing," she said, pushing him backward into his room and slamming the door behind them. His chambers were modest, containing nothing but a bed, neatly made with a fitted white sheet, and a chair, currently occupied by a pair of polished boots.

"If you wanted to see my bedroom," Tal said, pinching his nose to stanch the blood, "you could have just asked."

"This isn't funny," Elodie spat, shoving the general's letter into Tal's chest. "None of this is the least bit amusing."

Tal parsed the letter, his expression impassive. Finally, he looked up at her. "Surely you can appreciate your army finding solace in the word of the Second Son?" He watched her carefully, urging her toward a carefully laid trap.

"I do not criticize my constituents," Elodie said. "The fault I find is with you."

"Oh?" Tal smirked, sinking onto the bed. "And what have I done to displease Her Majesty?"

"You speak for the Second Son. Which means you held the power to stop the threats from the Republics. You simply chose not to." She knocked the boots from his chair so that she might sit.

Tal's expression was impossible to read. "So, she did tell you."

"Of course she told me," Elodie snapped. "But you've revealed yourself much more. You have taken my soldiers, further weakening my geopolitical position, all because the Second Son is threatened by the New Maiden's light."

"I was trying to save you, Lo." Tal leaned forward, looking wounded. "You are so determined not to see me that you fail to realize you have put your faith in the wrong person."

"Of course I see you," Elodie said, shaking her head at his baseless accusation. They had been friends for more than half their lives. "I have always seen you."

"You haven't," Tal whispered, so quietly the queen had to strain to hear. "You did not know what to do with my pain, and so you ignored my bruises and my burns. You did not want to lose my affection, and so you strung me along with just enough hope to get what you wanted from me. You never needed to lie in order to keep my loyalty, Lo. You always had it. And on my life, you always will."

The queen shifted in the unforgiving wooden seat. Tal was right. She had not known how to handle his magnitude of hurt. She had simply hoped her friendship would be enough.

"But He *sees* me," Tal continued, eyes glassy. "With Him, I am not damaged. My hurt was not earned. My pain is no longer proof that I am unworthy of love. And so," Tal said, sounding almost apologetic, "what He commands, I will do."

"You would abandon me for Him, then?" Her reign would be ruined.

"You abandoned me for Her," Tal countered. "Relationships go both ways, Elodie, whether you wish to admit it or not. Even if you did not return my affections, you might have stopped to consider what darkness might live within me, too. Might have accounted for me, the way you did for the New Maiden."

He got to his feet. The room was not large enough to pace. Now that he had drawn her attention to his hurt, Elodie could see it radiating from him. She had been too wrapped up in herself to notice that he was desperate for an escape. So hopeless that he'd been willing to pledge his fealty to an unknown evil that now resided in his heart.

"We are not so different, Sabine and me," Tal continued. "We come from similar shadows, carry similar scars. Neither one of us stands to improve your ranks. So imagine my surprise when I learned you had given your heart to her. It proved to me that you *could* have loved me; you merely chose not to."

"Just because you see me as an object to be desired," Elodie said, looking up at him, "does not mean that is my only purpose."

"Perhaps I do see you as a prize, but I treat my possessions with tenderness and consideration," Tal said sharply. "You've never deemed me worthy of the same, and so who among us is the true villain?"

Elodie gaped at the venom in his voice. Tal had never before demonstrated this precise a cruelty.

"Still, I am willing to offer you one final chance at redemption." Tal's smile was all teeth. "An opportunity to end the embargo and silence Edgar DeVos for good."

The queen clutched the seat of the chair with white knuckles. This was exactly what Velle needed in order to prepare for the coming winter. Exactly what Elodie required to turn her reign around. She held her breath, waiting for the catch.

"Give up Sabine, and all this strife can be forgotten," Tal demanded, his eyes glittering gold. "Offer me the New Maiden, and Velle will rise again."

21

Morning on the Lower Banks dawned cold and gray. After the effort exerted the day before, Sabine could not bear to wake her companions from their various states of sleep, so she slipped noiselessly out of their tent into the day's first light. She rolled out her neck, wincing as she poked tentatively at the knots in her shoulders.

The ache in her muscles was strangely satisfying. It was proof—definitive, tangible proof—of the work she had orchestrated and the relationships she had built. Sabine, who had spent years fearing that she could not trust her mind, found assurance in her body instead. This was a different kind of power. Not magic, but strength.

Still, as she surveyed the hole in the ground, she wondered how much farther she could burrow. The earth was packed more tightly the deeper she dug, each strike of the shovel meeting more resistance. Sabine couldn't help but fear that she was making too much of a mark on this earth. The New Maiden might have been born in the Lower Banks, but Sabine was merely a visitor, still getting to know the land and the people who inhabited it. She slipped the New Maiden's journal out of her pocket and settled herself on the sand, hoping She might offer Sabine words of wisdom in this trying time.

Some days I fear the duality of power. Before, when I was not yet Her— the New Maiden had underlined the capital letter three times—*I craved the attention, the understanding of others. Now that I possess it, I must confront my own inexperience. What type of person would wish to bear such crushing responsibility—to be remembered for decisions made out of necessity rather than idealism?*

Yet, whenever I doubt, I know where to turn. Every leader deserves an equal who can see beyond the choices you make, who challenges you and sharpens your convictions through debate.

Sabine smiled despite herself as she thought of Elodie, the way the Queen of Velle would tug on the short baby hairs that curled about Sabine's ears, grinning as they kissed. It was wonderful to be challenged. Delightful to be deemed worthy enough to polish.

It is especially challenging when the power that makes you valuable is a force you don't fully understand. I was not born the New Maiden. For years, I was nothing but a girl. And some days, I wonder what the difference is, if my tears were truly a magic salve to bring back the waters, to revive my homeland, or if a single bolt of luck struck me just once, and I will spend my life in the expectant shadows of one incredible, impossible mistake.

The New Maiden's words settled into the corner of Sabine's heart with a resounding ache. She, too, had no control over her power, had so many questions about its origins, and had no understanding of why it had chosen her as its host. She had not known what she was doing, had possessed no grand plan. Instead, she had incidentally performed a miracle and fumbled forward from that point on.

It was a relief Sabine could hardly name, a loosening of tension all the way down her spine. It was not possible to disappoint the New Maiden if the New Maiden Herself did not know what Her word meant. She knew only that She wished to do good. To channel Her influence toward benevolence. To matter.

The New Maiden had not known that one day, centuries into the future, She would be worshipped, had never imagined Her word lasting so staunchly after She'd passed. In fact, it was only after Sebastien proposed the idea that Ruti took up the pen to scribe Her teachings.

Even the New Maiden's archival image had been directed by a boy who would one day become the Second Son.

I am no God, She had written, *not like the ones of yore who light the sun and turn the tides. I am simply a girl who stayed, who planted her feet in the earth and waited, who wept with such conviction that her own prayers were answered.*

Do I confess I am a fraud? Or transform myself into whoever they need me to be?

Sabine's focus was interrupted by the soft footsteps of the red-headed attendant emerging from a tent. "You're up early." The girl smiled, gesturing to the clouds that were obscuring most of the sunrise.

"Couldn't sleep any longer."

"The water will do that to you." The attendant sighed, stretching her arms toward the sky.

"How do you mean?"

"If you listen closely, you can still hear Her crying," the girl said, holding up a hand to invite Sabine's silence.

Sabine listened intently. At first, all she could hear was the rhythmic shifting of the water sloshing against the shoreline. But the longer she listened, the more deeply she focused, the clearer she could make out the sobs.

Her chest tightened, familiarity flooding her senses. It was the sound not just of the New Maiden's sadness, but of Sabine's, too. Judging by the redheaded girl's expression, she recognized that sound as well.

"Which do you think came first," Sabine asked, "sadness, or the New Maiden?"

The attendant considered her question. "Sadness has always been." She looked up at the clouds, which hung heavy, threatening rain. "I think that part of Her power, part of Her *gift*, really, was holding it for us all."

But Sabine had often seen tears streaking the cheeks of Her most devout worshippers. "You think the New Maiden *saved* you from sadness?"

The attendant shook her head. "You misunderstand." She smiled softly. "I think She made sure that when it was our time to feel sadness, we did not do so alone."

A lump formed in Sabine's throat. She had never considered her impact in such a way. Perhaps the feelings she had once perceived as weakness were, in fact, a comfort. A way to offer connection to others when they suffered their own heavy hearts.

"Thank you," Sabine whispered, a ray of light breaking through the clouds to glitter against the water. "Truly."

"It is the least that I can do, Maiden." The attendant smiled before departing, robe fluttering behind her.

When Sabine turned away from the shore, her vision was still dotted with sparks of light. She scrubbed her hands against her eyes, hoping to clear her view. But one glittering dot stayed, sparkling up through the silt. Sabine knelt, using her thumb to clear away the dirt. A gold coin stared up at her, unique in shape, with hammered edges and a smooth face.

She turned it over in her hand. On the back were three numerals: VII.

Sabine turned the coin again to its blank face. The gold shimmered even in the tiny shred of sunlight the morning offered. She could not believe they had missed it the day before. The coin was a sign, encouragement from above. Sabine was not alone. This was not yet finished.

Before any others could meaningfully devote themselves to her, Sabine needed to prove herself to them. Being a leader meant setting an example. And so she sank her hands in the earth and again began to dig, energized by serendipity and a stranger's kindness.

The silt was cool between her fingers, tiny grains wedged themselves beneath her nails, landing on her lips, scratching at her eyes. She ignored all offers of assistance, waved away ladles of water and bowls of stew. She did not need sustenance today. Not when she had momentum.

By the time Katrynn and Brianne emerged from their tent, Sabine was up to her ears in soil.

"Bet?" Her elder sister stared down at Sabine with concern. "What are you doing?"

"I'm nearly there," Sabine panted, grasping another handful of dirt.

"And where might *there* be?" Brianne looked pointedly at her own pit, which was nearly three times the size of Sabine's.

Before she could answer, Sabine's hand struck something sharp, and she hissed through the pain. A bright stripe of blood bloomed across her palm. She held her right hand aloft as she excavated the offending item carefully with her left.

It was a shard of earth-red clay, striped with the same gold sheen of the coin. It was slightly rounded—like a jug or a vase— and clearly shattered. Sabine scraped off the sand that stuck to the shard. To Katrynn's horror, she sniffed it. The faintest odor of alcohol clung to its pores, as though it had once held a spirit or wine. Sabine placed the clay carefully beside the coin.

"Offerings," Genevar said, confirming her suspicion. Sabine looked up, the skin on the back of her neck aching with obvious sunburn. She had not noticed the Archivist join the crowd of observers.

"From her followers?"

"From her Favoreds." Genevar indicated the coin. "That is a token the Maiden forged, for Her Seven. Ruti wrote of them."

The surrounding crowd was quiet, and once again, Sabine could hear the faint strains of sadness coursing through the Lower Banks.

The artifacts were proof Sabine was inching toward even more momentous discoveries. It was only now that she welcomed assistance from the onlookers. And so it was that Her altar was excavated by the residents of the Lower Banks, the New Maiden's second coming by their side.

Tal

Tal had not expected Sabine. With Brianne, the plan of attack was clear. Tal would usurp René as head of the Church, install Elodie on the throne, and ensure that the New Maiden remained suspended in sleep for all eternity. It was effortless, to line up the pieces and watch them fall into place.

But when Sabine called forth the darkness in the city square, Tal began to squirm. The girl was a stranger, but her power left a familiar tang on his tongue. It tasted of saline and starlight.

Sinister machinations were afoot. Tal's heart urged him to protect Elodie from it all. So, when Sabine's shadow rushed toward him, fangs bared, ready to strike, Tal offered himself up to the darkness, and the shadow accepted his sacrifice.

At once, impossible pain. Every ounce of emotion Tal had carefully released slammed right back into him. He was again a trembling child at the mercy of his father's hands. A lovesick adolescent, forced to stew in his unrequited adoration. Worse—the Second Son's voice, which had once been a guiding light, now began to hiss.

Foolish to believe you could ever escape me, it said. *Foolish to think you would ever be free.*

This was not Sebastien, for his savior could never be so cruel. No, this darkness had come from the New Maiden, which meant She was using Her unwieldy emotions to undo His rightful teachings. It was just as the Second Son had warned: The New Maiden brandished emotion like a weapon.

The dark-haired girl on the cobblestones below would be His undoing unless Tal silenced her.

He concocted a plan to infiltrate her trust. All went as intended, save for a single hitch: The closer Tal grew to Sabine, the more she felt like home.

He had not intended to find comfort in her. The breadth of her feelings was off-putting, her earnestness irritating, her kindness exhausting. Yet there was a connection between them. Something precious. With Sabine, Tal was seen, was known, just as he had been with the Second Son.

You are allowing yourself to be corrupted, the darkness hissed at him. To compensate for his occasional weakness, Tal's sermons became more charged. He would stop at nothing to turn Velle's favor away from Sabine. To prove to Sebastien that he was a worthy executor of His legacy. To make Elodie see how brittle the New Maiden truly was.

The intimacy the queen shared with the New Maiden was a dagger in his back. But the blacksmith's son was now well-versed in healing. Like Sebastien had taught him, Tal sucked the poison from his wound and spat the venom out.

PART FOUR

The Second Son's freedom, his lightness, was short-lived.
While the New Maiden's sacrifice opened his eyes to the truth
of Her word, it also changed Her. Where once She was the sun,
now She was a new moon—a notable absence where there
ought to be light. Day by day, She grew diminished.

Gone was the thoughtful, enigmatic leader whose followers
clung to every word. Now She skipped sermons, Her legacy
unraveling stitch by stitch as She retreated inward to battle
the demons inside. Sebastien begged Her to return his pain,
but despite their repeated attempts, She could not dislodge the
darkness that had corrupted Her will.

Sebastien feared what this evil—his evil—could do in the
hands of one so influential. He knew the burden of this anger
and helplessness. If his pain infiltrated the New Maiden's
word, it could bleed into future generations and destroy Her
original vision, poisoning Her legacy.

The world would not survive a New Maiden dampened by
darkness. For the good of all creation, the Second Son needed
to rescue the New Maiden's soul.

—Psalm of the Second Son

22

Tal's proposition gave Elodie pause. As the Queen of Velle, her duty was first and foremost to her people. What was best for her constituents was to align herself with the Republics by way of Tal and the Second Son. But to do so meant turning her back on the New Maiden.

It was the same struggle Maxine had refused to face at Elodie's behest: comrades versus country. Elodie's love for Sabine, while new, was immense and undeniable. But love for her country had been instilled in her from birth. One was profoundly hers. The other, for everyone.

Country above all, Tera Warnou had taught her daughter. Above even her family. Above even her heart. Tal knew this. He was likely counting on it.

But it was not only Tal she would be saying yes to. He carried with him Sebastien, the Second Son. His purpose was nebulous, His word agitating and unclear. Elodie could not place her faith—already a fragile thing—in what she did not understand. But she could attest to Sabine's gentle instincts and her careful heart. The New Maiden's power would only ever be used for good. The queen could not say the same for Tal and the Second Son.

Elodie crossed the room in three steps. "No."

The word itself was simple, but the emotion it held was not. With that single syllable, their relationship shattered like a crystal goblet against a marble floor. The fragments lay at their feet, the shards so sharp, the slivers so thin, that there was no way it could ever be pieced back together.

If Tal was surprised, his face did not show it. "As you wish."

It broke her heart to look at him. It instilled in her an impossible rage. Their friendship had been meant to last a lifetime and instead was ending with stones thrown. She reached for the doorknob.

"Lo?" She paused but did not turn around. "When I see you next," Tal told her, "I cannot promise you will walk away unscathed." He sounded truly sorry.

He was not fully gone, then. Tal was in tune with himself enough to feel remorse. Which meant that while Elodie had not been able to get through to him, there was one other person who might.

Elodie ran all the way to her brother's room. Outside Rob's door she heard the telltale signs of his composing. Cymbals crashed, followed by long bouts of silence. Staccato notes rang out from the piano, as though he were testing flavors of icing for a cake. The queen did not bother to knock. He would not have been able to hear her anyway.

Rob had one foot on his sofa and a violin tucked beneath his chin. "Really, Elodie," he said, twisting a tuning peg errantly and then plucking the string to confirm its pitch, "your lack of consideration for other people's privacy is astonishing."

She did not take the bait. "I need your help."

"What gives you the idea that I'd be willing to assist?" Rob placed the violin back in its velvet case and scribbled six notes onto the staff paper in front of him.

"Because I am your sister."

Her brother met her eyes. "I don't find that a particularly compelling reason."

"Enough," Elodie snapped. "If you will not help me out of love, then help me out of loyalty. I am your queen. Assist me, or I will have no choice but to charge you with treason."

It pained her to be resorting to baseless threats to get her brother's attention. They had once been so close. As they stood in Rob's chambers, surrounded by his instruments and the songs that filled his head, their strained relationship reverberated like a dissonant chord.

He sighed, world-weary. "What do you *want*, Elodie?"

"I need you to reason with Tal," she said. "He plans to invade Velle with an army from the Republics in order to apprehend the New Maiden."

"You did not give her up?" Rob eyed her curiously. "I had thought you might. You've been so willing to sacrifice whatever is needed to protect your reign." His tone was bitter as citrus pith.

Her brother already knew of Tal's plans, then. Knew, and had done nothing to intervene.

"You would let the Republics wage war?" She could not believe that Rob, who abhorred the military, could have abandoned his pacifist heart so freely. "You would let him take Sabine?"

"*I* would do nothing," her brother said, "because *I* have no influence. But I see no reason why you are so adamant about protecting

197

her. Times are worse, under the New Maiden, than they've ever been before."

"Yes," Elodie said, rolling her eyes, "because your life has been such a dizzying maze of unfavorable circumstances."

"What do *you* know about hardship?" Rob spat back. "You received all our mother's attention, stood self-important in every circumstance, and now, as queen, you float around like your actions have no consequences. Frankly, it's insulting to those of us who will have to pay for your mistakes."

It was the cruelest thing her brother had ever said to her. It was also the most honest. Rob had always been that way, full of contradictions, knowing how to both rile her up and calm her down. But the intention behind his words was darker than ever before.

"*My* mistakes?" Elodie was furious, her voice taking on the particularly high pitch of near hysteria. "I have done nothing but protect this country since Mother's death."

"You put Brianne to sleep so that you might claim the crown," Rob accused, "then gallivanted about with Sabine, playacting a commoner in order to find a cure. You did not marry Edgar, and now he has enacted his revenge on the entire country." He fiddled with the lute leaned against his bed so that he would not have to look at his sister. "You abandoned me here, and you never once apologized." His bitterness hung about the room like a tapestry.

"Do you know how much I despise these castle walls, Elodie? How much the monarchy feels like a noose around my neck? I am a prince born to command orchestras, rather than armies. A boy who lusts after his best friend instead of his ladies-in-waiting. My father, my mother, and my sister have all made it clear: Velle's court holds no place for me. *That* is why I have aligned myself with Him,"

Rob said, tears welling in his eyes. "His word founded the Republics, who believe in the dissolution of the monarchy. If it weren't for the crown, I would be free. If it weren't for the throne, I might have a family."

Elodie's heart snapped like an overtightened viola string. Twice today, she had been presented with the insurmountable pain of a person whose soul she thought she'd known. That both Tal and Rob had been able to keep such hurt a secret from her left her frightened at the other intimations in her life she might have missed.

"I am sorry you are so unhappy," Elodie said softly. "I wish that you had told me sooner."

"I wish I had not needed to."

He struck an errant lute string. The note was quickly consumed by the uneasiness between them.

"You will not stop Him, then?"

That same syllable that had shattered Elodie's relationship with Tal was now employed against her: "No."

The queen's fury was so great she was overcome by an improbable veil of calm. "Very well," she said, sweeping out of Rob's rooms, sending a pile of sheet music scattering as she went.

Elodie stalked the corridors, fuming. She had been placed in an impossible position, and although she had tried her best to choose wisely, people she loved had still been hurt in the process.

Each flash of a red uniform set her skin prickling as she moved about the palace. She could only imagine the whispers that had spread due to her outburst in the Loyalist barracks. The queen—mad with rage—had attacked a guard, just like the New Maiden in the training room.

How long before Tal's public sermons berated Elodie, too?

While she was grateful Sabine had fled the castle, Elodie greatly wished she could seek the New Maiden's advice. In the absence of her physical presence, the queen made for the royal chapel.

The Maiden's inner sanctum had dulled since Elodie's last visit. It was quiet inside, the pews empty, the hymnals closed. The light through the windows illuminated dancing motes of dust, coating the room like a blanket of snow. She paused at the entryway, the wicks of the devotional candles bright white and unburned.

Elodie held her breath as she ushered a flame from the match to the taper. Sabine had always held a soft spot for the lights lit by worshippers. Elodie had never truly understood the sentiment, but as the wick caught, she was filled with quiet comfort. A radiance, where once there had been nothing at all.

"What did you pray for?"

Elodie jumped. She had thought herself alone.

The voice came from Silas, the towering Royal Chaplain.

"I fear prayer may not be powerful enough for what I currently require," Elodie said derisively. At the Chaplain's soft chuckle, her face flushed. "I'm sorry," the queen said, embarrassed by her blasphemy. "I forget myself."

"It's all right." Silas's voice was gentle. "Faith does not look the same for everyone."

Elodie sank down onto the nearest pew. The woman's kindness threatened to undo her. The queen leaned forward, resting her elbows on the back of the pews in front of her, and placed her head in her hands.

"May I join you, Majesty?" the Royal Chaplain asked. "I cannot bear to leave you in such distress."

"Certainly," Elodie said, voice muffled. "But I must warn you, I am poor company."

The Chaplain joined the queen on the pew, leaving a person's worth of space between them. "I'm certain that is not so."

"I've been told so many times today that I am self-serving and cruel," Elodie said, lifting her head from her hands to glance at the portrait of the New Maiden above the altar, "I am starting to believe it myself."

"The role of queen is a burden unfathomable to those who do not hold it." It was a relief to hear someone acknowledge the crown's unbearable weight. "But sometimes it is worth examining those inner anxieties." She was quiet for a moment. "I could take your confession if you'd like."

"Oh no, thank you," Elodie answered quickly. She had never found much comfort in stating her failures aloud.

"You do not need to speak your sins," the Chaplain coaxed, "only your fears. I will not judge you. I only mean to offer you sanctuary."

Elodie's eyes were fixed on the portrait of the New Maiden on the back wall. Although her stomach turned at the idea of spilling her secrets to Silas, she had come here to seek counsel. It seemed a shame to turn away from a helping hand in her time of need.

"I was faced with an impossible decision today," Elodie said, turning her attention to her skirt so that she would not have to meet the Royal Chaplain's eyes. "The choice I made does not serve my people. But I cannot fault myself for it." She swallowed thickly. "Others can." She chuckled humorlessly. "They have told me as much. But I do not feel guilty for wanting to protect the New Maiden at all costs."

"It is an honorable calling," Silas said, solemnly.

"You are perhaps a bit biased," Elodie said, glancing at the Chaplain's robes. Even so, it was a relief to hear her decision praised.

"Perhaps," Silas said. "But Her cause is righteous. Her pursuits, just."

Elodie's intentions were hardly so noble. "Why did *you* pledge your life to Her, Chaplain?"

"Ah." The woman's face shuttered. "A complicated story." She waged an internal battle before continuing to speak. "Actually, it involves your mother."

That piqued Elodie's interest. "You knew my mother?" She had not known Tera Warnou to hold connections to the clergy beyond René.

"Oh yes." The woman nodded. "Very well."

Elodie scoured her mother's anecdotes for someone who fit the woman's description, but she came up empty-handed. "My mother never mentioned a Silas."

"She wouldn't have." The woman chuckled dryly. "But you may have heard me mentioned by a different name."

The church was so quiet Elodie could hear the wind whistling through the hedges in the royal garden. "What name might that be?" she asked, even as she held the hopeful answer on her tongue.

"My given name was Rowan Warnou," the Chaplain said. "But that was a very long time ago."

23

While the people of the Lower Banks worked to carefully excavate each splintered piece of the New Maiden's altar, Sabine slipped away to the water's edge. She walked along the shoreline until she was out of sight, each step like a stitch tying water to earth and back again.

She had been so certain there would be a shift. That her veins would change color, or a familiar voice would tickle her ear. But she was still alone amidst the gaping expanse of numbness, a stretch of fog over the ocean that dimmed the stars above.

In a small grove—little more than two trees and a stump for sitting—she paused to comb through the New Maiden's journal again.

I'm afraid, the New Maiden had written, over and over. At first, Sabine had found relief in that recognizable phrase. But now it was a slap in the face, an empty bowl offered to someone withering away from hunger. She did not have the time to flip slowly through its contents, searching languidly for some hidden meaning. She needed answers.

Help me, she pleaded. But there was no response. No gust of wind rustled through the book's pages, guiding her to the entry that would call her magic back. There was no tingling in Sabine's fingers, no static on her skin. Nothing and no one were there to help her. Despite her best efforts to open her heart and build community, she was still devastatingly, impossibly alone.

It took all her self-restraint not to fling the journal into the water. "Why did you even *want* to come back?" Sabine shouted to the sky. She began to weep, her grief palpable in every drop of salt that fell from her cheeks. Sabine's tears splattered the pages below, seeping into the parchment and smearing the ink.

But the water did not erase the New Maiden's words. It changed them.

If you are reading this, then I am dead, and you are burdened. I am sorry for what I have done. I would not wish your lot in life on anyone.

Sabine wiped away her tears, the better to read the unexpected words.

I only meant to save him, the New Maiden had written. *I thought if I drove away his hurt, I would be worthy of the accolades offered to me. But when I opened myself up to his darkness, I did not know that it would sink its feral teeth into me, that it would shock me to my very core.*

People are so quick to inflict pain, to take the scars from their hearts and carve them onto another's. The world is dark and terrible. I do not know how anyone is meant to survive it.

It was a sentiment with which Sabine was intimately familiar, one she had considered time and time again beneath the blankets in her family home.

Sebastien is desperate to reclaim the darkness, to extract it from me at any cost. He is embarrassed by his hurt. But what he does not understand is that it does not define him. There is no use in him carrying this darkness alone. His scars only prove how poorly he was loved.

Yet as I sought to offer him salvation, I damned you in my stead. My time on earth is coming to an end. I have promised to return, but when I do, this darkness will belong to you.

As the New Maiden, I was always going to hold the burdens of those I loved. I made that decision. I chose that path for myself. But you, dear one . . . if you are reading this, you did not ask for my fate. You have inherited the consequences of my decisions, have held the pain of others without understanding why.

Your life has never been your own. Your soul was never yours alone. How frightened you must have been. How angry you surely are now.

Sabine could barely breathe. Anger was not an emotion she had ever permitted herself to embrace. Anger was for a father who had lost next quarter's rent to a card game. Anger was for a Loyalist guard who did not receive due deference. Anger was not for a girl with a family who loved her and a roof above her head. Sabine had always erred, instead, on the side of despair.

But sadness and anger were intrinsically linked. And if a person was allowed to feel only the half of it, the rest would echo emptily.

Do not shy from that rage. Cradle it carefully in your hands. Direct it toward that which has held you in place. And then, the New Maiden had written, *let it burn.*

Sabine raced barefoot through the water, her toes screaming with cold as she returned to the encampment. She arrived out of breath, scanning the crowd for Genevar, but Brianne found her first.

"Look what we've uncovered," she said, starry-eyed, pulling Sabine toward the mishmash of splintered wood, gold objects, and shattered ceramics. "All of this, for the New Maiden."

The attendants were placing rocks around the excavated area to denote the space where the altar had once been. As though guided by an invisible hand, Sabine stepped over the border. The red-haired attendant placed the final stone, sealing the New Maiden in the center.

Sabine knelt before the altar. The people of the Lower Banks encircled her, watching tenderly from all sides. She was not alone— not here. Not anymore.

Her lips were numb with purpose, her skin prickled, charged like the breath before a lightning strike. She dug her fingers into the earth and squeezed shards of clay and broken glass until her palms bled. She felt no pain, only purpose. Finally, she knew what to do.

Sabine let the broken offerings fall to the ground. Then she pressed her bloody hands to the earth, and she screamed.

She screamed for the New Maiden, carrying the pain of those She loved. She screamed for the third daughters before her, lost before they could live. She screamed for Brianne, a pawn in the clergy's hands, a sacrifice for Church and country, both of which had failed her. And she screamed for herself, a brutal, feral shriek, for the life she had lost and the life she still had to live, for her sadness and anger and everything in between.

It was Brianne who joined her first. Her small voice, usually so sweet and soft, turned raw as she shouted her fury. When Sabine turned toward her, Brianne's blue eyes sparkled. Genevar joined in next, her brittle voice low but surprisingly robust. Then the redheaded attendant, then another white-robed follower, then more and more— until the entire circle screamed to the sky, to the earth, to the sea.

Only Katrynn remained quiet, looking uncertain. Sabine got to her feet and stood before her sister on the other side of the circle.

"We deserve to be angry, Rynn." Sabine said the word with such tenderness, as though it was a breakable object rather than a feeling. For so many years, the Anders sisters had been taught just that. When their father lost the rent at the gambling table, that was anger for him alone to feel. Orla Anders was tasked instead with the quiet suffering that came later, the all-encompassing sadness at what was lost, not the fury at finding out who had done the losing.

Katrynn looked at Sabine warily. The sisters had followed their mother's example, were quick to bite their tongues when those feelings sparked. It was safer to suppress. But hiding in the shadows was no way to live, not when life had battered them and left them bruised.

Their hurt mattered, too.

Sabine held out her hand. Katrynn took it, unbothered by the dirt and the blood. She squeezed her sister's fingers, and then she opened her mouth and shrieked, the final voice in a chorus of chaos. The entirety of the Lower Banks raged as one.

Thunder rumbled in the distance, a response to their furious cries. The skies opened up, and in seconds they were soaked to the bone. Screams turned to shrieks turned to laughter. Anger became joy in one spectacular swoop. Sabine's skin sparked as the air before her swirled. Power crackled in her fingers, in her heart, in her toes, shimmering and iridescent as the emotion that nestled within her. She let out a whoop, laughter sacred on her lips.

Genevar crossed the stone border to stand by Sabine. "I knew that you would find your way."

"Thank you for bringing me here." The New Maiden squeezed

her hands into fists, unfurling her fingers one by one, reveling in the unfamiliar feeling of agency coursing through her.

"It was always my dream to live out my days in the place where Ruti wrote," the old woman said. "I think, perhaps, that when you take your leave, I will remain. I've spent too long in the depths of a cellar. I want to feel the sand beneath my toes."

"But—your records," Sabine stammered, too ashamed to speak her true denunciation: Genevar was abandoning *her*.

"Recordkeeping is not an art, child," the old woman said, smiling softly. "Anyone can do it if sufficiently devoted."

"I am," said the youngest Warnou. Her hair was plastered to her forehead, her smile so big she might have been the sun. Brianne had been born into the Church's tangled web. It only made sense that she would want to spend her days making order of disarray. The Archivist did not look surprised, as though this conclusion was not only expected but planned.

"You are," Genevar agreed, her shaking fingers working to unhook the clasp of a chain around her neck. On it hung a key with sharp teeth and a curved head. "History now belongs to you." Brianne beamed as she accepted the necklace.

"You'll be all right here?" Katrynn eyed the attendants defensively. She grabbed the arm of a white-robed man, who had opened his mouth to let the rain fall on his tongue. "You'll make sure she's safe?"

"We'll take good care of her," he confirmed, winking at Genevar. "We are a small but loyal community."

Sabine smiled. "I know." In a matter of days, she had wept, had sweated, had wedged dirt beneath her fingernails with the people of the Lower Banks. Because of them, she had what she needed to return to Velle triumphant. Or, at the very least, to put up a valiant fight.

And wasn't that the New Maiden's only wish for her? To embrace her anger and point it in the direction most warranted?

She considered this, as they planned their departure. She could not say for certain where the emotion truly belonged. The Second Son had earned some for the murders of third daughters and this vendetta against her. But there were many others who deserved her ire. Her father, for his inability to keep his family's hard-earned coin in his pocket. The Loyalists for their targeted scrutiny of people from her neighborhood. Chaplain René, who had barred all of Harborside from entering Her churches. Elodie, for not realizing the truth about Tal. Even Sabine herself, for acting weak when all along there had been magic running through her veins.

The New Maiden was due Sabine's anger, too.

Without Her, Sabine might have floated through life freely, might have flounced and flirted like Katrynn, might have been crafty and light-fingered like Artur. She might have met a nice girl, and settled down, Velle none the wiser to her sorry existence. But Sabine's soul had never been hers alone. Her mind, her magic, and her sadness had come from an enigmatic deity; her destiny had been set from the moment of her birth.

Just as the trip to the Lower Banks had lulled Sabine's travel companions to sleep, so did their return. One dusty lantern hung above her shoulder, jostling with each curve in the road, casting light across the carriage's quilted doors and the slack expressions of Katrynn and Brianne.

Again, Sabine did not rest. This time, however, she was not reading the New Maiden's confessions. Instead, she wrote her own.

It is a heavy weight. Her handwriting was uneven as the coach lumbered toward Velle. *I don't yet know where this feeling will fit, and if it will hinder or help me. But I will learn how to hold it, like the dagger that at first was awkward in my hand. I shall wield my anger like a weapon and use it to protect myself.*

"What are you writing?" Brianne's voice startled Sabine out of her musings. The youngest Warnou's eyes were heavy with sleep, her hair still matted with the ocean air.

"None of your business," Sabine said gently.

"Not *yet*, anyway," Brianne countered, letting her grin take over her entire face as she dangled the key before Sabine. "But one day, it'll be recorded in the Archives. I'm bound to outlive you."

She said it sweetly, but the truth of it sent Sabine reeling like a ship on stormy seas. The New Maiden had died at seventeen, the same age she was now. Although her magic had returned, she still did not know how this fight would end. If the Second Son had His way, Sabine might not live to see her eighteenth year. There was so little life to make a legacy.

24

Elodie's first reaction was not to embrace her aunt, but to berate her.

"Where have you *been?*" she howled, voice reverberating through the eaves. She had been struggling desperately to maintain control of her country, and all the while a Warnou elder looked on from behind the white robe of the clergy.

Silas looked taken aback. "In Adeya," she said, naming a small province on the border of Velle and the First Republic. "They needed help building a church, training the clergy folk, spreading Her word. I was there for three years. I only returned to the city upon hearing of your mother's death. I'd been away for so long that the Harborside chapel was the only one that would have me."

"Three years doesn't seem so long," Elodie said, her voice chilly.

"You misunderstand," Silas said softly. "I fled the palace more than thirty years ago. I swore then that as long as my sister was alive, I would never return to Velle."

"Why not?"

Silas exhaled slowly. "If you did not know of my existence, I suppose I am not surprised your mother kept her path to the throne from you, too."

"Tell me." Elodie's fingers gripped the pew in front of her. She could not stomach any more secrets. "Please."

"You already know," Silas said, eyes on the pulpit, "that your mother was a third daughter."

"None would let me forget it," Elodie chuckled softly.

"Then you also know," Silas continued, "that the third in line to the throne hardly ever sees it."

Elodie could not imagine her mother as anything other than a monarch. Tera Warnou had been shrewd and vindictive and incredibly persuasive. Her mind would have been wasted as a perennial princess. But the circumstances surrounding her mother's rule were shrouded in loss.

"One dead young queen is odd," Silas said, "especially for a girl under protection night and day. But two dead queens," she continued, "is beyond suspect. There was only one person my sisters' deaths would benefit."

The skin on Elodie's arms crawled. Silas spoke with such gravitas that she could not help but fear what the woman would say next.

"It was no coincidence that my sisters did not live more than a handful of months after the crown touched their heads," the Royal Chaplain said. "Tera was willing to do whatever it took to be queen. Sororicide was no exception."

Elodie pried her white knuckles from the pew. Her mother had murdered her own sisters in order to gain control of Velle's throne. Years later, Elodie had poisoned Brianne with sadness for the very

212

same reason. Once, Elodie had been proud to be compared to her mother. Now, the association felt like a curse.

"So she was a monster."

"It's never so simple as that, Elodie," her aunt said plainly. "Your mother was my greatest friend and confidant. She always took two of everything: cakes, flowers, jewels—*just in case*, she'd always say, though in case of what I never knew. She taught me how to enjoy something in the moment while also keeping it carefully preserved for the future." Silas laughed gently, a tinkling sound like chimes. "Perhaps that is what readied me to spread the New Maiden's word more effectively than most in Her Church. Knowing that what I felt each time I read Her word was never mine alone, but a treasure that could and should be shared."

"Were you always called to the Church?"

"Certainly not," Silas said, sounding affronted. "The clergy was not a suitable calling for a Warnou woman. 'Why give up your own lineage of power to amplify someone else's?' my mother always said."

"Then why . . . ?"

"Absolution," she answered simply. "I wanted to earn my sister the forgiveness she required but would never seek." She shifted on the pew. Her gray eyes were darker than Elodie's own, but the queen recognized the quiet determination behind her aunt's expression.

"Tera spent her childhood preparing to serve at the right hand of the queen. 'Our sisters were going to need it,' she claimed, and privately, I agreed. I liked Aurielle and Ursula well enough," Silas said, chuckling at Elodie's expression, "but they were terribly dull and prone to whims. If the Second Son had been campaigning this viciously back then, well," she sighed, "the whole country would have converted long ago."

Shame rose like a lump in Elodie's throat. "I haven't done much better," she admitted, gesturing to the royal chapel's empty pews. "If I had not been so distracted by the threats from the Republics, I might have identified His prophet sooner. It is my own weakness that allowed Him to rise so swiftly."

"Perhaps," the Chaplain said. "But past failings do not dictate future actions. What matters now is that you have chosen to make amends. Besides," she added, "the crown is far too heavy for a girl so young. You have been doing your best with the resources provided you. None can fault you for that."

"How would you know?" Elodie asked darkly. The compliment was not reassuring. Her aunt had been close enough to observe her struggle, but not invested enough to step forward and intercede.

The woman looked uncomfortable. "I have, on occasion, stopped by the queen's study to observe your work."

Elodie raised her eyebrows. It was disquieting, to know that she had been unwittingly perceived. "I beg your pardon?"

"I just wanted to ensure you were managing." Pink flushed the woman's cheeks. Her face held more wrinkles than Tera's had, but then Elodie's mother had not been expressive. Her face had not aged because she had not offered the world access to her heart.

"And no one noticed you lurking outside the door to the queen's study?" Elodie asked, incredulous. "Surely even New Maiden's cloth does not pardon you from such scrutiny?"

"It was not my status that protected me from onlookers, Majesty," Silas said, "but my vantage point." At her niece's bewildered expression, Silas got heavily to her feet. "It seems this castle has carefully guarded its secrets. Come with me."

Elodie followed Silas through a cramped hallway hung with fresh white robes, a lineup of ghosts patiently awaiting their turn to be resurrected. The queen expected her aunt to lead her into the office where René had once lorded over the parish, making unique and increasingly expensive demands in the name of the New Maiden. Instead, they stopped before a stone wall.

Silas produced a strange, knifelike key from her pocket, which she jammed into the shadowy crevice beneath a loose brick. She fiddled softly for several seconds before the rock emitted a mechanical *click* and the wall swung forward to reveal a cavernous darkness.

Elodie gasped.

"I suppose I'd better lead the way," the Chaplain said measuredly. "Watch your step. We're going down." She descended into darkness. Elodie followed carefully, holding her hands out in front of her lest she walk face-first into a wall.

"You're not like I thought you'd be," the queen said, after a moment of silence. It was indelicate, but the truth. When she'd imagined her mother's secret sister, she'd pictured Cleo's conviviality with a hint of Brianne's tenderness. But Silas—Rowan—was none of those things. She was terse and sharp, expressive but judgmental. She was nothing like Elodie had pictured a woman of the cloth or a fourth Warnou daughter to be.

"Well, expectations are a breeding ground for disappointment," Silas replied, sounding unconcerned. "How *did* you imagine me?"

"When my mother wrote to you, she made you sound—"

"She wrote to me?" Her aunt's voice came out strangled. Elodie was lucky her hands were still out in front of her, or the two of them would have collided.

"I found letters," Elodie admitted as they continued onward, "written to someone, begging for help. It was because of them that I learned of your existence. It was my father who revealed to me your name."

"Which one is your father again?"

"Antony."

"Ah, yes." Silas made a soft sound. "Always liked him. He deserved better than my sister." Elodie had secretly felt the same. "Where are these letters?"

"In her study," Elodie said. "I mean, *my* study. The queen's study?" The desk behind which Elodie's mother so often sat had never truly felt like hers to claim.

"Struggling to accept your title is nothing to be ashamed of, Elodie," Silas said gently. "The monarchy as a whole is a rather unethical system of governance."

"Oh?" The sentiment reminded Elodie of her brother's angry words, and thus she was inclined not to consider it. But beneath her resentment, she was beginning to see Rob's point. The longer she held the crown, the more she questioned what gave her the right to make decisions with such life-altering ramifications. She did not want that responsibility, nor had she earned it.

"While I was in Adeya, I learned more about how the Republics structure their administration," the Chaplain said, huffing as the path they followed grew steeper.

"Curse the Republics," Elodie said, voice dripping with venom. "They worship the Second Son and have stolen all my soldiers."

"They are not righteous examples," Silas conceded, "but their systems are worthy of consideration. What gives Warnou women the right to absolute rule? What philosophy do we hold that others do not?"

"Country above all," Elodie said, but the familiar phrase had turned rancid on her tongue.

"Tera taught you that one, did she?" Elodie could hear Silas's smile. "That is too heavy a weight for one person. I should know." She stopped walking, causing Elodie to run into her again. "We're here."

"Where?"

Metal scraped against stone. Hinges squawked, and a faint trickle of light illuminated a set of steep steps. Faint light glowed through the cracks in the wall to reveal the outline of a door. At the top of the stairs, Silas bade her niece to peer through the gap. On the other side was the queen's study.

"Lady above and among us," Elodie breathed. "You were spying on me."

"Just to see that you were all right. You're only a child," Silas said, looking apologetic. She unlatched a small lock and pushed the wall forward. Silas stepped over the books that had fallen to the floor, their pages crumpled, their spines cracked. "This is too much for any one person, let alone a girl of seventeen failed by a mother who was fixated on absolute control."

"She wasn't so terrible," Elodie argued. "She let me choose my own outfits. Most days."

Silas chuckled darkly. "You're funny. You must get that from me. Now let's see those letters."

Elodie procured the correspondence from its hiding place and handed them over to Silas. Her aunt sank into the desk chair and began to pore over Tera's words. Elodie, wanting to give her some privacy, collected the scattered tomes and fitted them back into their place on the false bookshelf.

As Silas worked her way through the many pieces of parchment, Elodie reflected again on her aunt's distaste for the monarchy. Her views were similar to Rob's, but Elodie was now disillusioned enough with the crown to take the questions seriously. What *might* her country look like if decisions included its people? How might its economic structure, its creativity, its position of power change?

Tera Warnou had fought so hard to instill in Elodie a reverence for the crown—had touted it as absolute and essential—that the eldest Warnou daughter had never taken the time to wonder if it really was worthy of her devotion. What's more, she had never offered herself a chance to question if she truly wished to bear the brunt of its weight. Instead, she had simply followed her mother's directives, much the way that Tal might have done with the Second Son.

She was no better than he. No less corrupted by power.

"There isn't anything revolutionary in there," Elodie said, when she could stand the silence no longer.

"On the contrary, Elodie dear," said Silas, who had taken up a pen and was scribbling onto a spare scrap of parchment. "There is much within these pages if you know your mother's cipher." She looked up, her gray eyes sparkling. "Which luckily, I do. These three letters offer up a message that is quite unexpected indeed. It says: *While I had a hand in our sisters' murders, I was not the one who killed them.*"

Elodie fiddled with her sleeves. Tera's confession did very little to absolve her of such a heinous crime. Elodie did not think it mattered much whether her aunts had died by her mother's hand, if Tera Warnou was the one who had set their murders in motion.

"That's not all," Silas said, pen scratching the parchment even more quickly. "The final four missives encrypt something even more relevant." She put her pen down with a *thunk*. "Your mother entered into an agreement with an unlikely ally. It says here," Silas said, her face a ghostly white, "that my sisters were murdered by a man named Ludwig. He was once the prophet of the Second Son."

25

The air was thick with the threat of rain as the carriage rumbled into Velle's city proper. Clouds hung low, shadows stretching long and lean across the cobblestones.

On the other side of the coach, Katrynn shivered. "This weather feels ominous."

Brianne did not respond. She was pressed against the carriage window, staring at the posters hung in every window. The moths were uniformly sketched—the curve of their bodies, their drooping antennae, the spotted markings drawn on their wings. It was clear these symbols had been printed and distributed. Every single building in the Commerce District boasted one.

"It's a pestilence," the youngest Warnou whispered, eyes so wide Sabine feared they might fall from her face. The New Maiden crossed her arms, trying to breathe through her rising panic. He had been busy in her absence.

They turned toward the Manufacturing District and were met

with a grim scene. People filled the road, squabbling over wood and stone, some wielding their wares as weapons. Their anxiety was tangible, a bitter, metallic tang that coated Sabine's tongue and left her unsettled.

The message on the posters was new: *First came fire, then famine and flood. When war and death are all that's left, which side will you fight for?*

Their driver called out to the horses, drawing the attention of the rambunctious crowd. The mob lunged for the vehicle housing the three girls. Hands slapped against the carriage windows, clambered for the door handles; some even clutched the spokes of the wheels until they began to splinter. The horses let out shrieks of panic, their whinnies shrill and fearsome. The carriage driver shouted as a stone shattered the window. Shards of glass fell at Brianne's feet.

"Where is the New Maiden?" Dirty hands scrabbled inside the broken window, skin sliced by the slivers of glass. Blood stained the carriage's upholstery.

Katrynn pounded on the roof, calling for the driver to move. "Run them down if you must," Sabine's sister shrieked.

"Give us the Maiden!" the crowd demanded.

"She isn't here," Brianne shouted, her voice breaking. Sabine pulled the young girl away from the window.

"We must deliver Her to Him!"

The momentum of bodies caused the carriage to sway. The crowd was too big. The coach would topple, and then those scrambling, squabbling hands would pull the girls from the wreckage. The New Maiden would be harmed in unimaginable ways because the onlookers were afraid.

But Sabine was not frightened. She was furious. *"Leave us!"* she shrieked, Katrynn and Brianne howling with her. A burst of lightning struck a tree, setting the brittle, bare branches alight. The crowd paused their onslaught to watch the fire, awestruck.

"Flying fish, Bet," Katrynn whispered. "Did *you* do that?"

"Did *we* do that?" Brianne asked, almost hopefully, as though her rage might hold power, too.

Sabine shook her head disbelievingly. "I have no idea." But there was no time for wonder. No point in mourning the fact that her darkness had not returned with her magic. "Go," she cried instead. The carriage driver did not need to be told twice. His horses barreled forward, leaving the dismal scene behind.

When the coach pulled up to the north gate, Sabine hid within the depths of her cloak, shrinking beneath its hood like a child behind a panel of curtains, face pressed to fabric, huddling in the dark. She could not risk being identified again. If the fervor in the streets was that intense, she was loath to face the frenzy within the palace walls. But the coach was waved through with no inspection, and the courtyard was all but abandoned. A stable boy hurried forward to take the horses, and a steward frowned at the state of the coach, but the usual bustle of Castle Warnou was nowhere to be found.

"Perhaps everyone has taken shelter from the thunder?" Katrynn suggested, glancing at the sky.

Sabine kept her hood up as she disembarked from the carriage. It was too quiet, like the surface of the ocean before a storm.

The girls hurried through the gardens toward the royal chapel, wind whipping through their hair, shaking loose dying leaves from withering branches. Water splattered from the fountain onto the earth below. Although a grumble of thunder began in the distance, the skies did not open up until the three of them were safely harbored in the sanctuary. Giant droplets of rain pounded against the tall windows, shutters clattering as the thunder rumbled closer, shaking the earth beneath their feet. The lightning was infrequent but dazzling, the sharp cracks lighting up the sky like a sunny day before plunging the world back into night.

Brianne frowned as she emerged from the Chaplain's office. "Silas isn't here."

"I'm sure she's all right," Katrynn said gently.

"Where would she go?" The youngest Warnou looked close to tears. Brianne had lost so much in her short lifetime—her mother, trust in her father and sister, her role as the New Maiden—that it was now a reflex to always assume the worst.

"Silas is strong, Brianne," Sabine said. "I'm certain that whatever she is doing is for the good of us all."

"I am grateful you think so highly of me, Maiden." Silas's steady voice floated toward them from the pulpit.

"Where did you come from?" Brianne strode forward accusingly. "I was just in that room, and there was no one there."

"That's quite the walk," came the breathless voice of the queen. "Really, Silas, how did you take that route every—" She stopped speaking the moment she saw Sabine.

Elodie looked exhausted. Her slumped shoulders were a jarring contrast to her usually impeccable posture. Her starlight hair had lost some of its sheen, and her bottom lip was chapped from where she had worried it between her teeth. But her eyes took on new life the moment she met Sabine's gaze.

The Queen of Velle walked purposefully down the aisle of the royal chapel and fell to her knees before the New Maiden's feet.

"Elodie, what are you—"

The queen reached for Sabine's hands, entangling their fingers together. "I pledge myself to your cause, heart and mind. Body and soul. I am yours, even if you are not mine."

Warmth flooded Sabine's cheeks, swirled gently in her chest. "I know not what I have done to deserve such allegiance."

"Which is exactly why you are owed it," Elodie said. "You do not beg loyalty. You earn it. I am only sorry I did not pledge it sooner."

"I know where your loyalty lies," Sabine said, pulling the queen to her feet. Elodie put a hand to her cheek affectionately. "But I fear why you feel so compelled to remind me. What has happened in my absence?"

"Tal offered me a choice," Elodie said darkly, avoiding everyone's eyes. "Velle, or the New Maiden."

"And you chose Sabine?" Brianne asked her eldest sister with trepidation.

"I chose Sabine," Elodie confirmed. Sabine's stomach twisted uncomfortably. It made no sense to value one person above the lives of thousands.

"What does that mean for Velle?" she asked, fidgeting with her hair.

"Tal has taken to the Republics," Elodie said, expression crumpling. "When he returns to Velle, it will be with an army in tow."

Despite the unfavorable news, a strange peace settled in Sabine's chest. An altercation with the Second Son had been inevitable from the moment she had identified His prophet. It had only ever been a matter of time. "What is it that he wishes to conquer?"

The queen trembled as she answered: "You."

It was almost calming to hear her greatest fear spoken aloud. "If that is the case," the New Maiden said, inhaling the last breath she would take in this time of peace, "we have no alternative but to recruit an army of our own."

26

After a short night of fitful sleep, Elodie gathered her most trusted advisers in the War Room. Between the unpredictable hostile acts and impending threats from Edgar and the Second Son, it was almost a relief to call the brewing battle what it was.

She pinned up the map of the Republics, pointing out the many places where their borders intersected with Velle's.

"This is what we're up against," the queen said. The ink-darkened outlines of the enemy states loomed above Velle like a rain cloud. "We're surrounded, which means they can invade from all sides."

"Do we need to worry about the water?" Artur Anders had come along with Cleo, and although he was the only boy in the room, he did not appear uncomfortable or overwhelmed. On the contrary, he seemed proud to prove his loyalty to Sabine, the way Elodie's own brother had been proud to demonstrate his betrayal.

Elodie shook her head. "Thankfully, that's not an option. It would take months for any invaders to make it through the Jvin Channel now that winter is nearly upon us." Artur looked relieved. Elodie shared his sentiment. She was already out of her depths on land. She could not handle a navy, too.

"There's truly no army left?" Cleo fretted, picking at a loose thread on her gown's sleeve.

"We'll have to recruit our own, Princess," Silas said.

From across the table, Cleo narrowed her eyes at the Chaplain. "Who are you, again?"

Silas turned to Elodie, a question in her eyes. The queen sighed. She supposed this was as good a time as any for the truth.

"Silas is our aunt," Elodie said. "Mother's younger sister, Rowan. The fourth Warnou daughter."

The room was silent as the group digested the information. Elodie's sisters reexamined Silas's face with their mother's memory in mind. There was a similarity in the eyes, the curve of the nose, and the set of the jaw. Just enough that one might miss it. Just enough to be recognizable once a person knew to look. Cleo squinted at the Chaplain suspiciously. Brianne stared at Silas with a mix of wonder and confusion.

"I apologize for my absence and my disguise," Silas said, breaking the silence, "but believe me when I say I had my reasons. I am here for you now—to defeat this darkness—and vow to explain everything afterward."

"If there even *is* an afterward," Cleo said ominously.

"Speaking of which"—Elodie clapped her hands to return the group's attention to the maps—"Velle has no army to mobilize, while the Second Son has conjured a tidal wave of soldiers. How do we fight it?"

The queen stared at the gathered group, all of whom looked uncomfortable.

"*Can* we fight it?" Katrynn asked eventually.

"Yes," Sabine said, speaking slowly, as though still formulating her thoughts. "My magic has returned in the form of anger. So long as I am surrounded by those with righteous fury, we have supplies enough to fight."

"Is there so much rage to harness?" Her brother looked at her with concern. "What's more, will you be able to control it?"

Artur was surely remembering the hours Sabine had spent grappling with her sadness. But that was before she had been offered the New Maiden's guidance. Before she knew who—and what—she was.

"Think about Ma," she said, speaking in terms her brother would understand. "Da gambled away all our money, and although she suffered through it, did she truly believe that what he said or did was *right*? Or did she believe that her only option was to submit to him?"

"Ma kept secret savings stored behind a loose stone in the hearth," Artur said, understanding dawning on his face. "She tucked away an extra coin here and there, because if Da didn't know about it, he couldn't lose it at the card table."

"One time, Ma told me that she left him in the Loyalists' possession a night longer than she needed to, hoping that would scare him straight," Katrynn admitted. "Didn't work, but at least he couldn't incur any additional debt in captivity."

"Exactly," Sabine said, looking at the assembled audience. "She resisted every chance she had. Most people have only their faith to trade on. No tithings, no land, no legacy. Some would give up their rights for proximity to power. But many more are like Ma, righteously angry with the meager choices they have, ready to step out of line and resist."

"I don't know," Cleo said, shifting uncomfortably. "That's a lot of speculation." Privately, Elodie was inclined to agree.

"Only because you haven't suffered," Katrynn said, not unkindly. "You are not used to being hurt or controlled by others; you are not used to barely scraping by. You have not sacrificed daily for the dream of something better, a dream that can be stolen by an ill-fated decision or too much drink. Your provenance makes you secure, and therefore ill-equipped to understand."

Elodie felt properly chastised, even though she had not been the one to receive the lecture. To Cleo's credit, she merely nodded and looked at her hands. Elodie was proud of both Cleo and Katrynn. This was the sort of energy—the sort of candor—required to honor the experiences of citizens from all walks of life. They would need to build their underground networks thoughtfully and strategically. Match the right messenger to each district.

"How will we find those willing to join us?" Brianne chimed in.

"We take a page out of the Second Son's book," Sabine said. "We put out the call and then let followers come to us."

"We distribute posters." Elodie nodded with understanding. "Hang them in every corner of the city and every house of worship. Present the people with another option and let them decide." It was a first step toward autonomy. Even if her people did not join them, the choice was more than they had ever been offered before.

"Will that be enough?" Artur asked. "No offense, Bet, but does anyone still believe in the New Maiden?"

"Faith can be shaken," Silas said, "but it is not so easily lost.

Sometimes, people simply need a reminder. Need to be forgiven and welcomed back with open arms."

"We know that there are faithfuls still," Katrynn added, "in the Lower Banks. Those people would have done anything for you, Bet. We could call on them."

"Wasn't one of the attendants a descendent of Beck?" Brianne asked.

"Of course." Silas's eyes went wide. "Descendants of Her Favoreds will be vital to our cause. Their connection to Her will only serve to make Sabine stronger. Once we locate them, they will recruit others." She smiled at Brianne. "This is a powerful start."

Brianne fiddled with a silver chain around her neck, pulling out a key. "I know how to find them."

"What is that?" Elodie questioned her sister. Brianne had changed: her dresses traded in for trousers and boots, her once styled hair now slicked back into a tight bun. She looked steadier in her body. Seemed more comfortable and in control. It was a wonder to watch her grow into herself.

"A key to the Archives," Brianne said. "I made a vow to protect and preserve the knowledge of the New Maiden."

"Genevar was a diligent record keeper," Sabine added. "As a descendent of Ruti herself, she will have traced the lineage of the others."

Warmth spread through Elodie's chest. Until now, her time as queen had been nothing but a constant, bitter battle. But the people in this room were proof that she was part of something greater than herself, that she could use her power to bring people together and accomplish true good despite the hurdles of the crown.

"Bri, you and Silas will go to the Archives," the queen commanded. "Pull as many records as you can about the Favoreds and their descendants and bring them back here." The two of them nodded and rose to their feet. Elodie admired their parallels. Both were the youngest of four, both had witnessed a sister harness her basest instincts to reach the throne. Both had found comfort in their faith. It was right that Brianne should have a proper adult to offer her guidance.

"Cleo"—Elodie turned to her middle sister, so inspired when it came to aesthetics and perception—"you start work on the posters. Be persuasive, funny, whatever you need to make it clear that we will not back down. We are just as much a force as those who whisper His word in the shadows."

She turned to Artur, the boy with mischief in his eyes. "Artur," she said, steeling herself for Sabine's reaction, "I need you to find out everything you can about explosives."

"Cool!" Artur grinned, while Sabine looked on with horror.

"The Second Son fights dirty," Elodie explained. "We must be prepared."

"Don't bother talking me out of it, Bet," Artur said, pushing back his chair and jumping to his feet. "The queen *commands* it." He winked and headed for the door, Cleo at his heels.

"Katrynn." Elodie turned to Sabine's sister. "We need to identify as many potential members of our resistance as possible. You spoke of your mother's quiet rage, which is precisely the weapon we'll need to channel as a collective. Do you think anyone else in Harborside would be willing to take up the call?" The Anders sisters exchanged a knowing look.

"We can find you recruits," Katrynn answered immediately.

"I'll go talk to Ma." Sabine's sister squeezed her hand before she departed.

Only the queen and the New Maiden remained.

Sabine fussed with her braid, looking troubled. "You sound so certain of our success."

Elodie sighed. "Does it help or hurt if I tell you that I am not as sure as I sound?"

"Helps," Sabine said. "It makes me less afraid that I will disappoint you."

Elodie drew the New Maiden near, cupping Sabine's cheeks between her palms. "This mess has no reflection upon you. If anything," she said, eyes flitting to the other girl's lips so that she might find relief from the depths of her eyes, "the fault is mine."

Sabine bit her bottom lip. "What could you possibly have done?"

"It is my world who stands against you," Elodie admitted, moving her hands from Sabine's face to clasp her hands. "My best friend, my brother—both are staunchly devoted to His cause and wish to eradicate the New Maiden."

"You truly had no idea," Sabine asked searchingly, "about Tal?"

Elodie hesitated. It was too late for a lie, too ill-timed for the entire truth. "He told me of his allegiance, but not his role. I should have shared my suspicions with you sooner."

Sabine's brown eyes took on a deep sorrow. "As long as you are with me now," she said softly, "that is all that I can ask for."

It was so simple, compared to the recent demands that had been made of her. She was moved to kneel again, but Sabine stopped her.

"Stay with me," she said, not quite smiling. "Right here, eye to eye."

Elodie lost herself in Sabine's fraught expression. There was no telling what the outcome of this fight with their enemies would be, but in this moment, it did not matter. They were equals in their power, in their anger, in their fear.

They were lucky to have in each other such a strong counterpart. They were compromised, too, for such love left a person vulnerable to impossible loss.

Elodie Warnou could only hope that after all was said and done, she would have another chance to drown in Sabine Anders's eyes.

27

Orla Anders would not allow her daughters to return to Harborside without her. "If my children are embroiled in battle," Sabine's mother said, "then I must stand by their side." When Sabine tried to protest, her mother held up a hand. "Who better to recruit for an army of anger than the person who spent her life among her neighbors, privy to their fears, their failures, and their concerns?"

To that, Sabine could not object. Her mother traded in potions that made life in Harborside just the slightest bit easier. While it was Sabine's magic that gave them potency, it was Orla's hand that formed their foundation. It was her mother who brewed elixirs for luck and for fortune, who snuck salve to battered partners and who crafted tonics to cure maladies when a doctor demanded too much coin.

Orla Anders had offered the people of Harborside shelter in the storm of life. Sabine and Katrynn's recruitment efforts would only benefit from her counsel.

"Harborsiders are proud, mind," their mother warned as the coach swept through the city, "so do not give them reason to be defensive. You are not there to apportion judgment, nor to tell them how to feel. You are simply there to offer them sanctuary."

Sabine's heart twisted in her chest, the same way it had when she'd received her neighbors' confessions. It had been a relief to hold out her hands and help her neighbors carry the weight of their woes. It was not dissimilar to the New Maiden's calling, to the way She had opened up Her heart to the burdens of Her followers.

"What will we do once they've agreed to join us?" Katrynn asked, fiddling with the buttons on her dress.

Sabine hummed tunelessly, searching for a solution. They needed a way to identify their recruits, to organize those willing to fight for Her cause. This task would require diligence, devotion, and an innocuous meeting place.

"Send them to the church in the Arts District," Sabine said, thinking fondly of the young girl who spent her days in the sanctuary. "Tell them to give their names to Freya. This way, we will have a record. We will know our numbers. We will be prepared."

Orla Anders reached both hands across the carriage, offering one to each daughter. "I am so lucky," she said, "to have raised two powerful girls. You both are extraordinary. Every single piece of you, from your tears to your toes."

Sabine reached for her sister's hand to complete the circle. She was grateful to belong to such wonderful women, to those who took the time to care for others not because they had to, but because they could. Even in the darkest times, when the Anders family had no money and very little hope, Orla had always ensured that her children had known love.

The carriage slowed as they turned onto the streets of Harborside. In the daylight, the cobblestones were calm, and to Sabine's relief, the moth iconography was far less prevalent in this district. The neighborhood was loyal. Harborside knew she belonged to them, knew it was divinely right that the New Maiden had risen from sea and salt. Sabine could only hope that devotion would translate to support when the time for battle came.

The Anders women split up. Orla took the winding streets nearest the family home, Katrynn claimed the east side of the harbor, and Sabine set off south. The New Maiden shook off her nerves as she approached a small residence with dusty windows and red-checkered curtains. She rapped lightly on the weathered front door.

The man who answered stared at Sabine with wide eyes. He was a decade older than Katrynn, with a baby balanced on his hip.

"Hello." Sabine beamed as the baby swatted the man's left ear. "Do you have a few minutes to talk about Her word?"

"You're not selling something, are you?" The man grimaced. "Rent is due, and I've got nothing to spare."

"The only thing I have to peddle," Sabine said gently, "is a place to release your anger."

And so, the New Maiden spent the day conversing with the people of her neighborhood, asking questions regarding their health and happiness, inquiring delicately about red handkerchiefs and to whom they offered their daily prayers.

"We keep our faiths separate," one woman said, at mention of the Second Son. "It keeps the peace."

"Do you know what the Second Son preaches?" Sabine inquired. "Are you comfortable with your husband's hatred of the same divinity you worship?"

The woman looked flummoxed. "I, well, that isn't really my responsibility, is it?"

"No," Sabine agreed. "But its consequences will come for you, someday soon. I urge you to consider, if you have ever found comfort in Her word, joining me in this fight."

The woman stared at her hands. "I can't."

"I understand," Sabine said graciously, remembering her mother's warning. "If ever that changes, we welcome you with open arms."

Others were far more willing to take up the call. In the next apartment, Sabine came face-to-face with a pair of young sisters, showcasing gap-toothed grins as they found a deity standing on their front steps.

"Gran!" one of the sisters shrieked. "She's here. The New Maiden! In our kitchen!"

"Nonsense," called a gruff voice. "The New Maiden doesn't want anything t'do with us."

"I swear it!" The other sister's voice was deeper but no less excited. "She's here!"

When their grandmother hobbled into the room and saw Sabine, she shrieked. "Why didn't you tell me?" She chastised her grand-daughters, who rolled their eyes. "I would have gotten dressed."

"It's a lovely nightgown." Sabine bit back a grin. "I particularly favor the lace. Now tell me," she said, accepting a mug of tea from the older sister, "have the moths come for you?"

"Pesky things," the grandmother said. "Always eating through my clothes."

"She means the posters, Gran," the little sister said.

"Oh, those," the old woman said darkly. "Fools, the lot of them."

237

"Happy to hear you say so," Sabine said, "because I have a proposition."

By the end of the afternoon, the New Maiden's voice was hoarse, but her army had grown. She'd garnered verbal commitments from half the harbor and had directed her people to the church in the Arts District where they could officially devote themselves to her army.

Harborsiders were starved for community and comfort. Her neighbors were good folk, and Sabine had been destined for exactly this—to pry open the floodgates and bring them a bounty in exchange for their suffering.

That was the true prophecy of the New Maiden. To make those without power or influence feel less alone. To amplify their voices and validate their reactions. With their anger on her side, Sabine would sow the seeds of their frustration and coax those precious blooms to life.

The New Maiden was not weak for giving in to emotion. If anything, it was proof of her strength. She would tend to the garden of Harborside's ire and let its fury unfurl. Then she could confirm what the world pretended not to know: Those who spent their days in the dirt would be first in line for the harvest.

28

While the rest of her compatriots enacted their assigned duties, Elodie Warnou stared at the map of the Republics. In a crowded War Room, her ideas had seemed sound. But alone, with the ghosts of battles past, she was beginning to doubt herself. Rob had once accused Elodie of never having to face the consequences of her actions. This time, there was no escaping them.

Her military inexperience left her paranoid that she was not considering all necessary angles of the impending warfare. With Velle's troops so scarce at the border, Elodie could not afford to remove General Garvey from his post in order to seek his counsel, nor could she risk having their correspondence intercepted by followers of the Second Son. In the past, she would have consulted with Tal on strategy. Once, she might have even called on Rob. While her brother was not a soldier at heart, his father had spent the last decade trying to win him over to the cause. Rob held valuable knowledge, no matter how little he wished to use it.

Still, there had to be *someone* left within the walls of Castle Warnou who could advise Elodie, however grudgingly, on how best to steel herself for battle.

The queen was shocked when she discovered that person to be Maxine.

Elodie stumbled upon the soldier as she wandered past the west tower. The guard was still at her post, hair braided down her back as usual. But her expression was different, the air about her less exacting and spiteful. Instead, Elodie read a different emotion, one closer to concern.

"Maxine," Elodie said, offering the guard a curtsy. "At ease."

"Majesty." Maxine dipped her head but did not relax. "What business have you here?"

"Inventory of the guard," Elodie lied, glancing down the hallway at the many open doors of the barracks. "Tal has gone, and with him half my Loyalists." She noted the polished buttons on Maxine's uniform. "Honestly, I'm surprised to find you here."

The Loyalist rolled her eyes. "Frankly, Majesty, I find that assumption insulting."

"You've not been moved by the word of the Second Son?"

Maxine let out a sharp laugh devoid of any humor. "I've spent my life in the military and the guard. I do not need to devote myself to a deity to hear criticism about emotional women."

Elodie had never considered that Maxine's icy exterior might be a front put up for her own protection. "I cannot imagine what that must have felt like, all those years surrounded by a suffocating layer of doubt from your peers."

Maxine snorted. "Yes you can. It's been happening to you since the moment you took the throne." She was not wrong. Still, it irked Elodie to hear the truth stated so plainly. "Now tell me, Majesty, what are you are really doing in this wing?"

The queen met the girl's brown eyes. "What can you tell me about combat?"

For the first time in their years of interaction, Maxine looked truly surprised. "I do not know that it is simple enough to summarize," she said, frowning. "It is messy, complex, and ultimately fruitless. No one wins a war, Majesty. There is always something irreparably broken. Always something irrevocably lost."

"But is it not exhilarating?" Elodie urged. "I remember the tales you told upon your return from the training grounds. Tal was so inspired by the decorated soldiers you had learned from. You lauded the virtues of the men on the front lines."

These were the stories that had ultimately convinced Tal to enlist. He had extolled Maxine's proximity to valor, and promised Elodie that he, too, would return with tales worth telling.

"We are instructed to shield new recruits from the truth," Maxine said, her voice unbearably pained. "Sometimes, one must turn horror into heroics in order to survive."

The hall was quiet as the guard's words seeped into Elodie's skin. "How can anyone emerge victorious?" The queen was not certain if that was her true question, but it was the only one she could manage.

"You sacrifice only what you are willing to lose," Maxine said, simply. "That way, regardless of the outcome, you can stand by your decisions. Which is more than most generals can claim. More than most commanders are willing to consider."

Elodie tamped down the well of emotion that threatened to spurt from her chest. She had come here looking for guidance, and instead had been offered an intimate glimpse of a woman harboring a great deal of hurt. Elodie could not change what Maxine had witnessed, could not fix what had been broken within, but she could take her advice and ensure she learned from the mistakes of others.

"Thank you." The words felt too small for the magnitude of trust that had passed between them, but she could not let the moment go unnoticed.

"I'm sure I don't know what for."

"Your honesty," Elodie said. "Your trust. And your willingness to do what I ask of you next." She grimaced. She had been concerned by their lack of military leadership, unable to rally fighters and plot against an organized army on her own. Now she knew exactly who might lead.

Maxine raised her eyebrows.

"You're being promoted," Elodie said. "Effective immediately, you are the commander of Velle's city military. The country's army has failed, and now we are under imminent threat of invasion from the Republics. I need you to organize our homegrown militia and engineer new ways to fight back. We cannot lose the New Maiden to the Second Son. I won't allow it. And now I know that you won't, either."

Maxine's eyes glittered curiously. "Majesty, are you sure?"

Elodie nodded. "Your loyalty is sound, your sword is strong, and your anger is sharp. I've never been more certain. Now, will you fight with me?"

"It would be my honor." Maxine offered the queen a taut salute. "Let's give Him hell."

Tal

His rage alone could not sustain him. Tal needed the anger of others if he was going to survive the darkness poisoning his mind.

With Tal's renewed focus on His mission came an increase in converts. Loyalists, citizens, and soldiers alike all joined His cause. As Tal had done once in the training yard, he traded the Second Son's teachings for their bitterness. He shuddered at the contents of their hearts. Some held cruelty that rivaled his father's. Others were broken, drenched in embarrassment disguised as rage. He could not empathize with those whose anger derived from perceived slights or entitlement. Bruised egos were not adequate fuel against Her torrent of profound emotion. The Second Son's word was meant to protect the world from Her darkness.

No matter their mettle, each new follower's offering provided Tal relief. A counterpoint to the slippery voice that had taken residence inside his head.

You haven't the faintest idea what you're up against, the voice would berate him. *You know not for whom you fight.*

The voice was wrong. Tal fought for himself. Just like Sebastien, he had been punished for his emotions while people like Elodie and Sabine could flaunt their feelings any way they wished. The Queen of Velle had proved she could love, so long as the object of her affection was not him. The New Maiden reincarnated was allowed to weep, using magic tears to manipulate the masses, emoting in ways Tal never could.

That inequity violated justice. It set them firmly on opposite sides. And even if Tal's allies did not have the purest of hearts, they understood one vital truth: The New Maiden would be His undoing, unless he undid Her first.

PART FIVE

*He had not meant to kill Her. The Second Son only meant
to siphon the darkness from Her soul as She slept. But just
as he felt the familiar twinge of pain, the slithering shadow
returning to its owner, the New Maiden awoke.*

*She did not recognize his silhouette. She fought and She
flailed. Sebastien tried to silence Her, and he did not notice his
fingers tighten around Her throat until She stopped moving.
Until the life was extinguished from Her eyes.*

*The Second Son had not expected the New Maiden to
break so easily. He had tried to help Her. Instead, She made
him a murderer.*

*If She had not been so fragile, his darkness would not
have corrupted Her so easily. If She had trusted him, he
might have saved Her. If She had not coerced him into being
vulnerable, She could have survived.*

*Sebastien finally understood his father's teachings. Feelings
made you a victim. Emotions led to corruption. Love only
ever led to loss.*

*The Second Son could not undo his mistakes, but he could
ensure that his fate befell no others. He would save the world
from hurt. He would protect Her Favoreds from the truth of the
New Maiden's death, from the fact of Her weakness. And then
perhaps, one day, he could wash Her blood from his hands.*

—Psalm of the Second Son

29

Their patchwork army assembled in waves.

First came the people of Velle, answering the call of the whisper networks and the posters designed by Cleo, which hung in every apothecary, laundry, seamstress shop, and bakery.

Second came clergy members from Silas's tenure in the Church. These were the folk from outside the city who had remained faithful despite their denied promotions, who were bolstered by the New Maiden's resurrection and Silas's new position of power. They embraced the Royal Chaplain with kisses on weathered cheeks, and fell to their knees to press their foreheads to the hem of the New Maiden's gown fussing over her hair and hands and smile. Their robes were a nearly translucent white, so well-worn that the fabric hung from their shoulders like butterfly wings waiting to be unfurled.

Next came the pragmatists, an eclectic mass from all corners of the country who had not been seduced by the Second Son's goading.

Elodie's father was among them, bringing with him a community of farmers whose embittered reactions to the embargo made them excellent conduits of anger. The New Maiden especially liked Duke Antony, a humble, funny man who proposed, somewhat seriously, that they ought to skewer the whole invading force with pitchforks.

"You ever try to lift a barrel of hay?" he asked Sabine, who admitted she had not. "Those prongs have quite a bit of power."

Then came the descendants of the New Maiden's Favoreds, some from beyond Velle's borders. Petra's and Hera's family lines arrived together, a gaggle of cousins who marched forward in lockstep—their actions, words, and expressions mirror images of one another. Petra's family of healers had brought with them tinctures and salves and would handle all triage and injuries garnered in warfare. Hera's family were hunters, bringing with them preserved meats to keep the army well-nourished and energized throughout the uncertainty.

Beck's descendant Envin, the woman from the Lower Banks, brought with her not only others in her line but also the entire fleet of attendants from the New Maiden's pilgrimage site, who embraced Sabine, Katrynn, and Brianne warmly.

"It is an honor to fight with you, Maiden," Envin said. "As She welcomed Beck with open arms, so, too, do we commit to your battle. We will station ourselves wherever you need us, will organize and build and barter. Employ us how you will."

Genevar returned, too, with cousins in the line descended from Ruti. "I have spent my life protecting the New Maiden's secrets," the old woman said. "I would not miss my chance to defend her legacy, too."

Theo's descendants were carpenters, who set to work building a barricade at the city's western gate in hopes of deterring the invading army.

Mol's descendants were fighters, and for that Sabine was especially grateful. While Maxine had enlisted a handful of Loyalists to join the queen and the New Maiden, she had banished even more of them as punishment for their affiliation with the Second Son. So Mol's descendants were a blessing, with their gunpowder and their axes as well as an ox-drawn carriage towing a cannon.

"The New Maiden need only ask, and we are at Her service," one of Mol's great-grand nephews said, eyes twinkling with the same particular mischief Artur possessed. Sabine's brother was instantly drawn to their camp, refining his homemade explosives under the watchful eye of experts who had been blowing things up for centuries.

There were no descendants of Sebastien. He had never invested in his own filial line.

All in all, they had assembled nearly one thousand people. Upon first hearing the number, Sabine's heart leapt. There was a time when she could not have fathomed even ten people devoted to her defense, let alone one hundred times that. But one look at Elodie's and Maxine's expressions told her that the news she found so joyous was, in reality, a tragedy.

"Velle's army used to outfit ten thousand men," Maxine said, pounding her fist against the glossy wooden table of the War Room. "The Republics' population is in the hundred thousands. There's no way we can overpower them." She hung her head in her hands.

"Do we *need* to overpower them?" Katrynn asked, timidly.

"We most certainly do need to overpower them," Maxine said, eyes alight. "We want to win, don't we?"

"Well," Sabine said carefully, "what does it mean to win?"

"We win if the city does not fall," Elodie said. "If we can outlast them and withstand their attacks. If we can prove that our core is stronger than outside threats. We must show them that our army will not lie down at the first sign of danger."

But Maxine shook her head. "We won't be able to hold them back," she said, referring to their own paltry numbers. "We can stall them, but we cannot stop them."

"If that's the case," Cleo said skeptically, "what's the point of fighting at all?" Brianne nodded in agreement. Silas was silent.

"The point is to make them think they've won," Sabine said, quietly with trepidation. "It's exactly what they'll expect. They do not believe that we can withstand their brute force, so we prove them right. Let the barricade fall, let the army enter the city, make them believe that they have bested us."

"And then what?" Elodie looked at her incredulously.

"We follow His instruction," Sabine said. All seven pairs of eyes stared at her as though she'd lost her mind. "We call the moths to us—and then we set them ablaze."

"We cut off the alleyways," Maxine said, nodding with understanding. "We direct them toward a place of our choosing, which we've rigged with explosives." She turned to Artur. "How's that going, by the way?"

Sabine's brother's eyes lit up. "Mol's descendants are experts. We have everything we need."

"Excellent." Maxine nodded tersely. "So we direct them toward a district, and then . . . boom." She paused, the room hanging on every word. "Some will get caught in the destruction. The others will be frightened and retreat, while my army is safely stowed far from the blast. It's risky, but it's all we have." She met Sabine's eyes with a nod of gratitude before turning toward Elodie. "Now—which neighborhood do we sacrifice?"

The queen's face paled. Elodie, who had worked so hard to do right by her people, would never be able to offer up one of her city's districts. It would tear at her heart, knowing that she had made yet another decision that harmed the people she had sworn to serve.

"Harborside," the New Maiden answered for her. "We lead the troops toward the water." Elodie opened her mouth to protest, but Sabine continued to speak. "The infrastructure is already faulty, and the harbor itself is the farthest point from the rest of the city— the destruction will be isolated. Besides," she said softly, "my neighbors have aligned themselves with the New Maiden in the highest numbers. It will make it easier to ensure that all civilians have been evacuated."

Her stomach squirmed even as the rest of the group agreed. It felt like a betrayal of her community, to recommend the destruction of their homes. But she could see no other way to make the greatest impact with the fewest casualties. Once the battle had ended, she would rebuild Harborside better than before, just as the New Maiden had revitalized the Lower Banks once upon a time.

Elodie, who still looked pained, turned to Katrynn and Artur for confirmation before agreeing. "All right," the queen said, once the Anders siblings had acquiesced. "If we must."

"Only as a last resort," Maxine chimed in. "Perhaps our barricade will be sufficient enough to restrain them." But she did not sound convinced. "Those on the front lines will take a defensive approach. We'll arm them with explosives and take hostage anyone who tries to fight against us on the inside."

"Except for Tal." Sabine knew that he would find a way beyond their barricade, no matter how carefully they protected the perimeter. It was not a question of *if* she would come face-to-face with the Second Son's prophet, but *when*. "If you see him, do not harm him." She swallowed resolutely. "He is mine."

30

The bells began at sunrise. Elodie, who had spent the entire night at the hazy edge of sleep, was on her feet in seconds. She shrugged on a dressing gown and raced to the top of the east tower, the better to witness the invasion that was heading for the city below.

The Republics' army crawled toward Velle's capital like an endless line of ants, the soldiers' uniforms black as midnight, swords glittering silver at their sides. They marched two by two, kept in line by commanders on horseback. From her height, Elodie could not make out the faces of the commanders, although she caught a glint of bright red hair from beneath a black cap.

Their numbers were impossibly mismatched. Elodie's scrappy legion stood no chance against the rigid, well-trained force at their door. Their only true asset was the element of surprise in their defense plan. Still, she was not convinced it would be enough.

The bells continued to toll. An attendant from the Lower Banks had been stationed in the bell tower at the city's center to ring the alarm at the first sign of invasion. Across the city, their makeshift army would be moving into place. The time for strategizing had ended. Now Elodie could only hope their execution would be enough.

Dizzy from the height and the impending battle, Elodie retreated from the tower. The corridors bustled with activity, servants hurrying to their own stations, as Elodie returned to her rooms to dress. She pulled on a basic white frock, signaling her loyalty to the Maiden, and then ran for the War Room. The rest of her council was already there, bleary eyed and frightened. They were all so young, awaiting a ruthless enemy.

"It is time," Maxine said, her face set. "Majesty?"

"Let Her will be done," Elodie said simply. She had pledged herself to the New Maiden, heart, body, and soul. In Her name, they would fight, and in Her name—Elodie hoped—they would win. As the people in the room rose to steel themselves for battle, Elodie reached for Sabine. "Be safe," she said, pressing a swift kiss to the girl's temple.

"And you," Sabine said, her expression unbearably tender. "I'll see you on the other side." Then the New Maiden took her leave from the War Room, flanked by Silas, Artur, and Katrynn.

"Majesty." Maxine bowed. "It has been an honor—"

"And it will *remain* an honor," Elodie interjected. She could not tolerate goodbyes, however precautionary. Maxine had told her only to sacrifice what she was willing to lose, but the Queen of Velle was not prepared to give up anything, certainly not the people she loved most. "Her will be done," she repeated to Maxine.

The commander nodded, clearing her throat gruffly. "Her will be done."

At last, only the three Warnou sisters remained. Brianne and Cleo had protested when Elodie first told them her plan. They wanted to be on the ground in the middle of the action, but the queen would not hear of it. She needed them safe, would not—*could not*—be like her mother, willing to sacrifice her sisters in favor of herself. But now that the cursed day had arrived, the queen thought she could see relief in their eyes at the prospect of staying by Elodie's side as she played the most infuriating role in the entire operation: sitting duck.

"Let's go," Elodie said, leading the way to the queen's study. Tal had given her an ultimatum: Let him in or die fighting. She knew the barricade the army would face at the city's western gate would only serve as a distraction. She expected that Tal would come for her directly, would demand she surrender to him face-to-face. And so the Queen of Velle settled herself behind her desk to wait.

She did not expect the knock to come so quickly. At the sharp rap of knuckles against the oak door, Elodie froze. Cleo shook her head emphatically, but Brianne peered through the keyhole. "It's Rob."

Elodie tapped her fingernails against the desktop. She had not spoken to her brother since their altercation in his apartments, had pointedly kept him far from their plans, for fear he would leak intelligence to the other side. But the urgent tolling of the bells was unmistakable. It stood to reason that he would have questions. "Let him in."

Cleo arched an eyebrow but said nothing as Brianne unlocked the door.

Rob stormed in, hair wild and eyes wide. "What's happening? Why aren't we evacuating? Where *is* everyone?"

"At war, dear brother," Elodie said carefully. "We are at war."

Rob spluttered incredulously. "I think I would know if we were under attack."

Elodie pursed her lips and gestured to the window. "See for yourself." The bells continued to clang.

Rob strode across the room to peer out of the study's small window, which overlooked the royal garden. Below, Silas and the Anders siblings were organizing the Favoreds' descendants, stationing them at every gate to welcome those evacuated from Harborside.

"Is that...a cannon?" Rob turned to face them, bewildered.

"That," Cleo confirmed brightly, "is a cannon."

"How did you manage to—"

"I am so tired of being underestimated," Elodie snapped. "No one doubted Mother this way."

"That's not an entirely fair comparison," came a reedy voice. Elodie's siblings jumped as the bookshelf moved forward—and René stepped out from the shadows.

"What are you doing here?" Elodie gaped at Brianne's father. This was not the ambush she had expected.

"Oh, come now, Elodie." René looked at her mockingly. "Surely my presence is not such a surprise, considering my true allegiances."

Brianne scowled at her father's mention of the Second Son. Cleo slipped an arm protectively around her younger sister's shoulders.

"How did you know about this passageway?"

René chuckled. "I have utilized it for years. Particularly useful to ensure the crown kept the Church's best interests in mind. And to intercede when it came time for debts to be paid." His eyes sparkled with malice.

It dawned on her like a brittle blue morning. Her mother had entered into some kind of contract with the Second Son. René, who served Him, even as he playacted devotion to the New Maiden, would have known the details of that agreement. The passage would have allowed René to pass unnoticed between chapel and castle, watching her mother, waiting for the perfect opportunity to collect what He was owed. It would have been so simple to poison a teacup left on an unobserved tray, to clear the throne for his daughter and the Second Son.

Elodie turned to her siblings. She could not subject them to the possibility of their mother's murder. "Pray, leave us a moment," the queen said. "I'd like to have a word with René alone." Her siblings exchanged curious looks but, in the end, obeyed. When the door had closed behind them, Elodie leveled her gaze on the former Chaplain. "Did you murder my mother in the name of the Second Son?"

"Yes," he said easily, as though accepting a tea biscuit. Elodie had anticipated his answer, but it still left a bitter taste on her tongue. "If it's any consolation," he added, "she should have known to expect it. The parameters of their agreement were very clear."

The hairs on the back of Elodie's neck stood straight like soldiers. "And what might those parameters have been?"

"He would clear your mother's path to the throne, and in return, she would bear three daughters."

Elodie made a strangled sound. She had always known Tera Warnou to be a reluctant mother, but she could not have imagined that even her children were born as pawns in her quest for power.

"This trade was most beneficial to the both of them," Brianne's father continued. "The Second Son had been eliminating third daughters for centuries, but He grew weary of the chase. He wanted to raise Her and nurture Her in order to abolish Her, once and for all." René offered the queen a catlike grin. "Which is where I came in. And why your mother was so . . . cooperative when it came to the custody of Brianne."

"She wouldn't have allowed it," Elodie argued, even as her heart sank with the weight of the truth. Tera Warnou had always kept her distance from her youngest daughter, but Elodie had never imagined the reason to be so sinister.

"Faith requires absolute commitment," René said. "And getting what you want demands sacrifice." He shrugged softly. "Your mother sought power above all, and she was willing to betray her children to get it. So, no, Elodie, no one ever doubted Tera's prowess, but that was because they knew the true power came from Him."

He continued, "You, however, have been most irritating. Meddlesome and headstrong. Impossible to wrangle, despite the prophet's best efforts."

Elodie looked about the room suspiciously. "And where *is* Tal?"

"Tallon sends his apologies, but he has"—René cleared his throat—"more important matters to attend to."

"More important matters than a war he incited?" Elodie snapped. She had been preparing for a very different battle and was now struggling to maintain the upper hand.

"I think what René is saying," came a new voice, "is that *you* are not important to the Second Son. But," the lilting voice continued, as it drew nearer, "you are rather important to me."

A shadow stepped forth from the passageway, revealing himself as none other than Edgar DeVos. "Many thanks, René," Edgar said, handing the man a bag of clinking coins. "You have been so very helpful."

"I'll leave you to her, then," René sneered, slithering back into the shadows as though he had not changed Elodie's world forever. When he was gone, Edgar strode around the desk, settling himself on the tabletop, with no regard for the documents and inkwells, which he disturbed with a great clatter.

"Don't you look lovely." His eyes raked over Elodie slowly, setting her skin crawling. "Ours has been quite the untraditional courtship, but I am a bit sorry to see it end. I've had a wonderful time, illustrating for you my affections." He nudged her knee with his foot, his smile sickly sweet. She shuddered.

"Do not touch me, Edgar."

"Oh, come." Edgar's face fell. "I understood your aloofness via letters, but I had hoped for a more passionate reunion in the heat of war. I can offer you safety, Elodie, in exchange for love. There is no stronger bond than survival."

Elodie snickered. "Be serious, Edgar."

"Do not laugh at me," Edgar shouted. "Everyone is always laughing at me. I will not allow my wife to find amusement at my expense."

"I would rather die than be your wife," Elodie said, each word filled with enough venom that she hoped Edgar would choke on it.

"And I would rather you die than deny me again," Edgar said, his voice just as poisonous. "So it seems we are in agreement."

In one swift motion, Edgar had her out of her chair and pinned against the wall. His fingers wrapped around her throat, crushing her windpipe, sending spots skittering across her vision. Elodie gasped desperately, clawing at him, but his hands might as well have been iron cuffs. Tears streamed down her face; her ears rang with the rush of her blood and the desperate pounding of her heart. Her lungs were going to burst. No matter how hard she tried to beg, no matter how hard she thrashed, Edgar would not let her go.

"I had hoped it would not come to this, my love," Edgar said, his breath hot on her cheek. "But if I cannot have you, no one will."

Even when Elodie went limp, when she began to slip into the sweet relief of unconsciousness, he continued to squeeze, his face twisted with regret, sweat pooling on his upper lip. It was a miserable way for her life to end, at the hands of a boy with wounded pride. What a waste of her brain, her ambition, her existence.

Elodie Warnou had deserved so much more.

31

The docks were deserted as the Anders siblings led Hera's and Petra's descendents through Harborside, the water surprisingly calm. Gulls swooped low, picking through piles of trash for food scraps. All the while, bells tolled ominously in the background. The group needed to rouse the neighborhood's residents, to evacuate the area before the Republics' army breached the barricade. Artur ushered Petra's family to the south side, filled with taverns and gambling halls, while Katrynn led Hera's kin east toward the residential quarters.

"Direct them to the castle," Sabine shouted to her sister. "The gates are open, ready to offer Velle's citizens shelter. And don't forget to check on the orphanage beneath the tavern next to the tannery," she called to her brother. "They won't answer the first time you knock, but if you tap three times softly, they'll know you can be trusted."

Sabine took the north side of the harbor. There were few

inhabitants in this sector—instead, the dockside was littered with storehouses where cargo was kept. Bins, containers, and crates were stacked impossibly high, waiting for their ships and crew. Yet it was not entirely abandoned. Atop the cavernous rooms and empty offices were the crowded barracks where sea merchants kept their debtors. Sabine's own father had been held in such a hovel, a dark, dusty place that stank of sweat. He was still at sea, crammed onto a ship with others who had put their faith in cards and dice, whose only value now was in what they owed to someone else.

The tolling of the bells was fainter here, the sound drowned out by the roaring wind and the rolling waves. She ran through the streets, pounding on every storeroom door until her palms ached and her knuckles were raw. She screamed until she shuddered and her voice broke. But she was not certain anyone heard her.

She stopped to catch her breath, a hand resting on a rusted shovel stuck upright between the slats of the dock. The old harbor bell had long lost its clapper, but the bowl remained, hollowed out like an empty shell shed from an insect. Salt air had tinged the copper green. But the shovel still boasted steel. She could make a riotous sound, if only she tried.

Unwedging the shovel from between the warped boards required an ungodly noise from the back of her throat and a seesawing motion that took far longer than she had to spare. But once it was finally free, she struck the hunk of metal ferociously and furiously. It emitted a *thunk, thwipp, thwapping* that reverberated in her teeth.

If nothing else, it was sure to garner attention, a girl smacking a shovel against the empty bell while clouds swirled above, turning the sky gray. And indeed, Sabine's hair had just only begun sticking to the sweat on her forehead when a man peered out of a door half off its hinges, blinking sleepily.

"What in the twelve hells are you doin', girl?"

Relief spread through Sabine like spilled water. "You must get away from the harbor, now," she croaked. "Velle is at war, and Harborside will be its first casualty. There's fire coming. Destruction. Ruin."

The man scratched at his head, his wiry hair sticking out at all angles. "You make it sound like Death himself is on his way."

"He very well may be," Sabine said darkly. "Please," she urged the man, voice at full force. "Listen to me. You have to get out of here. You and whoever else might reside inside."

"How do you know?" He studied her openly.

"The Republics are invading the city," Sabine said plainly. "We've rigged the harbor with explosives to cut them off."

The man made a face. "If I wake up my crew on account of a rumor, there's going to be hell to pay. Sailors need their sleep."

His calm interrogation flustered Sabine. She had not expected it to be so difficult to lead people to safety.

"If you *don't* wake them, they'll be straight *in* hell," she snapped. "And we all know Death's price is steeper than a merchant sailor's."

The man laughed outright, thunder no longer far away, but above them. "Suppose I do listen to you," he said, stroking his beard with one hand, "where would you have me go? My ships need ten men apiece to crew them. I don't have those numbers."

"Gather everyone up from the north side and have them sail with you to safety," Sabine said, reaching for the man, her fingers closing around his forearm. "That way your ships stay safe, and you've helped your neighbors, too."

At this suggestion, the man hesitated. "I don't know..."

His lack of urgency was as painful as peeling off a toenail. "Don't believe me, then," she said sharply, patience wearing thin. "If I were you, I'd take my chances and trust the New Maiden, even if you've been converted to another faith."

The man examined her with revitalized interest. "Maiden?" His fingers gripped the doorway.

"I am just as frightened as you," she said gently, holding the man's gaze. "I care just as much for my family, my neighbors, the salt of the sea. I must be going, but I pray you choose to care. I pray you remember that She came to save you. *I* came to save you."

The man's eyes softened. "Her will be done," he whispered.

Sabine dared not say more lest she break the tentative trust between them. She hurried onward, triumph flaring in her chest even as she continued her cries to evacuate. She hoped the man had taken up the call, too.

When she had covered the winding streets of the north side, she headed back toward her family home. To Sabine's relief, the windows of the apartments and the taverns she passed were empty. She saw no eyes peering out at the chaos, heard no frightened tears from lost children. She held tightly to the hope that her siblings had been successful and that her neighbors were gathered safely within the walls of Castle Warnou. Their tasks complete, Artur and Katrynn would be waiting for her at the bell tower. But before she joined them in the city's center, the New Maiden took one final detour.

Sabine ducked into the cool, cramped quarters of the Anders family apartment for what might be the very last time. She surveyed the small room, taking stock of the only home she had ever known. Despite its shabby disrepair, Sabine's family had built so many memories here, had laughed and cried and raged and screamed, had grown together and apart between these four walls. It was impossible to preserve it all. Still, Sabine wanted to ensure that her family had what they needed to remember.

She carefully enveloped her sister's silver-handled hairbrush in the midnight-blue scarf Katrynn had stolen off a noblewoman during a particularly windy season. She tucked both in the bucket of a fine wool hat that Artur had won from a visiting merchant during a card game. For her mother, Sabine extracted several jars of her rarest ingredients—beetles' wings and snake eyes and preserved lark hearts—tucking them into the folds of the hat. For her father, she even grabbed the last cigar that stank like a furnace, the one he said he'd smoke when he returned from sea.

She took nothing for herself. There was far too much their apartment held of her past—her days spent stewing beneath blankets, watching shadows stretch on the walls. Who Sabine had been, here, was not who she was, now. She wanted nothing by which to remember that other girl.

She had everything she needed within.

Her neighborhood now evacuated, Sabine took up watch in the bell tower. The clanging was dizzying, the noise so great she could not find space for her fear. Instead, she squinted down past the barricade at the invading army, at the tiny commanders dismounting from steeds and shouting for soldiers to fall into formation. Yet no matter how long the New Maiden watched and waited, she could not find the prophet's face.

Sabine traded her position in the tower for one atop the barricade, scrutinizing the soldiers whose jeers were drowned out by the endless tolling of bells. None of them had Tal's careful expression, his impossibly straight posture, his green and gold eyes. His absence left her perplexed.

Tal had been circling her since the moment they'd met, appearing everywhere the New Maiden went, arming Sabine with tiny daggers and emotional anecdotes, tugging on that invisible string that tied them together, body and soul, to the New Maiden and the Second Son. He would not hide from this final obligation. If anything, the soldier in Tal would have embraced it wholeheartedly. So where was he?

Sabine closed her eyes and caught a whiff of salt air off the water. If His prophet had not returned to the city, that meant the Second Son had another idea. He was sentimental and dramatic, and thus would surely demand that their final duel take place on sacred ground. The city held no special meaning to Sebastien or the New Maiden. Instead, he would wish to meet somewhere significant— the land where they both had been born, the land where they had learned to love, the land where they had lost so much. He would be waiting for her in the Lower Banks.

It was another of His careful cruelties. Sabine would have to leave Velle before the war had truly begun and sacrifice her curated supplies of anger. She would be forced to put the needs of the New Maiden before the needs of her kin, to let her followers fight without her by their side.

Just as she had imagined, her family's faces fell when she told them what she had to do. "I don't like the idea of you out there on your own with Him, Bet," her mother said.

"I have to go alone," Sabine said gently. "This is the way it must end."
Orla cupped her daughter's face in her hands. "Be careful, all right?"

Saying goodbye to her family suddenly felt important. This was not some ruse they were running off to play, coming back together an hour later with coins and an amusing anecdote. This was serious. This was dangerous. Worse, Sabine did not know how either battle was going to end.

"You too." She kissed her mother on the cheek, then turned to Artur. "Please, listen to Mol's descendants and keep yourself far away from the blast." Artur gave her a mock salute before enveloping her in a hug. Sabine squeezed him tightly. Then she rounded on Katrynn. "Rynn, I—"

But her sister did not let her finish. She squeezed Sabine's hand. "Burn Him to the ground."

A lump formed in Sabine's throat. Although she could not form the words, she hoped her eyes blazed with affirmation. She would not rest until it was finished. "*Tassi An*," she finally managed. Katrynn rewarded her with a smile like starlight.

Then Sabine took off running toward the city center. She stole a midnight-black mare from outside a tavern with a moth insignia and raced her out the southern gate, waved through by a group of Theo's and Beck's descendants. Sabine's jaw was tense, her knuckles white, as she clutched the reins. Although the creature moved faster than she could imagine, it wasn't quick enough to shake loose her feelings of guilt and regret at leaving behind the war waged in her name, at not having taken the chance to tell the queen she loved her.

But then, her power was in those feelings, in that emotionality. The New Maiden had told her as much. Sabine could not fathom what sort of fight the Second Son expected, what sort of strange reunion she and Tal would have upon the shore. However they dueled, it would end in blows. She could only hope that her anger would be weapon enough.

32

Elodie came crashing back to consciousness.

All at once, her airway was unrestricted and she took in great, gasping breaths, coughing through the shock of how simple it was to pull air in and out of her desperate lungs. She sank to her knees beside the limp body of her aggressor. Above Edgar stood Brianne, clutching a glass orb in her shaking hands.

The decorative ornament was painted to resemble the continents of the world. There was a smudge of blood next to the shape of the Sixth Republic.

"Bri?" Elodie croaked. "What are you—"

"We should probably restrain him," came the voice of the middle Warnou sister.

"Cleo?" Elodie tried to rise, but a wave of nausea sent her sinking back onto her heels.

"Should we tie him up?" Brianne turned to Cleo.

"I'm sure *I* don't know," Cleo said, her voice wavering at a pitch high enough to break glass. "You're the one who hit him with a paperweight."

"He was *strangling* Elodie." Brianne wiped the globe on her trousers—the red transferring to the sandy linen—before returning it to its place on the queen's desk.

"Bri…" Elodie's voice caught in her throat like gravel beneath a coach's wheel. It hurt to speak, to breathe, to think.

"No lectures, Ellie," her youngest sister said darkly. "If you need something done, best a Warnou woman does it."

Tears swam in Elodie's eyes, not from pain but pride. Her youngest sister was no longer the fumbling girl at the mercy of the Church. She was no longer controlled by even her family. Instead, she kept *them* safe. Brianne tucked a strand of hair behind her ear, then turned her attention back to Edgar. His breathing was quiet, but steady.

"I'm glad you didn't kill him." Cleo nudged his neck with the toe of her shoe.

"I'm sorry I didn't," Brianne said darkly. "He would have deserved it."

"Death is a very permanent punishment," Edgar said, his voice loose, eyes unfocused.

Elodie swore. She had been hoping to come up with a plan before Edgar came to. She glanced desperately at Rob, who hovered near the door looking uncomfortable.

Edgar noticed the prince at the same moment. "Help me, brother," he appealed to Rob, eyes wide. "In His name, please, let me go."

Rob stared at Edgar, looking thoughtful. Dread crept its way up Elodie's spine. Although she did not want to believe that Rob could betray all three of his sisters, she was unable to forget the anger he had expressed during their last conversation, the coolness with which he had dismissed her from his chambers.

"There's a good lad," Edgar said, latching on to her brother's hesitation. "We're the same. I knew it."

"We're not the same at all." The Prince of Velle's right hand closed around the glass paperweight on the queen's desk. "For when you threaten one Warnou, the others raise their hackles. As is one, so are we all. Which means"—Rob grimaced apologetically—"you had this coming."

Then he smashed the glass paperweight against Edgar's temple, and for the second time that morning, the senator of the Sixth Republic crumpled to the floor.

All three Warnou sisters shrieked. Brianne with surprise, Cleo with horror, and Elodie with relief.

"Bri," Rob called to his youngest sister, "hand me that curtain tie and come help me bind his feet."

Elodie watched her brother from where she sat, shaking, on the study floor. "What are you doing?" It was a complicated question with more than one answer. For now, Rob chose the most straightforward.

"He's useless to you up here," Rob said, speaking in a way that evoked his father's urgent, clipped tone. "In order to gain leverage, you'll want to flaunt him as a hostage and let the other side know your demands."

Elodie's heart leapt. With Edgar captive, they might be able to barter their way to peace, to prevent the death and destruction synonymous with their current strategy.

This was how Tera Warnou's four children found themselves

hauling the limp body of Edgar DeVos down the steps of the palace. A swell of appreciation rose in Elodie as she witnessed her siblings' determination and strength. She had been raised to believe that country and legacy were the two things that mattered most in the world. But her role model had been a cold, exacting monarch. A mother with secrets of her own, who had loved herself more than her children.

Yet the longer Elodie held the throne, the more apparent it became that a queen was nothing without allies. She needed the consultation of others, the insight and understanding of those who knew more—or at the very least, thought differently—than she.

Outside the confines of the castle, the air was charged with energy. Although the bells had finally stopped their ringing, the morning was still filled with noise. Shouts, pops, and the scrape of metal against metal rang out all around them, while the occasional *boom* echoed from the cannon a short distance away. A gray haze clung about the city below, and the breeze carried the stench of sulfur, bonfire, and the tang of steel. War was underway.

"It's going to take too long to carry him down to the city," Cleo moaned. "I'm exhausted already. Can't we just leave him here tied with really tight knots?"

"If they can't see him, they won't take us seriously," Brianne argued.

Elodie glanced down at her tormentor, at his freckle-spotted skin, his black suit, his distinctive, flame-red locks. "His hair!" She turned to her brother. "Rob, I need your sword."

Rob frowned at her. "I don't have a sword."

"Well, then, go get a sword," Elodie commanded, turning to her sisters. "Do either of you carry scissors?" Brianne shook her head, but the second Warnou sister shimmied something out of her stocking. "Cleo!" Elodie chastised as her sister handed over a dagger.

"Rob can have a sword," her middle sister pouted. "Why can't I have a knife?"

"I'm not angry at you for *having* a dagger," Elodie clarified, using the blade's edge to saw off a lock of Edgar's bright hair. "I'm angry at you for storing it in your stocking. One fall down a flight of stairs and you'll accidentally sever your tendon. You need to find a better place to secure it." She offered the dagger back to Cleo, who stuffed it theatrically in her waistband. Elodie pocketed the fiery curl.

After sealing the unconscious Edgar securely in the confessional of the royal chapel, the Warnou siblings headed down into the city proper. The smoke grew thicker with each step toward the bell tower, the air filled with the thrum of destruction: the cracking of wood and groaning of men and splitting of stone. Elodie took the lead, heading for the barricade at the western gate.

The cobblestones of the Commerce District were mostly deserted, although many eyes peered down at the Warnou siblings from the safety of their windows. Elodie committed these details to memory—taking note of who had joined their ranks and who had chosen to sit idly by. In contrast, the Arts District was electric with energy, the explosives there more fireworks than bombs, filling the air with brilliant flashes of color and light.

The scene at the western gate was grim. The barricade was under severe pressure from the battering rams and soldiers on the other side. Flashes of black uniforms and silver swords were visible through the cracks of the straining wood. Maxine was atop the blockade, shouting orders. When she caught sight of the queen, she scowled.

"I told you to stay in the palace," the commander shouted down at the queen, her voice hoarse.

"I have a hostage," Elodie said, waving the lock of Edgar's hair. "Of the highest rank. If we alert them, maybe we can negotiate their retreat."

Maxine descended the toppling structure to join her on solid ground. "What about Tal?"

"Tal isn't here," Katrynn said, extracting herself from the barricade and wiping sweat from her brow.

"He isn't?" Maxine frowned.

"Sabine is on her way to the Lower Banks," she said. "Where it all began."

Elodie swore. While it was a rather poetic place for their confrontation, she hated the idea of Sabine on her own against Tal and the Second Son. They had recruited an army of anger to bolster her power. Without it, Sabine had no support to rely on but herself.

Another gigantic, splintering crack. The western gate was beginning to give way. Katrynn chewed on her thumb, turning to Maxine. "We're going to have to sacrifice the harbor."

Elodie shook her head. "Not yet."

"We knew it might come to this," Katrynn reminded the queen gently. "Everyone is out—we made sure of it. Artur is in place with Mol's descendants. All we have to do now is let the soldiers follow the road to the water. And then"—she waggled her fingers—"boom."

"It's too risky," Elodie said, even as she glanced over her shoulder at the deteriorating blockade.

"War *is* the highest risk," Maxine said, nodding slightly at

Katrynn. "We go for the harbor. We hope for the best. We pray that it's the only thing we lose."

Elodie took a deep shuddering breath. She knew Maxine was right. They had missed the opportunity to negotiate over Edgar. There was no other choice but to relinquish Harborside, home of Velle's risen deity. "Do it."

Maxine sprang into action, shouting for their army to fall into position, to line the alleys, to direct all movement toward the water, to keep themselves out of harm's way.

"Majesty," Maxine shouted, "take shelter. Now!"

The Republics' army cascaded forth with thundering voices, sharp elbows, and even sharper swords. They came from all sides, blowing past the barricade as easily as a knife through butter. Somewhere to Elodie's left, Maxine was barking orders, shouting with all that was left of her voice. The queen reached for her youngest sister's hand, pulling Brianne toward the safety of the side streets. But Brianne was charged by a graceless soldier, his shoulder smacking her in the face, causing her to stumble. Elodie doubled back, pulling Brianne to her feet before she could be trampled by the army's polished leather boots.

The scuffle had cost them precious seconds, time they had needed to navigate out of harm's way. Elodie could no longer see Cleo, and though she called her sister's name, she could not hear her over the clamor of the crowd. Soldiers were still spilling into the city center, separating Elodie and Brianne in their wave of momentum, jostling forward, toward the harbor and its awaiting bombs.

Elodie shouted for her siblings, but the force of the crowd was too fearsome. She was headed toward danger, and no matter how hard she fought against the crush of bodies, they would not part. She had been a fool, to think herself strategic enough to wage war. A coward, to command grand plans for others to enforce. She had no business being queen. She could not protect her siblings, let alone an entire country. She had lost herself to hubris, and now Velle would pay the highest price.

The dock was drawing nearer, the salt air sharp in her nose. Then a glimmer of hope, as Elodie spotted Cleo's lithe fingers waving for help. The queen very nearly managed to grab her, felt the brush of her middle sister's soft skin. But just as she dared to believe that they might claw their way to safety, the cobblestones emitted a deep, low groan and Harborside exploded.

33

By the time Sabine arrived in the Lower Banks, out of breath and sun-flushed from the journey, the water glittered gold. The sky was streaked with pink, shadows swirling on the sand. The land was deserted. There were no bustling attendants ready to welcome her home. No sly-faced enemy awaiting his prey.

Sabine peeled off her boots and socks and wandered into the water. She was flooded with the same charged possibility she'd felt the first time she stepped foot on this soil. A knowing, all the way down to her bones. This place had birthed the New Maiden, and from the New Maiden was born Sabine.

"You came." Tal loped forward through the low tide, an unfamiliar smile on his lips. His eyes shone gold; no glimpse of green remained. His posture held no hint of the brash but unsteady boy beneath the noise. This was not the Second Son's prophet, but Sebastien Himself.

Rather than the dread Sabine had expected, she was engulfed

by a wave of nostalgia, like a scent that sparked a memory. As she took a step toward the Second Son, she felt not fear but familiarity.

"Sebastien," she called to Him, her voice even despite the thundering of her heart. To the shock of them both, Sabine held her hand out to Him. "Let me look at you." The gentle words felt right, as though the New Maiden was commanding her tongue.

"You delay the inevitable," Sebastien said, but still He stepped forward to place His hand in hers.

Sabine gasped at His touch. The air around them crackled, and clouds swirled in the sky above. Between them were many lifetimes of history, bleak and terrible yet wide and wonderful, too. They could both see it, memory made tangible, bitter like an herb on the tongue.

"You always were too defensive," Sabine said, glancing meaningfully at His other hand, which had moved instinctively to the hilt of Tal's sword. "Always too ready for a fight."

"How would you know what I was?" He breathed, but He did not sound angry. He sounded awed.

"I know you," Sabine replied just as calmly. His touch had woken up the darkest depths of her heart. "I have always known you."

"Then you know I have wronged you," the Second Son said, removing His hand from hers. "And you know I intend to wrong you again."

"You do not scare me, Sebastien," Sabine heard herself saying, and was even more surprised to find it was the truth. "You only make me sad."

His face clouded over, a storm beginning to brew. "That has always been your curse," He said, shaking His head. "Your softness makes you weak."

"Why does that anger you?" Sabine asked, frowning. "You, too, could be free, if only you allow yourself to feel."

"You speak as if it were easy," the Second Son said sharply, resentment blooming bold and bright. "But not all of us are entitled to that same release."

It was clear now where His shame stemmed from. The New Maiden had been a modest girl with magnificent feelings, who had never been cautioned against experiencing the full range of emotion. Sebastien's hurt—His envy—came from the fact that where He had been ridiculed for those feelings, She had been revered.

"Then I failed you," Sabine said gently.

"You did," He agreed, moving closer. "But not in the way you think. You failed me when you were unable to relinquish my darkness, when you were too weak to return my own pain to me. I never wanted to become a murderer." He clucked Tal's tongue against the roof of His borrowed mouth. "But that is what you made me."

"And from that accident, you continuously betrayed me," Sabine said. "You killed me a hundred times over. Every third daughter who died at your behest sent another piece of me off to sea. You chipped away at my soul until there was next to nothing left."

As soon as Sabine spoke of Her soul, she felt the final piece of it nestled inside her rib cage—hardened like crystal, its edges rough and jagged, no larger than a baby's tooth.

Tal's head nodded. "I know, though it pained me every time. I could not bear to see my darkness rise anew into the vessel of a third daughter." He pursed His lips in a muted frown.

"Oh, Seb." Sadness poured through Him, like a boat that had sprung a leak.

"This is exactly why I worked so hard to keep you from

returning," He accused softly, His expression shuttering. "I knew it would hurt too much to look at you. And I was right."

"It hurts me, too," Sabine said honestly. "Why did you not trust me with your darkness sooner? Why did you let it simmer and stew until you turned cold and cruel?"

Sebastien looked ashamed. "I did not tell you because of what it made me. For who could love someone so damaged as this?"

The Second Son extended Tal's arms out wide, as though they were wings. He closed Tal's eyes, clutched Tal's fingers into fists. And then darkness pushed its way to the surface.

At first, Sabine thought it was a trick of the light. The way the shadows curled gently about Him, wrapping around His wrists, shining across His skin. As the boy's fingers unfurled, the darkness leached outward, draping Him like a shroud. She knew exactly what sentiment He carried with Him, what slippery voice whispered in His ear.

Sabine could hardly find words through her astonishment. "You would wield my own darkness against me?"

"This magic is *mine*," the Second Son said, Tal's face twisted with frustration. "You could not bear it, and so I took it back." He flexed Tal's fingers, then clenched them again into fists. The darkness mirrored His actions, first swelling, then compacting. It followed His every breath, just as much a living creature as Sebastien once was.

But it moved inelegantly. Pain was written across Tal's borrowed face. It was so different from the way Sabine had contained that hurt.

She had learned to love the darkness. She had embraced it, let it settle within her in a way the Second Son had not. Even now, it slithered about the boy like a snake, rather than curling up like a house cat as it had done with her. There was a difference in how the two of them allowed such a force to live within. It bristled and snapped against Sebastien's skin. It welled and expanded within Sabine's veins.

She understood now why the New Maiden had first offered to hold the darkness for Him. He did not know how to nestle it beside His heart. It could only overtake Him. Harden Him. Hurt Him. The Second Son was fragile, aching to fill a most painful void.

"I cannot bear to look at you," Sebastien said, voice pained. "Please, let me end this."

Emotion rose in Sabine as He raised Tal's arms, as He dared to turn His hurt toward the only person who had ever offered Him comfort.

Sabine had not asked for this—any of this. She had not chosen to wage war with someone so frightened by the vastness of his feelings. She had not offered to carry the anger and darkness of another, had not planned to fall in love with the woman Tal had worshipped all his life.

She had simply lived, and by virtue of her existence, had been drawn into this tangled web of history and hurt. The New Maiden had cursed her. Had given her no choice but to fight.

This was the anger She had told Sabine to harness. But even without the New Maiden's pivotal instructions, in this moment Sabine was certain she would have known what to do.

Anger spiked within her, sharp as knives. Her ears buzzed with all the whispers in the world, everything that had been or ever might be. Her mouth was dry, but her eyes were not. They welled with rage, for all that had been taken from her. For the pounding, twisting wrongness Sabine had felt for simply existing, not knowing that it was the darkness she carried that made her special.

It was a gift, to be able to offer up space in one's heart for another. To protect them against the weight of the world. To be trusted enough with the truth of their hurt, and in sharing that burden, set them free. But she could not be expected to hold it without recognition. To let it root around inside her and then rot. It was a fine line. A tentative balance. One in which she deserved a say.

Sabine now contained enough anger to draw forth the swirling magic she had rediscovered in the place where the two of them now stood. It tingled in her fingers, begged to be let loose, to take its mark and strike. And yet, when Sebastien sent His darkness toward Sabine, instead of retaliating, she smiled.

Not His, it whispered in its glorious, terrible, beautiful voice. The one she had dreamed of every day since it first abandoned her. The one that was just as much a part of her as her heart or her mind or her bones. That voice was so welcomed after its prolonged silence that Sabine began to weep with relief. *Not His anymore*, the darkness promised, and then, more tentatively, not telling but asking: *Yours?*

Sabine did not know what she was doing. She knew only what she felt. Her emotions, which had once been so volatile as to leave her exhausted, frightened, and alone, had grown into instincts that she could trust, a compass she could follow.

Now that she knew she *could* exist without her darkness, Sabine found that she did not *want* to. And that made all the difference, didn't it? The choosing. The knowledge that she could cry, could rage, could laugh, could love, even while she held that sadness as an essential part of her. She could do it all.

And so, she whispered: "Yes."

"What are you doing?" Tal's voice held a high, desperate edge as He watched the darkness wrap itself around Sabine, watched it creep inside her and turn her blue veins black.

"I forgive you, Seb," she said, with a voice that was, but was not, hers. "For all you have done. Your pain did not define you. In fact, you were forged in spite of it. But now, it is time to relinquish your hurt. To let go of your fear and allow yourself to feel something else."

The Second Son's voice wavered. "I do not know how."

The New Maiden took His hand. "You do not let the darkness claim you. You acknowledge that you have known it, that you have held it, and that you have *survived* it. And then," she said, placing a hand on Tal's chest, just above his heart, "you set it free."

The tears that fell onto Sabine's cheeks tasted like salt and starlight. Even though it was darkness that seeped back into her, Sabine felt a warmth within. That precious jewel of the New Maiden's soul began to pulse a soft, careful rhythm in harmony with her own heartbeat. This was not only darkness, but hope. Sabine was still dark and light and everything in between.

Anger became acceptance.

She sank to her knees, her tears splattering the earth beneath her. The Second Son watched with something akin to awe. A single tear rolled down Tal's cheek. That drop contained the world, every hurt never spoken, all the pain never shared. Sebastien knelt beside the New Maiden, and, at long last, the Second Son wept.

When all His tears ran dry, Sebastien kissed the New Maiden softly, tender and chaste. "Your will be done, Isolde," He whispered, the gold nearly gone from Tal's eyes, and then, with a great shuddering breath, Tal's body crumpled onto the sand.

34

First pain. Then shrieking, splintering, ringing, roaring, keening, crying, and cursing. It hit Elodie all at once, so loud that she could hardly make sense of all the sounds. She struggled to open her eyes, to move her arms. She wished the screaming would stop—it was so piercing that she could not focus. Her head ached something terrible. Finally, she managed to make sense of the buzzing near her ear. Someone was calling her name.

"Elodie. Elodie? Elodie!" Elodie peeled her eyes open and took in the desperate, fearful face of her commander. "Majesty, get up," Maxine was saying, running a hand across the queen's forehead. It came back wet with blood. "Please, stop screaming. We need to get you out of here."

Elodie forced her mouth shut, and the screaming stopped. Her throat was raw, her lungs thick with smoke and dust. Her limbs were heavy and foreign as she fought to command them. She blinked rapidly, trying to focus on the scene before her, but she could not comprehend it.

The world was on fire. The dock around her was littered with debris: giant wooden planks, charred strips of sails, metal scraps twisted and melted grotesquely. The ships docked in the harbor were ablaze, and great plumes of thick, black smoke made the afternoon look like midnight. The air was sharp as a sword and hurt just as much to swallow. Beside her was what looked to be someone's front door. With dread, Elodie pushed herself to her knees and turned away from the water to face her city.

She started screaming again. Where once there had been buildings—tall and short, squat and wide—now was nothing but an endless plain of wreckage. Roofs sloped, lining the ground, while the bones of buildings smoked and sparked, exposed to every element. The castle, high on the hill, remained untouched even as the city below burned.

"Elodie!" Maxine's voice was sharp. "Help me. *Now.*"

She searched for the other girl, who was struggling to pull a wooden beam off a pile of rags. No, not rags. Bodies. Elodie's screams turned to shrieks as she rose to her feet. She had to find her family. Wood splintered into her skin, blood blooming bright on her palms, but she did not notice, did not care, as she helped Maxine unearth Brianne from beneath a crush of wood. The youngest Warnou was bleeding, her left arm at an odd angle, but she was breathing.

"Cleo," she was saying, tears mixing with the ash on her face to create a strange paste. "She was with me and then..."

But Maxine was quicker. "Over here!" she screamed, and the

Warnou siblings hobbled to where the middle sister's skirt stuck out from beneath a pile of debris.

"I can't…" Maxine was scrabbling desperately at the stone that sat atop the pile, but it would not budge. "Help, I'm—"

"Here," came Silas's gentle voice. Elodie's aunt stood beside Maxine and helped her roll away the rock, haul away a broken window and bricks from a toppled chimney, to reveal Rob and Cleo, huddled together in a cave of rubble, looking petrified but otherwise unharmed.

Elodie fell to the ground in relief. The smoke was thicker now, the char so biting that it was like trying to breathe beneath layers of blankets.

"Let's get you to the healers," Maxine said, holding out a hand to the middle Warnou sister.

"I can't move," Cleo said from where she was huddled, tears streaking her face. "I don't want…"

Maxine reached in to gather Cleo in her arms. Rob got shakily to his feet and followed, helping Brianne navigate the rubble without jostling her injured arm.

Elodie watched them go. Around her, the world moved slowly, the haze so thick it might have been a dream. Black-uniformed soldiers lay lifeless in the street, their faces soft in death, swords abandoned by their side. Others struggled to maintain consciousness, to claw their way free from the harbor and rejoin their retreating ranks.

Velle had won the battle, but at an impossible cost. There was blood on Elodie's hands, and no matter how desperately she scrubbed, they would never again be clean.

She did not move until she felt a gentle hand on her back.

"Elodie," Silas said softly. "It's time to go."

The queen shook her head. "This is…" She grasped desperately for a word that could encompass the damage, the terror, the fear she felt, but there was no way to describe it. She began again. "I was supposed to lead. I was supposed to keep my country safe, and I failed. What am I to do now?"

"You stay alive," Silas said, helping her move one foot in front of the other, guiding her over the shattered chair legs and twisted bed frames that littered the cobblestones. "You stay alive, you mourn the dead, and then," she said grimly, "you rebuild."

It was easier said than done. Elodie had much to examine and even more to repair. Her country was broken and hungry, her relationships strained and bruised. She focused her efforts externally first.

Before freeing Edgar from the chapel's confessional booth, Elodie presented him with a carefully worded declaration of peace that promised the reinstating of the Republics' imports.

"I'm not entirely authorized to sign such a sweeping proclamation," Edgar said, as the queen freed one of his freckled hands so that he could commit his name to the page in ink.

"You were able to instill enough passion in the Republics so as to cut off our resources," Elodie said sourly, as she offered him a quill. "I'm certain you can find it within yourself to be just as convincing with this new mandate."

She sent Edgar and the treaty back into the arms of the Republics' commanders, accompanied by Maxine. Velle's ruthlessness in the name of desperation had shaken the officers, and they were glad to take their leave and agree to Velle's terms of peace. It helped that the queen had offered to pay higher tariffs. It was astonishing how easily money made allies.

Next, Elodie turned her attention to the displaced people of Harborside. Before the neighborhood could be rebuilt, it needed to be treated, cleaned, and repaired. This left hundreds without homes. She offered these citizens damages, enough coin that they could leave the city behind if they wished, enough to survive if they planned to stay. Then the queen called for the local inns to open their doors to their neighbors. Once those rooms had all been filled, Elodie offered up Castle Warnou.

Suddenly, the palace was alive with people laughing in the corridors, running through the hallways, every room finally occupied. People were desperate to make themselves useful: cooking, cleaning, sharing in the burden of running house and home. Now, instead of looking down from a bell tower at her subjects, Elodie was living among them. She could speak to them night and day, ask for their opinions, listen to their worries, hear their prayers.

This lively immersion period brought her to an inevitable realization: Velle's people deserved much more than she could give them.

Tera Warnou had impressed upon her daughter to love her country, and Elodie did. She loved Velle more than anything—except perhaps her siblings and Sabine—but just because she loved a thing did not mean she had to control it. The pressures of the monarchy had made her tense and cruel, had caused her to lash out, to hold impossible expectations, and to exact her anger on those who did not deserve it. If Elodie Warnou wished to be good, she could not continue to wear the crown. But Velle's law stated that only a Warnou woman could take the throne. So, in order for Elodie to abdicate, she'd first need to find a successor.

"*I* certainly don't want it," Cleo said, looking horrified the minute the offer had left her sister's lips. "You've been miserable since the moment that crown touched your head. All that agony, and for what? No, thank you. If I ever need to supplement my lavish lifestyle, I'll simply marry rich."

Elodie went to the youngest Warnou next. "I have only just been released from a lifetime of tiaras and ball gowns," Brianne said. "Sorry, Ellie, but I don't think that's what I want. I don't even know if that's who I *am*," she added, shrugging the shoulder not done up in a sling. "One cursed reign was enough, thank you." She shivered. Elodie could not blame her. "Anyway," she said, gesturing to her desk covered with parchment, the ink-splattered pages laid out carefully to dry, "I already have a job. I'm the Archivist now. This is the first time in my life I've been able to choose who *I* want to be." She smiled softly. "I won't give that up."

Which left only one contender.

Elodie found Silas in the garden, pruning roses. "The church is rather full," the Royal Chaplain said. "I'm grateful to have so many worshippers," she said quickly. "But sometimes, I miss the quiet."

Her aunt's face gave nothing away as Elodie made her proposal. When she had finished speaking, Silas shook her head. "I would never be queen."

"Please," Elodie begged. "I can't bear it."

"Then why maintain the monarchy at all?" Silas asked simply. "If no one wishes to rule Velle, perhaps that is a sign that it deserves to be governed by the many instead."

Elodie chewed the inside of her cheek, hardly daring to let herself hope. "Would that work?"

"You've seen the way our citizens have banded together." Her aunt clipped a bright red bloom. "In the aftermath of tragedy, very often there is hope. Let your people speak for themselves. Let them speak for one another. Let the world belong to all of us, instead of just a few. That's what the New Maiden wanted, anyway." She smiled softly to herself.

Elodie found peace in such a meaningful thought. She also found relief. She could not bear the pressure the throne demanded, nor would she wish for such a curse to befall anyone else. Her brother was right—it was not ethical for a single person to hold absolute power, and certainly not Elodie, who was still learning to become herself.

Rob came to see her when plans of the political restructuring broke. It was odd to observe him in her apartments. Where once he had been so comfortable, now he hovered awkwardly near the window. "Sit," Elodie demanded, then paused. The time for her to command those around her had come to an end. "If you wish," she added quickly.

"Is it because of me?" Rob asked. "That you are giving up the throne?"

"Yes and no," Elodie answered him honestly. "Yes, because you were right, that the monarchy is antiquated and ill-matched for progress. No, because I want this, too. Velle deserves more than I can give it," she said softly. "So do you."

Rob sank onto a footstool, fiddling nervously with his sleeve. "I don't hate you," he said quietly.

"I should hope not," Elodie said, but her attempt at levity fell flat. "I'm sorry, Rob," she tried again, "that you felt abandoned. That you believed yourself alone. You never were. You never will be."

"I'm sorry, too," he said, unable to meet his sister's eyes. "I just needed to hear you say it. I just needed to know you cared."

"Our mother did not love you the way she should have," Elodie said fiercely, "but her failure is not a reflection on you. You matter to me. You, Cleo, and Brianne are my world. I won't let you doubt that again."

Rob was quiet for a long time. So long that Elodie feared she might have made a mistake. Perhaps this was not what he had wanted from her at all.

"He wants to see you," he said after a moment. Despite his best efforts, Rob could not entirely keep the bitterness from his voice. Elodie did not need to ask who her brother meant.

"I can't," she said simply. While Tal was not entirely responsible for the actions he had carried out in the name of the Second Son, their friendship still felt unsalvageable. They had exchanged unspeakably cruel words, had committed betrayals so fresh the wounds still wept. While their relationship would never be what it once was, perhaps one day Elodie would be ready to pick up the shattered pieces and hold them to the light. Their friendship might refract. But not yet.

Tal's only saving grace in Elodie's eyes was that he had not hurt Sabine. The New Maiden had returned to the castle's courtyard at dawn, Tal's limp body slumped against hers, exhaustion radiating from every limb. It was only after Tal and the horse had been tended to that Sabine collapsed.

The New Maiden slept for three days straight. On the afternoon of the fourth day, there came a knock on Elodie's door. On the other side was Katrynn Anders.

"She's awake?" Elodie asked instantly, hope fluttering in her chest.

Katrynn beamed. "She's asking for you."

A soft smile played about the New Maiden's lips as the queen approached her bedside. She looked radiant where she sat propped up by pillows, not at all like she had been lost to sleep for days. Her brown eyes were bright, her cheeks flushed. The veins in her left hand ran inky black beneath her skin.

"It's all right," Sabine said, when she saw where Elodie's attention lingered. Her voice was hoarse. "I chose this." She wiggled her fingers before slipping Elodie's hand in hers. "The darkness is mine to carry."

Elodie traced the lines of the other girl's veins. "I'm glad you're okay."

"Were you worried about me, Majesty?" Sabine teased.

"Yes," Elodie said solemnly. "But I'm not your queen anymore."

"Oh?" Sabine raised her eyebrows curiously. "And are you pleased with this particular outcome?"

"I chose this," Elodie said, echoing Sabine's sentiment. "The queendom was mine to abolish."

"Well, then," Sabine said, squeezing Elodie's hand, "I'm proud of you."

"You don't think less of me?" Elodie asked quietly, only now allowing herself to examine her own fear. So many before her had successfully shouldered the crown. It was only Elodie who had buckled beneath it.

"How could I?" the New Maiden asked, putting a hand to Elodie's cheek. "You are strong enough to know your limits. Thoughtful enough to protect your goodness. Wise enough to know the difference between power and righteousness." Sabine's eyes shone with such awe and appreciation that Elodie could hardly bear it.

Sabine made her feel so steady, so certain. So appreciated for the same things Elodie valued most about herself. There was no doubt, no misplaced feelings, no unsustainable affection. Sabine saw Elodie for who she was: a girl with ambition who had battled with her bloodline's most evil monsters and emerged triumphant.

"I love you," Elodie told her, the word filling her up with impossible warmth. Sabine was her equal in every sense, her goodness illuminating the path ahead, urging Elodie to become the best version of herself.

"I love *you*," Sabine said, and lady above, what a thrill to offer up her heart and have another hold it.

That was the difference between Elodie and her mother: Tera Warnou had been afraid to give away her love lest anyone use it against her. "Country above all" had been a shield to ensure she always maintained the upper hand. But love was not meant to possess or control. Love was freedom. Love was letting go. That was the greatness to which Elodie truly aspired, a power far more sustainable than crown or cult.

Love was the legacy Elodie Warnou wished to leave.

35

On the north side of the harbor, several men fiddled with a complicated contraption made of rope. Sailors tied knots and dockhands barked orders while Sabine and the rest of the assembled volunteers watched, open-mouthed, as a ship's intact rudder was extracted from the mountain of wreckage before them.

It was maddeningly slow work. They'd been excavating Harborside for nearly a week, yet the piles did not seem to deplete, the smoke had not entirely cleared, and the fatigue never faded from Sabine's bones.

"Feels a bit like we're back in the Lower Banks excavating sacred remains," Katrynn said, as she bent down to collect a perfectly usable metal tankard from beneath a pile of glass.

It was true, only this time Sabine's anger had no target but herself. Harborside's destruction had been her idea. While ultimately she had hoped the resistance would not need to employ the tactic, if she had not offered up the option of sacrifice, her neighbors would not be displaced.

You have taken your calling too literally, her darkness teased. *The New Maiden rebuilt the Lower Banks from the ashes, but She did not set them on fire Herself.*

Sabine swatted its taunting away. Once, she had believed that she was at the mercy of her darkness. That she was a failure for her feelings and that anger had no place in her life. But then she had slipped a princess a vial of tears, had fulfilled an ancient prophecy, had set off a chain reaction that changed her country—changed her life—forever. Now she had settled into a comfortable coexistence, choosing when and how the darkness gained access to her heart. It currently nestled itself in the hollow of her ribs, wrapped around the pulsing gem of the New Maiden's soul. Its presence was steadying. Sabine was whole once again.

When the mix of sunlight and sweat grew too much for her to bear, Sabine went in search of drinking water. A stall had been set up in what was once an alleyway, with jugs of water and ladles for the taking.

Sabine slipped into line, grateful for a moment of inactivity. She was still exhausted from her time in the Lower Banks, from the emotions she had wrenched forth and the anger she had released. The darkness had taken its toll on her, too, forcing her into a strange, fitful sleep as it worked to find its place within her again.

Someone stepped into the queue behind her, jostling her slightly. "Pardon me," the person said, as she glanced over her shoulder. "I didn't mean to—" But the speaker fell silent as soon as he saw her face.

Tal looked a wreck, as depleted and worn down as Sabine felt.

He had traded his uniform for plain clothes, his sword nowhere in sight. His eyes were sunken and held a deep discomfort. Before she could talk herself out of it, Sabine wrapped him in a tight embrace.

"What are you...?" But when Tal realized she did not mean to harm him, he stopped struggling and allowed himself to be held.

You would comfort your enemy? her darkness asked. But Tal was not Sabine's enemy, just as Sebastien had not been Hers. They had both been impossibly marked, had found shame in their emotions and comfort in a darkness few others could understand.

When at last Sabine released him, Tal looked relieved. Their touch no longer held the electricity of the past; no danger swirled about them, big and bright. They were simply two people who bore similar scars.

"What are you doing here?" Sabine asked, glancing around at the bustle of the harbor. It was strange, after their rivalry, that Tal would participate in something so close to Sabine's heart.

"Searching for steel," Tal said. "I'm taking over my father's forge." He shifted uncomfortably. "He was lost in the blast. Good riddance, I suppose." His face twisted in a scowl, his demons still scrabbling for space. Sabine dared not poke such a tender bruise.

"If you ever need to talk...," she offered, but Tal shook his head.

"I've done enough."

"Not so," Sabine argued. "We both have been cursed with a burden too much for one person to hold. There is no need to suffer alone."

"It's the only way I know how," Tal said softly. He tried to smile. Failed. "I thought He would free me. Instead, I'm more lost than ever." He looked at Sabine desperately. "I was born into so much anger and pain. Where am I supposed to go from here?"

"You were not made to hurt," she said gently, "but you *were* hurt. You deserve to heal."

Tal pursed his lips. "That might take the rest of my life."

"That's all right," Sabine said. "All any of us can do is survive, one day at a time."

Eight days after her clash with the Second Son, Sabine returned to the First Church of the New Maiden. The doors were locked. She pulled a small key from her pocket, fiddling about until she heard a soft *click*. The tiny chapel, tucked away behind the rolling hills now brown with frost, looked just as it had the first time Sabine had stumbled across its threshold, her darkness screaming, her vision spotting. It had been a refuge then, as it was now. She pushed open the door, which groaned familiarly. The sanctuary was quiet as death inside, and just as cold. Very few feet had passed through to disturb the dust.

Sabine sank into the nearest pew and sighed. The sound echoed softly, like the scratch of pen to parchment. This made her laugh, thinking of the new Archivist. Brianne was now perpetually painted in ink. Her tongue, her fingertips, her sleeves were covered in the stuff, an ironic parallel to the way Sabine's own darkness manifested. She'd tried to wipe away a blot that had dried on Brianne's cheek, but the youngest Warnou had waved her away. "Don't bother," Brianne had said upon their visit days prior. "It'll only come back. Now, tell me why you're here." While Brianne had handed over the key willingly, she had still examined Sabine with curiosity. "What are you going there to do?"

"I just need a place to clear my head," Sabine had mumbled. "I'm surrounded by so many people lately, I need somewhere to simply... exist."

But that wasn't the entire truth. Before the Second Son had perished, He had whispered a final word. A name.

For as long as Sabine had known of Her, the New Maiden had only ever been referred to by Her title. This made Her sacred, untouchable, inhuman. This left Her isolated, and trapped.

The New Maiden was more than Her word. The New Maiden was more than Her magic. The New Maiden had first been a girl with a name. A name that had been kept secret for centuries.

Sabine knelt at the altar of the First Church. Her hands shook as she kissed her thumb, precisely the way she had seen Silas do. Inside the chapel, her darkness was silent.

It was only Sabine and the scrap of Her soul that she carried within. A soul that belonged to a girl named Isolde.

Now that she could name the New Maiden, Sabine felt less strange speaking to Her.

"I still don't know why You chose me," she said, her voice louder than she'd expected in the small room. "I don't know if I did right by You, or by the world. I might have made our burdens worse. But the war is done. It is finished, and..." She trailed off, worrying her bottom lip between her teeth. "I think You might be, too."

The Second Son was vanquished, or at the very least, distilled. Brianne held the key to the Archives, would keep Her memory alive, while Silas helmed Her Church. Her word had been returned to its intended usage: inspiring good works and good acts—acts and works that Sabine would continue. She did not need to be the second coming of the New Maiden to do good. More importantly, she did not *want* to be the New Maiden. She wanted to be Sabine—tinged with darkness, filled with light.

It was time to return Her title. Which Sabine could not do until she returned Her name.

Sabine spoke the New Maiden's name like a prayer. She sang it like a hymn. She let it fill up the chapel around her, let it drape across her tongue and linger on her lips. Sabine let Isolde exist, the way She once had. Let Isolde live, the way She had never been allowed.

With every syllabic refrain, Sabine worked to dislodge the shard of Her soul, wiggling it out like a loose tooth, coaxing it forth like a frightened animal. Then Sabine spoke the New Maiden's name one final time. With a sound like a sigh, she felt her darkness release its hold on that small speck of diamond dust.

Sabine saw Her then, for a single second, as Isolde's soul burst forth to meet her. In that moment, she wanted to keep Her, for how could she live alone? But then Sabine caught sight of Her face. Isolde was smiling like She never had in the images hung above the altars. How good, how bright, how beautiful She had been.

A girl, never destined for anyone to own.

And so Sabine let the New Maiden go.

Author's Note

My sadness is a great and terrible thing, beautiful and often impossible for me to hold.

For a long time, this emotion felt unearned—my life is good, therefore I should have no reason to feel this way. My brain could not figure out how to make the feeling fit. And so, I ran from it. Throughout my teenaged years—while I held my friends' hands as we navigated their own sadness, as we screamed and cried together at their suffering—I let my own darkness devour me and did not say a word.

I was diagnosed with depression in college. I then experienced a panic attack so vivid I took myself to the emergency room in my early twenties. There were months at a time when I was twenty-five where I existed within a fog, hardly able to walk down the street without the pavement spinning beneath my feet, my vision going black, my heart hammering so hard I thought it might burst out my chest. I was getting older, but not wiser. Weaker, it seemed.

I was too proud to ask for help. Was certain I could make it through if I just kept going. Kept pushing forward. Continued to bottle up my emotions. Denied myself the truth. It took me a long time to embrace medication and therapy. Longer, still, to believe I deserved to find a careful coexistence with my sadness.

It wasn't until I had fully embraced this piece of myself that I realized how different my life might have been if I was brave enough to face my darkness. To ask for help naming it. To get the support I needed to finally understand that there was nothing wrong with me for holding it. That it was a part of me, just like my heart and brain and soul. That I could do more than just endure it. That I could exist alongside of it, rather than in spite of it.

This is how Sabine was born. A girl who *literally* bottled up her emotions, whose depression existed as a tangible, shadowy thing. It was only by learning how to live with her darkness that Sabine's true power was unlocked. It was only by speaking her emotions out loud that her destiny revealed itself. Sabine did what I could not at seventeen: She embraced her sadness as an intrinsic part of her. But instead of bending to its whims, she claimed it as her own.

The darkness does not own us. It does not command us. It's simply a part of us. If it ever feels like too much to hold, say something. Ask for help. You are never alone in this.

You are more than your darkness. Don't let it eclipse you. Each of you contains light.

SAMHSA's National Helpline is a confidential, free 24/7 information service, in English and Spanish, for individuals and family members facing mental and/or substance use disorders. This group provides referrals to local treatment facilities, support groups, and community-based organizations. Visit samhsa.gov or call 1-800-662-HELP (4357).

ACKNOWLEDGMENTS

I am so grateful to have the opportunity to offer my continued thanks to (and for) the following folks: To Jessica Anderson and Jim McCarthy for absolutely everything all of the time. To the team at Christy Ottaviano Books. To the folks at Little, Brown Books for Young Readers/Hachette, including Janelle DeLuise, Hannah Koerner, Esther Reisberg, Cassie Malmo, and Kelly Moran; copy editor Richard Slovak; and proofreaders Kelley Frodel and Su Wu. To Karina Granda for the art direction and Gemma O'Brien for the cover art. To Calah Singleton and the Hodderscape team. To the booksellers, bloggers, and readers who have loved, shared, posted, or talked about one of my books. To the friends who let me scream, cry, rant, rage, celebrate—sometimes all in one breath. To the family who shows up, every single time, for me and my art. Finally, to Katie (& Kit). I'd do all of it again for you.

ADRIENNE TOOLEY grew up in Southern California, majored in musical theater in Pittsburgh, and now lives in Brooklyn with her wife; their dog, Biscuit; eight guitars; and a banjo. She's the author of the Betrayal Prophecies duology, which includes *The Third Daughter* and *The Second Son*; the Indie Next List selection *Sofi and the Bone Song*; and *Sweet & Bitter Magic*. In addition to writing books, she is a singer-songwriter and has released several EPs, which are available on Spotify and other streaming sites. She invites you to visit her online at adriennetooley.com and on social media @adriennetooley.